For Katy and Susan

SCRIBNER

A Division of Simon & Schuster, Inc.
1230 Avenue of the Americas
New York, NY 10020

First Scribner hardcover edition July 2010

SCRIBNER and design are registered trademarks of The Gale Group, Inc.,
used under license by Simon & Schuster, Inc., the publisher of this work.

For information about special discounts for bulk purchases,
please contact Simon & Schuster Special Sales at 1-866-506-1949
or business@simonandschuster.com.

The Simon & Schuster Speakers Bureau can bring authors to your live event.
For more information or to book an event, contact the Simon & Schuster Speakers Bureau
at 1-866-248-3049 or visit our website at www.simonspeakers.com.

DESIGNED BY ERICH HOBBING

Manufactured in the United States of America

3   5   7   9   10   8   6   4   2

Library of Congress Cataloging-in-Publication Data

Morais, Richard C., 1960–
The hundred-foot journey : a novel / by Richard C. Morais.
—1st Scribner hardcover ed.
p.   cm.
1. Cooks—Fiction. I. Title.
PS3613.O584H86   2010
813'.6—dc22   2009050619

ISBN 978-1-4391-6564-5
ISBN 978-1-4391-6566-9 (ebook)

The
Hundred-Foot
Journey

A Novel

Richard C. Morais

Scribner

New York   London   Toronto   Sydney

Contents

Mumbai

Chapter One

I, Hassan Haji, was born, the second of six children, above my grandfather's restaurant on the Napean Sea Road in what was then called West Bombay, two decades before the great city was renamed Mumbai. I suspect my destiny was written from the very start, for my first sensation of life was the smell of machli ka salan, a spicy fish curry, rising through the floorboards to the cot in my parents' room above the restaurant. To this day I can recall the sensation of those cot bars pressed up coldly against my toddler's face, my nose poked out as far as possible and searching the air for that aromatic packet of cardamom, fish heads, and palm oil, which, even at that young age, somehow suggested there were unfathomable riches to be discovered and savored in the free world beyond.

But let me start at the beginning. In 1934, my grandfather arrived in Bombay from Gujarat, a young man riding to the great city on the roof of a steam engine. These days in India many up-and-coming families have miraculously discovered noble backgrounds—famous relatives who worked with Mahatma Gandhi in the early days in South Africa—but I have no such genteel heritage. We were poor Muslims, subsistence farmers from dusty Bhavnagar, and a severe blight among the cotton fields in the 1930s left my starving seventeen-year-old grandfather no choice but to migrate to Bombay, that bustling metropolis where little people have long gone to make their mark.

My life in the kitchen, in short, starts way back with my grandfather's great hunger. And that three-day ride atop the train, baking in the fierce sun, clinging for dear life as the hot iron chugged across the plains of India, was the unpromising start of my family's journey. Grandfather never liked to talk about those early days in

Bombay, but I know from Ammi, my grandmother, that he slept rough in the streets for many years, earning his living delivering tiffin boxes to the Indian clerks running the back rooms of the British Empire.

To understand the Bombay from where I come, you must go to Victoria Terminus at rush hour. It is the very essence of Indian life. Coaches are split between men and women, and commuters literally hang from the windows and doors as the trains ratchet down the rails into the Victoria and Churchgate stations. The trains are so crowded there isn't even room for the commuters' lunch boxes, which arrive in separate trains after rush hour. These tiffin boxes—over two million battered tin cans with a lid—smelling of daal and gingery cabbage and black pepper rice and sent on by loyal wives—are sorted, stacked into trundle carts, and delivered with utmost precision to each insurance clerk and bank teller throughout Bombay.

That was what my grandfather did. He delivered lunch boxes.

A *dabba-wallah*. Nothing more. Nothing less.

Grandfather was quite a dour fellow. We called him Bapaji, and I remember him squatting on his haunches in the street near sunset during Ramadan, his face white with hunger and rage as he puffed on a beedi. I can still see the thin nose and iron-wire eyebrows, the soiled skullcap and kurta, his white scraggly beard.

Dour he was, but a good provider, too. By the age of twenty-three he was delivering nearly a thousand tiffin boxes a day. Fourteen runners worked for him, their pumping legs wrapped in lungi—the poor Indian man's skirt—trundling the carts through the congested streets of Bombay as they off-loaded tinned lunches at the Scottish Amicable and Eagle Star buildings.

It was 1938, I believe, when he finally summoned Ammi. The two had been married since they were fourteen and she arrived with her cheap bangles on the train from Gujarat, a tiny peasant with oiled black skin. The train station filled with steam, the urchins made toilet on the tracks, and the water boys cried out, a current of tired passengers and porters flowing down the platform. In the back, third-class with her bundles, my Ammi.

Grandfather barked something at her and they were off, the loyal village wife trailing several respectful steps behind her Bombay man.

It was on the eve of World War II that my grandparents set up a clapboard house in the slums off the Napean Sea Road. Bombay was the back room of the Allies' Asian war effort, and soon a million soldiers from around the world were passing through its gates. For many soldiers it was their last moments of peace before the torrid fighting of Burma and the Philippines, and the young men cavorted about Bombay's coastal roads, cigarettes hanging from their lips, ogling the prostitutes working Chowpatty Beach.

It was my grandmother's idea to sell them snacks, and my grandfather eventually agreed, adding to the tiffin business a string of food stalls on bicycles, mobile snack bars that rushed from the bathing soldiers at Juhu Beach to the Friday evening rush-hour crush outside the Churchgate train station. They sold sweets made of nuts and honey, milky tea, but mostly they sold bhelpuri, a newspaper cone of puffed rice, chutney, potatoes, onions, tomatoes, mint, and coriander, all mixed together and slathered with spices.

Delicious, I tell you, and not surprisingly the snack-bicycles became a commercial success. And so, encouraged by their good fortune, my grandparents cleared an abandoned lot on the far side of the Napean Sea Road. It was there that they erected a primitive roadside restaurant. They built a kitchen of three tandoori ovens—and a bank of charcoal fires on which rested iron kadais of mutton masala—all under a U.S. Army tent. In the shade of the banyan tree, they also set up some rough tables and slung hammocks. Grandmother employed Bappu, a cook from a village in Kerala, and to her northern repertoire she now added dishes like onion theal and spicy grilled prawns.

Soldiers and sailors and airmen washed their hands with English soap in an oil drum, dried themselves on the proffered towel, and then clambered up on the hammocks strung under the shady tree. By then some relatives from Gujarat had joined my grandparents, and these young men were our waiters. They slapped wooden boards, makeshift tables, across the hammocks and quickly covered them with bowls of skewered chicken and basmati and sweets made from butter and honey.

During slow moments Grandmother wandered out in the long shirt and trousers we call a *salwar kameez,* threading her way between the sagging hammocks and chatting with the homesick soldiers missing the dishes of their own countries. "What you like to eat?" she'd ask. "What you eat at home?"

And the British soldiers told her about steak-and-kidney pies, of the steam that arose when the knife first plunged into the crust and revealed the pie's lumpy viscera. Each soldier tried to outdo the other, and soon the tent filled with oohing and "cors" and excited palaver. And the Americans, not wishing to be outdone by the British, joined in, earnestly searching for the words that could describe a grilled steak coming from cattle fed on Florida swamp grass.

And so, armed with this intelligence she picked up in her walkabouts, Ammi retreated to the kitchen, re-creating in her tandoori oven interpretations of what she had heard. There was, for example, a kind of Indian bread-and-butter pudding, dusted with fresh nutmeg, that became a hit with the British soldiers; the Americans, she found, they were partial to peanut sauce and mango chutney folded in between a piece of naan. And so it wasn't long before news of our kitchen spread from Gurkha to British soldier, from barracks to warship, and all day long jeeps stopped outside our Napean Sea Road tent.

Ammi was quite remarkable and I cannot give her enough credit for what became of me. There is no dish finer than her pearlspot, a fish she dusted in a sweet-chili masala, wrapped in a banana leaf, and tawa-grilled with a spot of coconut oil. It is for me, well, the very height of Indian culture and civilization, both robust and refined, and everything that I have ever cooked since is held up against this benchmark, my grandmother's favorite dish. And she had that amazing capacity of the professional chef to perform several tasks at once. I grew up watching her tiny figure darting barefoot across the earthen kitchen floor, quickly dipping eggplant slices in chickpea flour and frying them in the kadai, cuffing a cook, passing me an almond wafer, screeching her disapproval at my aunt.

The point of all this, however, is Ammi's roadside tent quickly established itself as a cash cow and suddenly my grandparents were doing extremely well, the small fortune they amassed, the hard-currency residue of a million soldiers and sailors and airmen moving in and out of Bombay.

And with this came the problems of success. Bapaji was notoriously tightfisted. He was always yelling at us for the smallest thing, such as dabbing too much oil on the tawa grill. Really a bit mad for money. So, suspicious of the neighbors and our Gujarati relatives, Bapaji began hiding his savings in coffee tins, and every Sunday he traveled to a secret spot in the country where he buried his precious lucre in the ground.

My grandparents' break came in the fall of 1942 when the British administration, needing cash for the war effort, auctioned off tracts of Bombay real estate. Most of the property was in Salsette, the larger island on which Bombay was built, but awkward strips of land and vacant lots of Colaba were also disposed of. Among the land to be sold: the abandoned Napean Sea Road property on which my family was squatting.

Bapaji was essentially a peasant and like all peasants he respected land more than paper money. So one day he dug up all his hidden tins and went, with a literate neighbor at his side, to the Standard Chartered Bank. With the bank's help, Bapaji bought the four-acre plot on the Napean Sea Road, paying at auction 1,016 English pounds, 10 shillings, and 8 pence for land at the foot of Malabar Hill.

Then, and only then, my grandparents were blessed with children. Midwives delivered my father, Abbas Haji, the night of the famous wartime ammunition explosion at the Bombay Docks. The evening sky exploded with balls of fire, great eruptions shattering windows far across the city, and it was at that precise moment my grandmother let out a bloodcurdling scream and Papa popped out, yelling louder even than the explosions and his mother. We all laughed at this story, the way Ammi told it, for anyone who knew my father would agree it was a most appropriate backdrop to his arrival. Auntie, born two years later, arrived under much calmer circumstances.

Independence and Partition came and went. What precisely

happened to the family during that infamous time remains a mystery; none of the questions we asked Papa were ever given a straight answer. "Oh, you know, it was bad," he would say, when pressed. "But we managed. Now stop with the police interrogation. Go get me my newspaper."

We do know that my father's family, like many others, was split in two. Most of our relatives fled to Pakistan, but Bapaji stayed in Mumbai and hid his family in a Hindi business associate's warehouse basement. Ammi once told me they slept by day, because at night they were kept awake by the screams and throat-slitting taking place just outside the basement's door.

The point is Papa grew up in an India very different from the one his father knew. Grandfather was illiterate; Papa attended a local school, not very good, admittedly, but he still made it to the Institute of Catering Technology, a polytechnic in Ahmedabad.

Education makes the old tribal ways quite impossible, of course, and it was in Ahmedabad that Papa met Tahira, a light-skinned accounting student who would become my mother. Papa says he first fell in love with her smell. His head was down in a library book when he caught the most intoxicating whiff of chapatis and rose water.

That, he said, that was my mother.

One of my earliest memories is of Papa tightly squeezing my hand as we stood on the Mahatma Gandhi Road, staring in the direction of the fashionable Hyderabad Restaurant. Bombay's immensely wealthy Banaji family and their friends were unloading at curb edge from a chauffeur-driven Mercedes. The women squealed and kissed and remarked on one another's weight; behind them a Sikh doorman snapped open the glass door of the restaurant.

Hyderabad and its proprietor, a sort of Indian Douglas Fairbanks, Jr., called Uday Joshi, were frequently in the society pages of the *Times of India,* and each mention of Joshi made my father curse and rattle the paper. While our own restaurant was not in the same league as Hyderabad—we served good food at fair prices—Papa thought Uday Joshi was his great rival. And here now was this high-society crowd descending on the famous restaurant for a *mehndi,* a prenuptial tradition in which the bride and her women friends sit plumped on cushions and have their hands, palms, and feet intricately painted with henna. It meant fine food, lively music, spicy gossip. And it most certainly meant more press for Joshi.

"Look," Papa said suddenly. "Gopan Kalam."

Papa bit the corner of his mustache as he wetly clapped my hand in his paw. I will never forget his face. It was as if the clouds had suddenly parted and Allah himself stood before us. "He a billionaire," Papa whispered. "Make his money in petrochemicals and telecommunications. Look, look at that woman's emeralds. Aiiee. Size of plums."

Right then Uday Joshi emerged from the glass doors and stood among the elegant peach saris and silk Nehru suits as if he were their equal. Four or five newspaper photographers instantly called at him to turn this way and that. Joshi was famously smitten with all things European, and he stood perkily before the clicking cameras in a shiny black Pierre Cardin lounge suit, his capped white teeth flashing in the light.

The famous restaurateur commanded my attention, even at that tender age, like a Bollywood screen legend. Joshi's throat, I remember, was lusciously wrapped in a yellow silk ascot, and his hair was airily combed back in a silver pompadour, mightily secured with cans of hair spray. I don't think I had ever seen anyone so elegant.

"Look at him," Papa hissed. "Look at that little rooster."

Papa could not stand watching Joshi a moment longer, and he turned abruptly, yanking me toward the Suryodhaya Supermarket and its special on ten-gallon vats of vegetable oil. I was just eight and had to run to keep up with his long strides and flapping kurta.

"Listen to me, Hassan," he roared over the traffic. "One day the Haji name will be known far and wide, and no one will remember that rooster. Just you wait and see. Ask the people then, ask them who Uday Joshi is. *Who he?* they say. *But Haji? Haji,* they say, *Haji are very distinguished, very important family.*"

In short, Papa was a man of large appetites. He was fat but tall for an Indian, just six feet. Chubby-faced, with curly iron hair and a thick waxed mustache. And he was always dressed the old way, a kurta, over trousers.

But he was not what you would call refined. Papa ate, like all Muslim men, with his hands—his right hand, that is, the left resting on his lap. But instead of the decorous lifting of food to his lips, Papa stuck his head down in the plate and shoveled fatty mutton and rice into his face as if he'd never get another meal. And he sweated buckets while he ate, wet spots the size of dinner plates appearing under his arms. When he finally lifted his face from the food, he had the glassy-eyed look of a drunk, his chin and cheeks slicked with orange grease.

I loved him but even I must agree it was a frightful sight. After dinner Papa hobbled over to the couch, collapsed, and for the next half hour fanned himself and let everyone else in on his general satisfaction with loud belches and thunderous farts. My mother, coming from her respectable civil servant family in Delhi, closed her eyes with disgust at this after-dinner ritual. And she was always on him while he was eating. "Abbas," she'd say. "Slow down. You'll choke. Good heavens. Like eating with a donkey."

But you had to admire Papa, the charisma and determination behind his immense drive. By the time I came along in 1975, he was firmly in control of the family restaurant, my grandfather ailing from emphysema and largely confined, on his good days, to overseeing the tiffin delivery business from a stiff-backed chair in the courtyard.

Ammi's tent was retired for a gray concrete-and-brick compound. My family lived on the second floor of the main house, above our restaurant. My grandparents and childless aunt and uncle lived in the house one over, and down from them our family enclave was sealed off with a cube of wooden two-story shacks where our Kerala cook, Bappu, and the other servants slept on the floor.

It was the courtyard that was the heart and soul of the old family business. Tiffin carts and bicycle-snack-bars were stacked against the far wall, and under the shade of the saggy tarp were cauldrons of carp-head soup, stacks of banana leaves, and freshly made samosas on wax paper. The great iron vats of flecked rice, perfumed with bay leaf and cardamom, stood against the courtyard's opposite wall, and around these delicacies hummed a constant thrum of flies. A male servant usually sat on a canvas sack at the kitchen's back door, carefully picking out the black specks of dirt among the basmati kernels; and an oily-headed female, bent at the waist with her sari gathered between her legs, was brushing with a short broom the courtyard dirt, back and forth, back and forth. And I recall our yard as always full of life, filled with constant comings and goings that made the roosters and chickens jerk about, nervously clucking in the shadows of my childhood.

It was here, in the heat of the afternoon after school, that I would find Ammi working under the porch eaves overhanging the interior courtyard. I'd scramble atop a crate for a hot-faced sniff of her spicy fish soup, and we'd chat a bit about my day at school before she passed over to me the stirring of the cauldron. And I remember her gracefully gathering up the hem of her sari, retreating to the wall where she kept an eye on me as she smoked her iron pipe, a habit she kept from her village days in Gujarat.

I remember this as if it were yesterday: stirring and stirring to the city's beat, passing for the very first time into the magic trance that has ever since taken me when I cook. The balmy wind warbled across the courtyard, bringing the faraway yap of Bombay dogs and traffic and the smell of raw sewage into the family compound. Ammi squatted in the shady corner, her tiny wrinkled face disappearing behind contented claps of smoke; and, floating down from above, the girlish voices of my mother and aunt as they folded chickpea and chili into skirts of pastry on the first-floor veranda overhead. But most of all I recall the sound of my iron hoe grating rhythmically across the vessel's floor, bringing jewels up from the soup-deep: the bony fish heads and the white eyes rising to the surface on eddies ruby red.

I still dream of the place. If you stepped out of the immediate safety of our family compound you stood at the edge of the notorious Napean Sea Road shantytown. It was a sea of roof scraps atop rickety clapboard shacks, all crisscrossed by putrid streams. From the shantytown rose the pungent smells of charcoal fires and rotting garbage, and the hazy air itself was thick with the roar of roosters and bleating goats and the slap-thud of washing beaten on cement slabs. Here, children and adults shat in the streets.

But on the other side of us, a different India. As I grew up, so, too, did my country. Malabar Hill, towering above us, quickly filled with cranes as between the old gated villas white high-rises called Miramar and Palm Beach arose. I know not where they came from, but the affluent seemed to suddenly spring like gods from the very ground. Everywhere, the talk was of nothing but mint-fresh software engineers and scrap metal dealers and pashmina exporters and umbrella manufacturers and I know not what else. Millionaires, by the hundreds first, then by the thousands.

Once a month Papa paid Malabar Hill a visit. He would put on a fresh-washed kurta and take me by the hand up the hill so we could "pay our respects" to the powerful politicians. We gingerly made our way to the back doors of vanilla-colored villas, the white-gloved butler wordlessly pointing at a terra-cotta pot just inside the door. Papa dropped his brown paper bag among the heap of other paper bags, the door unceremoniously slammed shut in our face, and we were off with our rupee-stuffed paper bags to the next Bombay Regional Congress Committee official. But there were rules. Never to the front of the house. Always at the back.

And then, business done, humming a ghazal under his breath, Papa bought us, on the trip I am remembering, a mango juice and some grilled corn and we sat on a bench in the Hanging Gardens, the public park up on Malabar Hill. From our spot under palm trees and bougainvilleas we could see the comings and goings at Broadway, a spanking-new apartment building across the torrid green: the businessmen climbing into their Mercedes; the children emerging in school uniforms; the wives off for tennis and tea. A steady stream of wealthy Jains—silky robes, hairy chests, gold-rimmed glasses—headed past us to the Jain Mandir, a temple where they washed their idols in sandalwood paste.

Papa sank his teeth into the corn and violently mowed his way down the cob, bits of kernel sticking to his mustache and cheeks and hair. "Lots of money," he said, smacking his lips and gesturing across the street with the savaged cob. "Rich people."

A girl and her nanny, on their way to a birthday party, emerged from the apartment building and flagged down a taxi.

"That girl is in my school. See her in the playground."

Papa flung his finished corncob into the bushes and wiped his face with a handkerchief.

"Is that so?" he said. "She nice?"

"No. She think she spicy hot."

At that moment, I recall, a van pulled up to the apartment building's doors. It was the fabled restaurateur Uday Joshi, delivering his latest business, home catering, for those distressing times when servants had the day off. An enormous picture of a winking Joshi stared at us from the side of the van, a bubble erupting from his mouth. NO MESS. NO FUSS. WE DO IT FOR YOU, it said.

The doorman held open the door as the caterer, in white jacket, bolted from the back of the van with tin trays and lids and foil. And I remember the deep rumble of Papa's voice.

"What Joshi up to now?"

Father had long ago done away with the old U.S. Army tent, replacing it with a brick house and plastic tables. It was a cavernous hall, simple, boisterous with noise. When I was twelve, however, Papa decided to move upmarket, closer to Joshi's Hyderabad Restaurant, and he turned our old restaurant compound into the 365-seat Bollywood Nights.

In went a stone fountain. Over the center of the dining room, Papa hung a disco glitter-ball, made of mirrors, revolving over a tiny dance floor. He had the walls painted gold before covering them, just like he had seen in pictures of a Hollywood restaurant, with the signed photographs of Bollywood stars. Then he bribed starlets and their husbands to regularly drop by the restaurant a couple of times a month, and, miraculously, the glossy magazine *Hello Bombay!* always had a photographer there precisely at the right moment. And on weekends Papa hired singers who were the spitting image of the hugely popular Alka Yagnik and Udit Narayan.

So successful was the whole venture that, a few years after Bollywood Nights opened, Papa added a Chinese restaurant to our compound, and a real disco with smoke machines that—much to my annoyance—only my oldest brother, Umar, was allowed to operate. We occupied our entire four acres, the Chinese and Bollywood Nights restaurants seating 568, vibrant businesses catering to Bombay's upwardly mobile.

The restaurants reverberated with laughter and the thump of the disco, the smell of chilies and roast fish in the air wet and fecund with spilled Kingfisher beer. Papa—known to everyone as Big Abbas—was born for this work, and he waddled around his studio lot all day like some Bollywood producer, yelling orders, slapping up the head slovenly busboys, greeting guests. His foot always on the gas. "Come on, come on," was his constant cry. "Why so slow, like an old woman?"

My mother, by contrast, was the much-needed brake, always ready to bring Papa down to earth with a smack of common sense, and I recall her sitting coolly in a cage just upstairs from Bollywood Nights' main door, penciling in the accounts from her lofty perch.

But above us all, the vultures that fed off the bodies in the Tower of Silence, the Parsi burial grounds up on Malabar Hill.

The vultures I remember, too.

Always circling and circling and circling.

Chapter Two

Let me think happy thoughts. If I close my eyes I can picture our old kitchen now, smell the clove and bay leaf, hear the spitting of the kadai. Bappu's gas rings and tawa grills were off to the left as you entered, and you'd often see him sipping his milky tea, the four basic masalas of Indian cooking bubbling away under his watchful eye. On his head, the toque, the towering chef's hat of which he was so proud. Energetic cockroaches, antennae waving, scampered across the trays of raw shellfish and sea bream to his elbow, and at his fingertips were the little bowls of his trade—garlic water, green peas, a creamy coconut and cashew gruel, chili and ginger purees.

Bappu, seeing me at the door, signaled for me to come over to watch a platter of lamb brains slide into the kadai, the pink mass landing among prattling onions and furiously spitting lemongrass. Next to Bappu stood a fifty-gallon steel vat of cottage cheese and fenugreek, simmering, two boys evenly stirring the milky soup with wooden trowels, and to the far right huddled our cooks from Uttar Pradesh. Only these northerners—my grandmother decided—had the right feel for tandoori, the deep coal pots from which emerged toasted skewers of marinated eggplant and chicken and green peppers with prawns. And upstairs, the apprentices only slightly older than myself working under a yellow garland of flowers and smoking incense.

It was their job to strip leftover tandoori chicken from the bones, snap beans over a barrel, shave ginger until it liquified. These teenagers, when off-duty, smoked cigarettes in the alleys and hooted after girls, and they were my idols. I spent a good deal of my childhood sitting with them, on a footstool in the upstairs cold kitchen, chatting away as an apprentice neatly split okra with a knife, using his finger to smear a lurid red chili paste on the vegetable's white inner thighs. There are few things more elegant in this world than a coal black teenager from Kerala dicing coriander: a flurry of knife, a chopping roll, and the riot of awkward leaves and stems instantly reduced to a fine green mist. Such incomparable grace.

One of my favorite vacation pastimes, however, was accompanying Bappu on his morning trips to Bombay's Crawford Market. I went because he would buy me jalebi, a twist of fermented daal and flour that is deep-fried and then drenched in sugary syrup. But I wound up, without trying, picking up a most valuable skill for a chef, the art of selecting fresh produce.

We started at Crawford's fruit and vegetable stalls, baskets stacked high in between narrow walkways. Fruiterers delicately built pomegranate towers, a bed of purple tissue fanning out below them in the shape of lotus flowers. Baskets were filled with coconuts and star fruit and waxy beans, and they rose vertically, several floors up, creating a sweet-smelling tomb. And the corridors, always neat and tidy, the floor swept, the expensive fruit hand polished to a waxy gloss.

A boy my age squatted on his haunches high up on the shelves, and when Bappu stopped to try a new breed of seedless grape, the boy scuttled over to a brass water jug, washed three or four grapes quickly, and handed them down to us for a taste. "No seeds, you know," the stall boss yelled from his three-legged stool in the shade. "Brand-new ting. For you, Bappu, we make kilo cheap."

Sometimes Bappu would buy, and sometimes he would not, always playing the vendors off one another. We took a shortcut to the meat market, through the pet stalls and the cages filled with panting rabbits and shrieking parrots. The smell of chickens and turkeys hit you like a village latrine, the throbbing, clucking cages and the glimpse of bald rumps where feathers had fallen out in patches. The poultry butcher sang out from behind a red valley of slashes on the chopping block, a basket of bloodied heads and wattles at his feet.

This was where Bappu taught me how to look at the skin of a chicken to make sure it was smooth, and how to bend the wings and beak for flexibility to judge the chicken's age. And the clearest sign of a tasty chicken: plump knees.

Entering the meat market's cool hall, I erupted in goose bumps, my eyes adjusting slowly to the gloomy light. The first vision to emerge from the fetid air was a butcher mincing stringy meat with a massive knife. We passed rhythmic hacking, the air sickly sweet with death, the gutter-river red.

Sheep with their throats freshly cut hung from a chain of hooks at Akbar's halal meat shop, and Bappu threaded his way between these strange trees, slapping the meaty hides. He'd find one he liked and butcher Akbar and Bappu would haggle, roar, and spit until their fingertips touched. When Akbar lifted his hand an assistant dropped an ax into the animal we had purchased, and our sandals were suddenly awash in a crimson tide and the gray blue tubes of intestines shuddering to the floor.

I remember—as the butcher expertly cut and trimmed the mutton, wrapping the legs in wax paper—lifting my head to the blue black ravens that intensely stared down at us from the rafters directly overhead. They raucously cawed and ruffled wings, their white trails of shit splattering down the columns and onto the meat. And I hear them now, to this day, whenever I attempt something ludicrously "artistic" in my Paris kitchen, this raucous cry of Crawford ravens warning me to stay close to the earth.

My favorite stop at Crawford, however, was in the fish market. Bappu and I always made the fish market our last stop, hopping the fish-gut-clogged drains that had backed up into oily-gray seas, and laden down as we were with our purchases of the morning. Our goal was fishmonger Anwar and his stall in the back of the covered quarter.

Hindus hung yellow garlands and burned incense under pictures of Shirdi Sai Baba on the concrete columns that supported the fish market. Bins of fish came clattering in, a silvery blur of wide-eyed pomfrets and pearlspots and sea bream, and here and there stood sulfuric heaps of Bombay duck, the salted shiners that are a staple of Indian cooking. By nine in the morning the early shift of workers had finished their day, and they undressed modestly under a robe, washing in a rusted bucket and scrubbing their scale-flecked lungi with Rin soap. Black recesses of the market flickered with the glow of coal fires, delicately fanned alive for a simple meal of rice and lentils. And after the meal the rows of men, impervious to the noise, settled down one by one for a nap on burlap bags and cardboard flaps.

What glorious fish. We'd pass oily bonito, the silver bodies with the squashed, yellow-glazed heads. I loved the trays of squid, the skin purple and glistening like the tip of a penis, and the wicker baskets of sea urchins that were snipped open for the succulent orange eggs inside. And everywhere on the market's concrete floor, fish heads and fins sticking out at odd angles from man-high ice heaps. And the roar of Crawford was deafening, a crash of rattling chains and ice grinders and cawing ravens in the roof and the singsong of an auctioneer's voice. How could this world not enter me?

There, finally, in the back of Crawford, stood the world of Anwar. The fishmonger sat cross-legged, all in white, high up on an elevated metal desk amid a dozen chest-high heaps of ice and fish. Three phones stood beside him on the desk—one white, one red, and one black. I squinted the first time I saw him, for he was stroking something in his lap, and it took me a few moments to realize it was a cat. Then something else moved, and I suddenly realized his entire metal desktop was covered with a half dozen contented cats, lazily flipping their tails, licking paws, haughtily lifting their heads at our arrival.

But let me tell you. Anwar and his cats, they knew fish, and together they kept alert eyes on the crate-skidding work going on at their feet. Just a little wobble of Anwar's head or a soft click of his tongue sent workers scuttling over to a pink order slip or to a Koli fisherman's arriving catch. Anwar's workers were from the Muhammad Ali Road, fiercely loyal, and all day they remained bent at his feet, sorting lobsters and crabs, carving the beefy tuna, violently scaling carp.

Anwar said his prayers five times a day on a prayer rug furled out behind a column, but otherwise he could always be found cross-legged atop his battered metal desk in the back of the market. His feet ended in long, curly yellow toenails, and he had a habit of massaging his bare feet all day long.

"Hassan," he'd say, tugging at his big toe. "You still too small. Tell Big Abbas to feed you more fish. Got nice tuna here from Goa, man."

"That no decent fish, man. That cat food."

And from him would come the rasping cough and hiss that meant he was laughing at my cheek. On days when the phones were ringing—Bombay hotels and restaurants placing their orders—Anwar courteously offered Bappu and me milky tea, but otherwise filled out pink slips and watched stern-faced with concentration as his workers filled crates. On slow days, however, he'd take me aside to an arriving basket of fish and show me how to judge its quality.

"You want a clear eye, man, not like this," he'd say, a blackened nail tapping a pomfret's clouded eye. "See here. This one fresh. See the difference. Eyes bright and full open."

He'd turn to another basket. "Look here. It's an old trick. Top layer of fish very fresh. Nah? But look." He dug to the bottom of the basket and hauled a mashed fish out by its gills. "Look. Feel dat. Meat soft. And the gills, look, not red like this fresh one, but faded. Turning gray. And when you turn back the fin, should be stiff, not like this." Anwar flicked his hand and the young fisherman withdrew his basket. "And look at this. See here? See this tuna? Bad, man. Very bad.

"Bruised, like heavy battered, yaar? Some no-good wallah give him a big drop off the back of truck.

"Haar," he'd say, wobbling his head, delighted I had learned my lessons.

One monsoon afternoon I found myself with Papa and Ammi around a table in the back of the restaurant. They pored over the wad of chits on spikes that stood between them, determining in these scratched orders which dishes had moved more in the last week and which not. Bappu sat opposite us in a stiff-backed chair, like in a court of law, nervously stroking his colonel's mustache.

This was a weekly ritual at the restaurant, a constant pushing of Bappu to improve the old recipes. It was like that. Do better. You can always do better.

The offending item stood between them, a copper bowl of chicken. I reached over and dipped my fingers into the bowl, sucking in a piece of the crimson meat. The masala trickled down my throat, an oily paste of fine red chili, but softened by pinches of cardamom and cinnamon.

"Only three order dish last week," said Papa, glancing back and forth between Bappu and grandmother. He took a sip of his favorite beverage, tea spiked with a spoonful of garam masala. "We fix it now or I drop from menu."

Ammi picked up the ladle and poured a slop of the sauce on her palm, thoughtfully licking the slick and smacking her lips. She shook her finger at Bappu, the gold bracelets jangling menacingly.

"What's this? This not like I taught you."

"Wah?" said Bappu. "Last time you tell me to change. Add more star seed. Add more vanilla pod. Do this, do dat. And now you say it not like you teach me? How can I cook here with you changing mind all the time? Make me mad, all this knockabout. Maybe I go work for Joshi—"

"Aiieee," screamed my furious grandmother. "Threaten me? I make you what you are today and you tell me you go work for that man? I throw everyone of your family to the street—"

"Calm down, Ammi," Papa yelled. "And Bappu. Stop. Don't talk crazy. No one fault here. Just wan' to prove the dish. Could be better. You agree?"

Bappu straightened his chef's hat, as if repositioning his dignity, and took a sip of tea. "Yaar," he said.

"Haar," added grandmother.

They all stared at the offending dish and its failings.

"Make it drier," I said.

"Wah? Wah? Now I take order from boy?"

"Let him speak."

"Too oily, Papa. Bappu skims butter and oil off top. But much better he dry-fries. Make a little crunchy."

"No like my skimming now. That right? Boy know better—"

"Be quiet, Bappu," Papa yelled. "You always going on with your palaver. Why you always talk like that? You an old woman?"

Well, Bappu did follow my suggestion after Papa had finished his verbal battering, and it was the only hint of what would become of me, because the chicken dish established itself as one of our bestsellers, renamed, by my father, Hassan's Dry Chicken.

"Come, Hassan."

Mummy took my hand and we slipped out the back door, heading to the Number 37 bus.

"Where are we going?"

We both knew, of course, but we pretended. It was always like this.

"Oh, I don't know. To the shops, maybe. A little break from the routine."

My mother was shy, quietly clever with numbers, but always there to rein in my father when his exuberances got the better of him. She was, in her quiet way, the family's real ballast, more so than my father, despite all his noise. She made sure we children were always properly dressed and that we did our homework.

But that did not mean Mummy did not have her own secret hungers.

For scarves. My Mummy did like her *dupatta*.

For some reason—I am not exactly sure why—Mummy occasionally took me on her clandestine forages into town, as if I alone might understand her mad shopping moments. They were rather harmless excursions, really. A scarf or two here and there, maybe a pair of shoes, only rarely an expensive sari. And for me, a coloring book, or a comic, our shopping adventure always ending in a bang-up meal.

It was our secret bond, an adventure reserved exclusively for the two of us, a way, I think, she made sure I did not get lost in the shuffle of the restaurant, Papa's demands, the rest of her clamoring children. (And maybe I wasn't quite so special as I'd like to think. Mehtab later told me that Mummy used to secretly take her to the cinema, and Umar to the go-cart track.)

And, on occasion, it wasn't about a boost from shopping at all, but about some other hunger, something far deeper, because she'd hover before the shops, smack her lips in meditation, and then head us off in an entirely different direction, to the Prince of Wales Museum, perhaps, to pore over the Mughal miniatures, or to the Nehru Planetarium, which from the outside always looked to me like a giant filter from an industrial turbine stuck sideways into the ground.

On this particular day, Mummy had just worked very hard for two weeks closing the restaurant's year-end books, for the tax man, and so, task successfully completed, another profitable year put to rest, she rewarded us with a little foraging trip on the Number 37 bus. But this time we changed buses, journeyed farther into the roar of the city, and we wound up in a stretch of Mumbai where the boulevards were wide as the Ganges, and the streets lined with big glass shop fronts, doormen, and teak shelves polished to a shiny gloss.

The name of the sari shop was Hite of Fashion. My mother looked at the bolts of cloth stacked to the ceiling in a tower of electric blues and moleskin grays, her hands clasped together under her chin, just staring in wonder at the Parsi shopkeeper up on the ladder, as he handed down the most vibrant bundles of silk to the assistant at his feet. Her eyes were teary, as if the sheer beauty of the material were just too much to take in, like looking directly into the sun. And for me that day, we purchased a spanking-smart blue cotton jacket, with, for some reason, the gold seal of the Hong Kong Yacht Club stitched to its breast.

The shelves at the nearby attar shop were filled with amber- and blue-colored glass bottles, long-necked as swans and as elegantly shaped. A woman in a white lab coat dotted our wrists with oils saturated in sandalwood, coffee, ylang-ylang, honey, jasmine, and rose petals, until we were quite intoxicated, sickened really, and had to get some fresh air. And then it was off to look at the shoes, in a pish-posh palace, where we sat on gold couches, the gilt armrests and clawed feet shaped as lions, and where a diamanté-encrusted omega framed the shop's window, in which glass shelves displayed, as if they were the rarest of jewels, spiky heels, crocodile pumps, and sandals dyed hot purple. And I remember the shoe salesman kneeling at Mummy's feet, as if she were the Queen of Sheba, and my mother girlishly turning her ankle so I could see the gold sandal in silhouette, saying, "Nah? What d'you think, Hassan?"

But I remember most of all that when we were on our way back to the Number 37 bus, we passed an office high-rise where the ground-floor shops were taken up by a tailor and an office supply store and a strange-looking restaurant called La Fourchette, which was wrapped under a lip of cement, from which protruded a tired French flag.

"Come, Hassan," said Mummy. "Come. Let us give it a try."

We ran giggling up the steps with our bags, pushed through the heavy door, but instantly fell silent. The interior of the restaurant was mosque-like dark and gloomy, with a distinctly sour smell of wine-soaked beef and foreign cigarettes, the low-hanging and dim-watted orbs hanging over each table providing the only available light. A couple in shadow occupied a booth, and a few tip-top office workers in white shirts, their sleeves rolled up, were having a business lunch and sipping red wine—still an exotic rarity in India in those days. Neither Mummy nor I had ever been in a French restaurant, so to us the dining room looked terribly smart, and we soberly took a booth in the back, whispering to each other under the low-hanging copper lamp as if we were in a library. A lace curtain, gray with dust, blocked what little light penetrated the building's brown-tinted windows, so the restaurant's overall ambience was that of a den with a slightly seedy notoriety. We were thrilled.

An elderly woman, painfully thin, wearing a caftan and an armful of bangles, shuffled over to our table, instantly recognizable as one of those aging European hippies who had visited an ashram and never returned home. But Indian parasites and time had worked her over and she looked to me like a desiccated bug. The woman's sunken eyes were heavily lined with kohl, I remember, but in the heat the makeup had run into the creases of her face; red lipstick had been applied earlier in the day with a very shaky hand. So the overall affect, in the bad light, was rather frightening, like being served lunch by a cadaver.

But the woman's gravelly-voiced Hindi was lively, and she handed us some menus before shuffling off to make us mango lassi. The strangeness of the place overwhelmed me. I didn't know where to begin with this stiff menu—such exotic-sounding dishes like bouillabaisse and coq au vin—and I looked panic-stricken up at my mother. But Mummy smiled kindly and said, "Never be afraid of trying something new, Hassan. Very important. It is the spice of life." She pointed at a slip of paper. "Why don't we take the day's special? Do you agree? Dessert is included. Very good value. After our shopping, not such a bad thing."

I remember clearly the *menu complet* started with a *salade frisée* and mustard vinaigrette, followed by *frites* and a minute steak on which sat a dollop of Café de Paris (a delicious pat of herbs-and-garlic butter), and ended, finally, with a wet and wobbly crème brûlée. I'm sure it was a mediocre lunch—the steak as tough as Mummy's newly acquired footwear—but it was instantly elevated to my pantheon of unforgettable meals because of the overall magic of the day.

For the sweet caramel pudding that dissolved on my tongue is forever fused in my memory with the look on Mummy's face, a kindness graced by the inner glow of our carefree outing. And I can still see the twinkle in her eye as she leaned forward and whispered, "Let's tell your father French food is new favorite. Nah? Much better than Indian, we'll say. That should get him excited! What d'you think, Hassan?"

I was fourteen.

I was walking home from St. Xavier's, weighted down with my math and French books, picking away at a paper cone of bhelpuri. I lifted my head and saw a black-eyed boy my age staring back at me from the filthy shacks off the road. He was washing himself, from a cracked bucket, and his wet, brown skin was in places turned white by the blinding sun. A cow was collapsed at his feet. His sister squatted in a watery ditch nearby while a mat-haired woman behind them lined a concrete water pipe with ratty belongings.

The boy and I locked eyes, for a second, before he sneered,

reached down, and flapped his genitals at me. It was one of those moments of childhood when you realize the world is not as you assumed. There were people, I suddenly understood, people who hated me even though they did not know me.

A silver Toyota suddenly roared past us on its way up to Malabar Hill, breaking the boy's mean-eyed spell, and I gratefully turned my head to follow the shiny car's diesel wake. When I turned back, the boy was gone. Only the tail-twitching cow in the mud and the girl poking the wormy feces just squeezed from her bottom.

From inside the water pipe, shadowy rustlings.

Bapaji was a man of respect in the shantytown. He was one of those who had made it, and the poor used to press their palms together when he made his arrogant way through the barracks, tapping the heads of the strongest young men. The chosen tore through the clamoring crowds and jammed onto the back of his three-wheeler put-putting on the roadside. Bapaji always picked his tiffin delivery boys from the shantytown, and he was much revered because of it. "Cheapest workers I can find," he rasped at me.

When my father refocused the business on the higher-margin restaurants, however, he stopped hiring the young men from the slum. Papa said our middle-class clients wanted clean waiters, not the filthy rabble from the barracks. And that was that. But still they came, begging for work, their gaunt faces pressed against the back door, Papa chasing them away with a roar and a swift kick.

Papa was a complicated man, not easily put in a box. He could hardly be called a devout Muslim, but he was, paradoxically, careful about staying on the right side of Allah. Every Friday, for example, before the call of prayers, Papa and Mummy personally fed fifty of the very same slum dwellers from cauldrons at the restaurant's back door. But this was insurance for the afterlife. When it came to hiring staff for the business, Papa was ruthless. "Nothing but rubbish," he'd say. "Human rubbish."

One day a Hindu nationalist on a red motorbike roared into our world, and before our very eyes the Napean Sea Road–Malabar Hill division between rich and poor widened like a causeway. The

Shiv Sena was actively trying to "reform" itself at that time—the Bharatiya Janata Party was just a few years from power—but not all of the fiery extremists went quietly into the night, and one hot afternoon Papa came back into our compound with a clutch of flyers. He was grim-faced and tight-lipped and went up to his room to talk with Mummy.

My brother Umar and I studied the yellow papers he'd left curling on the rattan chair, the overhead fan making the paper shiver. The flyers singled us out—a Muslim family—as the root cause for the people's poverty and suffering. A cartoon depicted an immensely fat Papa drinking a bowl of cow's blood.

The images come now like postcards, such as the time my grandmother and I cracked nuts under the compound's porch. Behind us we could hear the nationalists shouting slogans into a megaphone. I looked up at Malabar Hill and saw two girls in white tennis outfits sipping juice drinks on a terrace. It was a very strange moment, for somehow I knew how it would end. We were not of the shantytown, or of the upper classes of Malabar Hill, but instead lived on the exposed fault line between these two worlds.

From that last summer of my childhood I can still extract sweet tastes. Late one afternoon Papa took us all out to Juhu Beach. We staggered with our beach bags and balls and blankets through an alleyway ripe with cow dung and frangipani, and out onto the boiling sand, dodging the tinseled horse carriages and their lumpy deposits of hot plop. Papa spread three tartan blankets out across the sand as we children tore down to the platinum blue water and back.

Mummy never looked so beautiful. She wore a pink sari, her gold-sandaled feet curled under the thigh, across her face the soft, sweet smile of ghee. Kites shaped like fish fluttered loudly above us, and the strong wind made Mummy's kohl-lined eyes run. I snuggled up against the soft heat of her leg as she rummaged in her string sack for a tissue, dabbing at herself in the pocket mirror.

Papa said he was going down to the water's edge to buy my youngest sister, Zainab, a feather boa from a hawker. Mukhtar and Zainab and Arash, the four of us, we ran after him. Paunchy old men tried to recapture their youth with a game of cricket; my oldest brother, Umar, did backflips across the sand, showing off with his teenage friends. Vendors lugged coolers and smoking trays down the beach, singing out their wares of sweet breads and cashews and Fanta and monkey balloons.

"Why only Zainab get something?" wailed Mukhtar. "Why, Papa?"

"One ting," Papa yelled. "One ting each. And then no more. You hear?"

The taut kite strings moaned in the wind.

Mummy sat on the blanket, curled into herself like a pink pomegranate. Something my auntie said must have made her laugh, for Mummy turned gaily, her teeth white, her hands stretched out to help my sister Mehtab thread a garland of white flowers through her hair. That is how I like to remember Mummy.

It was a hot and humid afternoon in August. I was playing backgammon with Bapaji in the compound courtyard. A chili-red sun had just dipped behind the backyard banyan and the mosquitoes whined furiously. I was about to tell him we should move indoors, when Bapaji suddenly jerked his head up—"Don't let me die," he rasped—and then violently pitched forward onto the spindly-legged table. He shuddered; he twitched. The table collapsed.

When Bapaji died, so, too, did the last scrap of respect we had in the shantytown, and two weeks after he was buried they came at night, their distorted, rubbery faces pressed up against Bollywood Nights' window. All I remember was the screaming, the terrible screaming. The torchlit mob pulled my mother from her cage while my father hustled us children and a stampede of restaurant guests out the back door and up to the Hanging Gardens and Malabar Hill. Papa rushed back to get Mummy, but by then flames and acrid smoke leaped from the windows.

Mother was bloodied and unconscious under a table in the downstairs restaurant, flames closing in all around her. Papa tried to enter, but his kurta caught fire and he had to retreat, slapping his blackened hands. We heard his terrible screams for help as he raced back and forth in front of the restaurant, helplessly watching Mummy's braid of hair, like a candlewick, catch fire. I never told anyone, because there is a chance it was my overactive imagination at work, but I swear I smelled her burning flesh, from our safe perch up on the hill.

The only thing I remember feeling afterward was a ravenous hunger. Normally, I am a moderate eater, but after Mummy's murder I spent days gorging on mutton masala and dumplings of fresh milk and egg biryani.

I refused to part with her shawl. I was in a torpor for days, Mummy's favorite silk shawl wrapped tightly around my shoulders, my head lowering again and again over lamb trotters soup. It was, of course, just a boy's desperate attempt to hold on to his mother's last presence, that fast-fading odor of rose water and fried bread wafting up from the diaphanous cloth around my head.

Mummy was buried, as is the Muslim tradition, within hours of her death. There was dust, a choking red-earth dust that got into the sinuses and made me wheeze, and I recall staring at the red poppies and ragweed next to the earth hole that swallowed her up. No feeling. Nothing. Papa beat his chest until his skin was red, his kurta soaked with sweat and tears, the air filling with his dramatic cries.

The night my mother was buried, my brother and I stared into the dark from our cots, listening to Papa as he paced back and forth behind the bedroom wall, bitterly cursing everyone and everything. The fans creaked; poisonous centipedes scurried across the cracked ceiling. We waited, on edge, then . . . wallop—the horrible clap that came each time he brought his bandaged hands violently together. And that night, through the door of his room, we heard Papa whisper, a kind of half moan, half chant, repeated over and over again, as he rocked back and forth on the edge of his bed: "Tahira, on your grave I promise, I will take our children from this cursed country that has killed you."

And during the day the fiery emotions in the compound were intolerable, like a vat boiling and boiling and boiling but never running dry. My little sister Zainab and I hid behind the upstairs steel Storwel closet, curled into balls and pressed against each other for comfort. There was a horrible wail from downstairs and the two of us, desperate to get away from the sound, climbed into the closet and buried ourselves in the hundred scarves that were Mother's simple vanity.

Mourners came, like vultures, to pick over us. Rooms filled with the deathly fug of sour body odor, cheap cigarettes, burning mosquito coils. The chatter was constant and high-pitched, and the mourners ate marzipan-filled dates while clucking over our misfortune.

Mummy's snooty Delhi relatives stood in silken finery in the corner, their backs to the room as they nibbled on crackling papad and grilled eggplant. Papa's Pakistani relatives loudly roved around the room, looking for trouble. A religious uncle wrapped his bony fingers around my arm and pulled me aside. "Allah's punishment," he hissed, his white head shaking with palsy. "Allah's punishing your family for staying behind during Partition."

Papa finally reached his limit with my great-aunt, and he dragged the shrieking woman out through the banging screen door, roughly shoving her into the courtyard. The dogs pricked up their ears and howled. Then he went back inside to kick her sack of belongings out after her. "Come back in here you old vulture, and I'll kick you back to Karachi," he yelled from the porch.

"Aaaiiee," screamed the old woman. She pressed her palms against her temples and strutted back and forth in front of the charred remains of the restaurant. The sun was still hard. "Wah I do?" she wailed. "Wah I do?"

"Wah you do? You come into my house, eat my food and drink, and then whisper insults about my wife? Think because you old you can say what you like?" He spat at her feet. "Low-class peasant. Get out of my house. Go home. I don't want to look at your donkey face anymore."

Ammi's scream suddenly hurtled through the air like an ax. In her hands she clutched clumps of her own white hair, like hairy-root onion grass, and she was bloodily raking her face with her nails. There was more roaring and confusion as Auntie and Uncle Mayur jumped on her, pinning down her arms so she wouldn't do more damage to herself. A blur of *salwar kameez,* a gasping scuffle, followed by a stunned silence as they dragged shrieking Ammi from the room. Papa, unable to take it anymore, stormed from the compound, leaving flapping chickens in his wake.

I was sitting on the couch next to Bappu the cook during all this, and he protectively put his arm around me as I pressed myself into his fleshy folds. And I remember the human crush in the living room stiffening momentarily during Papa's and Ammi's outbursts, samosas frozen halfway to open mouths. It looked like they were playing some parlor game. For as soon as Papa left, our guests looked furtively about from the corners of their eyes, reassuring themselves no other unhinged Haji was about to jump out at them, and then happily resumed their gold-toothed masticating and palaver and tea-slurping as if nothing had happened. I thought I might go mad.

A few days later a pudgy man with slicked-back hair and black-framed glasses appeared at our door, smelling of lilac water. He was a real estate developer. Others came after him, like betel-spitting bugs, often at the same time, outbidding one another on our front porch, each desperately trying to snatch Grandfather's four acres for another apartment high-rise.

It was destiny that our losses coincided with a brief period when Bombay real estate suddenly became the highest in the world, more expensive than New York, Tokyo, or Hong Kong. And we had four unencumbered acres of it.

Father turned icy. All afternoon, for several days, he sat pudgy on the damp couch under the porch, occasionally leaning forward to order the half-dozen developers shot glasses of tea. Papa said very little, just looked grave and clicked his worry beads. The less he said, the more frantic became the table-slapping and the red-juiced squirts of betel spit hitting the wall. Finally, however, exhaustion set in among the bidders, and Papa stood, nodded at the man with the hair doused in lilac water, and went indoors.

From one day to another, Mother was gone, forever, and we were millionaires.

Life is funny. No?

We boarded the Air India flight in the night, the sultry Bombay air pressing against our backs, the smell of humid gasoline and sewage in our hair. Bappu the cook and his cousins openly wept with their palms pressed against the airport glass, reminding me of geckos. Little did I know that was the last we would ever hear or see of Bappu. And the plane ride is largely a blur, although I do recall Mukhtar's head was in the airsick bag all through the night, our row of seats filled with his retching.

The shock of my mother's death lasted for some time, so my recollections of the period that followed are odd: I am left with weird, vivid sensations but no overall picture. But one thing is without doubt—my father stuck to the promise he made Mummy at her graveside, and in a stroke we wound up losing not only our beloved mother but also all that was home.

We—the six children ranging from ages five to nineteen; my widowed grandmother; Auntie and her husband, Uncle Mayur— we sat for hours on harshly lit plastic seats at Heathrow Airport as Papa bellowed and waved his bank statements at the pinched-faced immigration official deciding our fate. And it was on these seats that I had my first taste of England: a chilled and soggy egg-salad sandwich wrapped in a triangle of plastic. It is the bread, in particular, that I remember, the way it dissolved on my tongue.

Never before had I experienced anything so determinedly taste-less, wet, and white.

London

Chapter Three

The entire experience of leaving Bombay rather resembled a certain technique for catching octopus found in the Portuguese villages living off the rough waters of the Atlantic. Young fishermen tie pieces of cod to large treble hooks attached to ten-foot-long bamboo poles; at low tide, they work the rockiest shorelines, jabbing the cod under half-submerged rocks normally inaccessible under pounding surf. An octopus will suddenly shoot out from under the rock and latch on to the cod, and what ensues is an epic battle, the grunting fisherman trying to drag the octopus up onto the rock with the grappling hook secured at the end of the pole. More often than not the fisherman loses the battle in a squirt of ink. If the fisherman is successful, however, the stunned octopus is plopped on top of the exposed rocks. The fisherman darts in, grasps the octopus's gill-like opening on the side of its head, and turns the entire head inside out so the internal organs of the octopus are exposed to the air. Death is fairly quick.

That's what England felt like. Wrenched from the comfort of our rock, our heads were suddenly turned inside out. Of course, our two years in London were undoubtedly most necessary, for this period provided us with the time and space we needed to properly say our good-byes to Mummy and the Napean Sea Road before moving on with life. Mehtab correctly calls it our Period of Mourning. And Southall—not India but also not yet Europe—I suspect was the ideal holding tank as we became acclimatized to our new circumstances. But such is the benefit of hindsight. At the time it seemed as if we had wandered into hell. We were lost. Maybe even a little mad.

* * *

It was Uncle Sami, my mother's youngest brother, who picked us up at Heathrow Airport. I sat in the van's backseat, sandwiched between Auntie and my newly discovered cousin, Aziza. My London-born cousin was my age, but did not look at me, or talk, just put on Walkman earphones and beat her thigh to crashing dance music as she looked out the window.

"Southall very good neighborhood," Uncle Sami yelled from the front. "All the Indian shops, right at your fingertips. Best Asian shopping in all England. And I've found you a house, just around the corner from us. Very big. Six rooms. Needs a bit of work. But not to worry. Landlord said he would have everything tip-top."

Aziza was unlike any of the girls I had known in Bombay. There was nothing simpering or coquettish about her, and I stole glances at her from the corner of my eye. She wore, under her leather jacket, sexy things, ripped lace and a black leotard. She sent off heat, too, a powerful mix of teenage body odor and patchouli oil, and made us all jump to attention every time she cracked her gum like pistol shots.

"Just two more roundabouts," Uncle Sami said, as we once again screeched around a traffic circle on the Hayes Road. And as we leaned around the corner, I felt my cousin's hot knee push back against my thigh, and instantly a cricket bat was poking up through my pants. But my hawkeyed auntie seemed to read my thoughts, for she had a face on like a mouthful of lemons, and she leaned against me on the other side.

"Better Sami had stayed in India," she spat in my ear. "That girl. So young and already a dirty toilet seat."

"Shush, Auntie."

"Don't shush me! You stay away from her. You hear? She only make trouble."

Southall was the unofficial headquarters of Britain's Indian, Pakistani, and Bangladeshi community, a flatland in the armpit of Heathrow Airport, its Broadway High Street a glittering string of Bombay jewelers, Calcutta cash-and-carries, and Balti curry houses. It was terribly disorienting, this familiar noise under the gray skies of England. A sprawl of semidetached houses split into flats crowded the surrounding residential streets, and you could always tell who were the latest arrivals from Mother India by the dingy sheets hung across the leaky windows. And at night the sulfuric orbs of Southall's streetlamps glowed eerily through the evening fog, a permanent wetness that moved in from the marshes of Heathrow Airport, heavy with the smells of curry and diesel.

When we arrived, a few streets of Southall were also in the throes of gentrification, worked over by ambitious second-generation immigrants. Papa called them the "Anglo Peacocks," and their renovated white stucco houses rather looked as if they had been pumped up on steroids, massive extensions front and back rippling with mock-Tudor windows, satellite dishes, and glass conservatories. A secondhand Jag or Range Rover often straddled these crescent driveways.

Mummy's relatives had lived in Southall for thirty years, and they secured for us a large stucco house, just two streets over from the Broadway High Street. The house belonged to a Pakistani general, a bolt-hole the absentee landlord rented out while awaiting the day he might have to flee his country in a hurry. The house—which we quickly nicknamed the General's Hole—desperately wanted to be one of the grander Anglo Peacock homes, but failed to live up to its own ambition. It was squat and ugly, narrow in the front, but stretching back almost an entire block to a small garden where a rusted barbecue and a broken fence finished off the property. A sickly chestnut tree stood on the buckled street in front, and when we moved in, there was litter out front and litter out back. And I recall that the house was always filtered through gloomy light, hunkering as it was in the shadows of a local water tower, the rooms inside covered in tatty linoleum or threadbare rugs. Bits of glass-and-chrome furniture and wobbly lamps did little to cheer the place up.

That house was never home and I forever associate it with the constant din of a prison: the clanking radiators, the alarming shuddering of pipes throughout the house whenever a tap was turned on, the constant creaking and cracking of floorboards and glass. And every room soaked in a chilly damp.

Papa was obsessed with finding a new business he could build in England, only to abandon the idea a few weeks later when another bit of foolishness caught his attention. He imagined himself an import-exporter of firecrackers and party favors; then a wholesaler of copper kitchenware made in Uttar Pradesh; this was followed by an enthusiasm to sell frozen bhelpuri to the Sainsbury's supermarket chain.

Papa's final entrepreneurial brainstorm, however, came to him as he was sitting in the bath with Auntie's shower cap clapped over his head, his torso, like a hirsute iceberg, thrusting up from the milky-white water. A mug of his favorite tea spiked with garam masala stood at his elbow and his face was running with sweat.

"We must do research, Hassan. Research."

I sat perched on the laundry hamper, watching Papa as he feverishly washed his feet.

"On what, Papa?"

"On what? On new business. . . . Mehtab! Come here! Come. The back."

Mehtab came in from the bedroom and sat dutifully on the rim of the bath as Papa leaned forward and looked over his shoulder. "The left," he said. "Under the shoulder blade. No. No. Yaar. That one."

Papa was cursed, ever since he was a teenager, with an unattractive rash of blackheads, pimples, and boils across the broad expanse of his hairy back, and while Mummy was alive, the duty of popping the worst offenders fell on her.

"Squeeze," he yelled at Mehtab. "Squeeze."

Papa scrunched up his face, Mehtab pinching the boil hard between her painted nails, the two of them yelping with surprise when the offending item suddenly exploded.

Papa craned his head around to get a look at the proffered tissue.

"Lots come out, yaar?"

"But what business, Papa?"

"I am thinking sauces. Hot sauces."

From that moment on, the talk was of Madras sauces and nothing else. "Watch how I do this, Hassan," Papa exclaimed over the Broadway High Street's traffic. "Before you start business, always find out about competition. Nah? Market research."

The Shahee Supermarket was the prince of all Southall's shops. Owned by a wealthy Hindu family from East Africa, it took up the entire ground floor of a 1970s office tower at the end of the Broadway High Street. Sometimes the store dropped a half floor down into the basement, to frozen mint peas and chapatis, and sometimes it rose three steps to a reinforced platform that displayed nothing but five-kilo bags of broken basmati. Every inch of the shop was taken with floor-to-ceiling shelves of tins and sacks and boxes of what have you, and it was here displaced Indians like us bought aromatic reminiscences of home. Bags of butter beans and bottles of Thums Up; tins of coconut cream and pomegranate syrup; and colorful packets of sandalwood incense for our "pleasure and prayer."

"And what's this?" Papa demanded, pointing at a jar.

"Patak's Madras Curry Paste, sir."

"And this?"

"Rajah's Lime and Chili Pickle, sir."

And Papa went down the entire stock of shelves, blowing his stuffed nose, giving the poor shop assistant hell.

"And this is Shardee's, yaar?"

"No, sir, this is Sherwood's. And it isn't a pickle. It is a Balti curry paste."

"Is that so? Open a jar. I want to taste."

The shop assistant looked around for the manager, but the Sikh was out front on Broadway High Street, standing guard over shrink-wrapped stacks of pink toilet paper. With no help on hand, the young boy maneuvered himself safely behind cases of dented chickpea cans before he spoke again. "I am sorry, sir," he said politely. "We don't give tastes like that. You must buy the jar."

*　*　*

"We want proper service," Papa told Uncle Sami.

Aziza looked at me, signaled we should sneak out the back for a cigarette.

"Not these simple fellows from East Africa," continued Papa, tapping Uncle Sami's elbow so the poor fellow had to look up from his newspaper.

"My God. That stupid boy at Shahee's, like he had a bone through his nose."

"Yes, yes. Very good," said Uncle Sami. "Liverpool is up, two-to-one."

But Papa, he was like a dog after a rat, and "proper service" became our excuse for voyaging to that mysterious place Papa had heard so much about: Harrods Food Hall. It was a memorable event that day the entire family descended on the West End, the hustle and bustle of Knightsbridge momentarily warming us, reminding us of the car-tooting excitement of Bombay. For a few minutes we stood awestruck before the red-stone department store, gaping up at the Royal Warrants bolted to the side of the building. "Very important tings," Papa told us reverentially. "Means English Royal Family buy chutney here."

And then we plunged through Harrods' doors, through the leather handbags and china and past papier-mâché sphinxes, our heads bent all the way back as we stared up with awe at the mock-gold ceiling encrusted with stars.

The Food Hall smelled of roasting guinea fowl and sour pickles. Under a ceiling suitable for a mosque, we found a football pitch devoted entirely to food and engaged in a din of worldly commerce. Around us: Victorian nymphs in clamshells, ceramic boars, a purple-tiled peacock. An oyster bar stood beside hanging slabs of plastic meat, while the grounds were covered in a seemingly endless line of marble-and-glass counters. One entire counter, I recall, was filled with nothing but bacon—"Smoked Streaky," "Oyster-Back," and "Suffolk Sweet Cure."

"Look," Papa yelled, with a mixture of delight and disgust, at the trays of pig meat under glass. "Pork bellies. Haar. And here, look."

Papa roared with laughter at the silliness of the English, at the glistening carrots artfully displayed with a yard of their furiously green bush. "Look. Four carrots, £1.39 a bunch. Haahaa. Pay for the bush. Eat the whole ting. Like rabbits."

We passed from one room to another, under Victorian chandeliers, surveying produce from corners of the globe we had never even heard of, Papa's guffaws ever less frequent. And it's the confused expression on his face that I recall, while he tapped the glass, counting thirty-seven different types of goats' cheese, each with its own exotic name like Pouligny-Saint-Pierre and Sainte-Maure de Touraine.

The world was an awfully big place, we suddenly realized, and here was the evidence before us: gently smoked ostrich from Australia and Italian gnocchi and black potatoes from the Andes and Finnish herring and Cajun sausages. And perhaps, most shocking, but clear as can be, England's own rich vein of culinary deposits, wonderful-sounding creations like "Duckling, Apple & Calvados Pie" or "Beer-Marinated Rabbit Loins" or "Venison Sausage with Mushroom & Cranberry."

It was utterly overwhelming. A Harrods security officer, flak-jacketed and with wires in his ears, walked around us.

"Where the Indian sauces, please?" Papa asked meekly.

"Down in Pantry, sir, past Spices."

Past the Jelly Belly towers in Sweets, down the escalator, through Wines and into Spices. And there, Papa's hand raised, a brief glimmer of hope in Spices, but quickly dashed at the sight of more such cosmopolitan labels: French Thyme, Italian Marjoram, Dutch Juniper Berries, Egyptian Bay Leaf, English Black Mustard, and even—the ultimate slap—German Chives.

Papa let out his breath. And the sound, it broke my heart.

Squashed in the corner, almost hidden behind packages of Japanese seaweed and pink ginger, just token contributions from culinary India. Some bottles of Curry Club. A few baggies of chapatis. Papa's entire world reduced to next to nothing.

"Let's go," he said listlessly.

And that was that. The English schemes. Finished.

Harrods totally undid Papa, and shortly thereafter he succumbed to the depression that must have been lurking just below his manic search for a new occupation. Because from then on, right until we left, Papa spent his time in England sitting like a turnip on the Southall couch, wordlessly watching Urdu videos.

Chapter Four

When the low-hanging skies of Southall became too gray and oppressive and we craved the color and life of Mumbai, Umar and I took the tube into Central London, switched trains, and headed out to the Camden Locks of North London. The journey was quite long and uncomfortable, but emerging from the cavernous tunnels of the Northern Line, into the crowded streets of Camden, it was like being reborn.

Here the buildings were painted tarty pinks and blues, and under the row of saggy awnings were tattoo parlors and body-piercers, Dr. Martens boot dealers and handmade hippie jewelry, and musty little holes from which blared head-banging music from the Clash or the Eurythmics. As we walked down the High Street, a little bounce back in our walk, greasy-haired barkers tried to lure us into shops selling secondhand CDs and aromatherapy oils, vinyl miniskirts, and skateboards and tie-dye T-shirts. And the strange people thronging and jostling on the sidewalks—the ring-studded Goths in black leather and green Mohawks, the posh girls from private Hampstead day schools down for a bit of slumming, the winos lurching from rubbish bin to pub—all this sea of humanity reassured me that as alien as I felt, there were always others in the world far odder than I.

On this particular day, just over the central canal, Umar and I turned left into the covered markets for lunch, where the former brick warehouses along the locks, the stalls, the cobblestone lanes, were all jammed with inexpensive food stalls from around the globe. Asian girls wearing thick eyeglasses and paper hats called out—"Come here, boys, come"—beckoning us over to their tofu and green beans, to their Thai chicken skewers in satay, to the woks where a cross-looking chef was repeatedly plopping steamy portions of sweet-sour pork onto rice. We would wander in awe, peering, like at the zoo, into stalls selling Iranian barbecue, fish stews from Brazil, Caribbean pots of plantain and goat, and thick wedges of Italian pizza.

But my older brother, Umar, whom I followed sheeplike on these outings, led us straight to the Mumbai Grill, where laminated copies of Bollywood film posters, 1950s classics such as *Awara* or *Mother India,* decorated the booth. And from the vats of lamb Madras or chicken curry on the counter we would get a delicious dollop of rice and okra and chicken vindaloo, all unceremoniously smacked, for £2.80, into a Styrofoam pouch.

So, plastic forks and vindaloo in our hot hands, shoveling food in our mouths as we walked, we wandered deeper into the bowels of the Camden markets, drifting against our will to the stalls that would have drawn Mummy. There, the necklaces of colored glass beads; the Suzie Wong cocktail dresses in black-and-red satin; and the prayer shawls, pashmina silk, the Jamawars, all hanging like diaphanous vines from pegs, a riot of glittering colors that made us think of Mummy and Mumbai. At a corner stall, under an awning that was saggy and tired, I stopped to study rack upon rack of cheap cotton carryalls from India, each for just ninety-nine pence, that were a lively rust and maroon and aquamarine, embroidered with dainty little flowers or stitched with beads and bits of glass. They drew me in under the awning, under the elaborate cotton chandeliers with silk tassels and tubular insides, from which a low-watt bulb cast a yellow light. And there were the scarves, the *dupatta,* draped over racks or knotted and hanging like thick rope from pegs, pink and floral, psychedelic and striped. Up on the wall a fantastic quilt of colorful scarves, stitched together and hung across the entire shop, displaying the entire universe of *dupatta* on offer.

"Yes. Can I help you?"

And there she was, Abhidha, a name that literally means "longing," in tight-fitting jeans and a simple black V-neck wool sweater, offering to help me, with her curious smile.

I wanted to blurt out, *Yes, help me. Help me find my Mummy. Help me find myself.*

But what I said was, "Ummm . . . something for my aunt. Please."

I do not recall what all was said exactly, as she had me run my hand along a silk pashmina shawl in deep crimson, talking to me earnestly in that soft voice, my heart pounding. I kept on asking her to show me one more thing, so I could keep on talking to her, until her father in the back finally barked she was needed at the cashier, and she looked at me full of regret, and I followed her to the cash register, where I emptied out my pockets to buy my aunt that crimson shawl, until, at the end, I stuttered that I'd like to see her again, for a meal or a movie, and she answered, yes, she'd like that. And so that was how I found my first love, Abhidha, among the shawls, when I was seventeen.

Abhidha was by no means a classic beauty. She had, admittedly, quite a round face pocked by a few old acne scars here and there. When we got home that day, Umar told my sister Mehtab that I was in love, and then added unkindly, "Hot body, but face . . . face like an onion bhaji." But what Umar obviously didn't see, and I did, was that Abhidha's face was permanently lit by the most intriguing smile. I did not know where this smile came from, in a woman of twenty-three, but it was as if Allah had once whispered some cosmic joke into her ear, and from then on she walked through life filtering the world through this amusing take on events. Nor did I really care what Umar thought—or anyone else, for that matter— because from then on I was driven to seek out Abhidha, whenever our schedules or families permitted, because something in me knew she was a kindred soul, would bring out that driving ambition buried deep inside me, that part starved to taste the flavors of life far beyond the comfort zone of my heritage.

Abhidha's family was originally from Uttar Pradesh, lived in Golder's Green, and ran their import-export business from Camden. British-born and in her last year at Queen Mary College, University of London, Abhidha was frighteningly bright and ambitious, single-mindedly trying to improve herself. So she would agree to meet me—her purse slung over her shoulder, banging on her hip, always an inky pad and pen in her hand—but only for something educational, like a special exhibit at the British Museum or the Victoria Albert. And if we met in the evening, it was to see Aeschylus's *Oresteia* at the National Theatre, or an incomprehensible play—usually by some mad Irishman—in a hot and sticky room above a pub.

I resisted her at first, of course, all this high culture, which I didn't think was my thing, until that night we did a coin toss to see who got to decide what we were doing that Saturday. I was adamant we see a Bruce Willis film involving an unusually large number of helicopter chases and exploding office buildings, and she—almost knocked me over—she wanted to see a Soviet-era play, from the then dissident underground, about three homosexuals incarcerated in Siberia.

This, as Saturday evening entertainment, was as attractive to me as having all my teeth pulled, but she won the coin toss and I wanted to be with her, so we took the tube up to the Almeida Theatre in Islington, and sat for three hours in the dark, on a hard bench behind a pillar, constantly shifting our tingly bottoms.

Somewhere in the middle of the play tears began streaming down my face. I am not exactly sure what happened, but the play wasn't really about homosexuals, this I realized, but about the human soul when it has a destiny—at odds with the society around it—and how this destiny drove these Russian characters into exile. It was all about homesick men achingly missing their mothers and comforting foods from home and how this exile in Siberia brought them to the very edge of madness. But it was also about the majesty of their destiny to be homos, and that it was a force of its own and could not be denied, and that none of them in the end, no matter how they suffered, none of them would ever have traded in their destiny for the comfortable life they left behind in Moscow. And then they all died. Horribly.

Good heavens. What a mess I was in when we finally emerged into the dark and wet night of Islington. I was sullen, snappish, totally embarrassed for having blubbered like a girl during this strange play. But women—this I will never understand—they are touched by the oddest things, and Abhidha was on her cell phone, ringing a chum, and the next thing I knew she was shoving me into the back of a black taxi, and we were on our way to her friend's flat in Maida Vale.

The friend, she was out, just a cat on the windowsill looking rather offended by our arrival. There was a wooden bowl of bananas on the dining room table and the flat smelled of rotten fruit, cat litter, and moldy old carpet. But it was there, in the narrow bed under the dormer window, that Abhidha peeled off her V-neck sweater to give me a good nuzzle in her coconuts, while her hands down below tugged at my belt. And that night, after a good bounce, we slept with her bottom pushed up against my groin, contentedly curled together like a pair of Moroccan crescent pastries.

Time and gravity: several weeks later, one perfect day in April, Abhidha asked me to meet her at the Royal Academy of Arts on Piccadilly, for an exhibit on Jean-Siméon Chardin, an eighteenth-century French painter she was researching for a paper. We walked hand in hand through the gallery, eyes up on the walls at the thick crusts of paint portraying tables set with a Toledo orange, a pheasant, a piece of turbot hanging from a hook.

Abhidha walked smiling through the light-filled gallery—that incredible smile—clearly admiring Chardin's work, and I followed her, at a loss, scratching my head, until I finally blurted out, "Why you like these paintings so much? They're all just a bunch of dead rabbits on a table."

So she took me by the hand and showed me how Chardin painted, again and again, the same dead rabbit, partridge, and goblet—in the kitchen. The same wife and scullery maid and cellar boy—in the kitchen. Once I saw the pattern, she began reading to me—almost in an erotic whisper—from a pedantic text written by some old fossil of an art historian. " 'Chardin believed God was to be found in the mundane life before his eyes, in the domesticity of his own kitchen. He never looked for God anywhere else, just painted again and again, the same ledge and still life in the kitchen of his home.' "

Abhidha whispered, "I just love that."

And I remember wanting to say, it was at the edge of my lips, *And I just love you.*

But I didn't. And after the exhibit we dashed across Piccadilly, to eat the packed lunch she'd brought us from home, some sort of grilled chicken wrap, laughing and running across the street as the lights turned and the cars came roaring down at us.

St. James's Church, Piccadilly, facing the traffic but set slightly back, was a sooty gray brick building, by Christopher Wren, the flagstone courtyard out front occupied by a few antiques stalls selling china, stamps, and silver flatware. But the church's small garden, tucked around the corner, was deliciously British: wispy stalks of lavender, starwort, and granny's bonnets, all slightly messy and wild, growing between aged trees of oak and ash.

A woman—Mary, I suspect—stood in green bronze among the flowering shrubs, hands aloft, beckoning London's lost to this oasis in the hubbub, where at the edge of the pocket garden a green motor home was parked. And as we made our way to the bench, we passed the open door of the battered old caboose and furtively took a peek: a tousle-haired social worker was flipping through a glossy magazine, sitting patiently, we assumed, until the next homeless person dropped in for a cup of tea and an earful of advice.

It was in this idyllic garden, as we sat and ate our lunch, that Abhidha dropped her bomb. She asked me to come next Saturday to a poetry reading and dinner party in Whitechapel so I could meet her friends from the university. I immediately understood what she was saying, that this was no small thing she was asking me to do, trying me out with her college peers, and so I stammered in response, "Of course. With pleasure. I will be there."

But this you must know: the violent murder of a mother—when a boy is at that tender age, when he is just discovering girls—it is a terrible thing. Confusingly mixed up with all things feminine, it leaves a charred residue on the soul, like the black marks found at the bottom of a burned pot. No matter how much you scrub and scrub the pot bottom with steel wool and cleansers, the scars, they are permanent.

At the same time I was getting to know Abhidha, I was regularly dropping by the basement lair of Deepak, a boy from the neighborhood in Southall. Deepak was one of the Anglo Peacocks and his parents, wishing he would just go away, turned over their entire basement to their son, who promptly filled it with state-of-the-art

hi-fi and TV, the floor covered in fat beanbags. And in the corner—
a foosball table.

Foosball, I tell you, it is a devilish invention of the West. Makes
you forget everything in the world. Nothing but twirling that handle and smacking that little ball, just so you can hear the marvelous
sound of that white sphere whizzing through the air and smacking the back of the goal with a satisfying wooden *thwock*. Increas-
ingly I was down in Deepak's basement, the two of us first smoking
a couple of spleefs of hashish, and then, my God, four hours gone,
just like that, and we were still twirling handles and sending those
little wooden men into deadly head spins.

On the Friday before I was supposed to meet Abhidha's university friends in an East End flat, I went down to Deepak's basement, and there were two giggly English girls sunk like plump little
peaches among the beanbags. Deepak introduced me to Angie, a
chubby little thing with an upturned nose, her blond hair swirled
up in a kind of rat's nest and fastened atop her head with hairpins.
She wore a shiny black miniskirt, and the way she was reclined in
that beanbag, I kept on getting a peek of her blue cotton panties.
And those chubby white legs, I tell you, swinging open and shut,
banging up against my knee.

We chatted for I'm not sure how long, and then, when I passed
Angie the joint, she put her hand on my leg, ran her chipped nail
polish down the seam of my jeans, and I got all pokey down there.
In no time, heavy snogging. Well, I won't go into all the details, but
she and I, we eventually went over to her house—her parents were
gone for the weekend—and spent two days in bed.

I never went to Abhidha's party. I never even called to say
I wouldn't be there, just didn't show up. A few days later, full of
remorse, I did call, again and again. And when Abhidha finally
came to the phone, to listen to my groveling apologies, she was as
lovely as she always was.

"It's all right, Hassan," she said. "It's not the end of the world. I'm
a big girl. But I do think it's time you found someone your own age
to be with. Don't you agree?"

This, then, became my lifelong pattern with women: as soon as things between us were on the verge of becoming close, I withdrew. Difficult to admit, but my sister Mehtab—who oversees the restaurant's accounts and maintains my flat—is really the only woman I have ever maintained a relationship with over time. And she insists my emotional clock stopped, that part to do with women, when Mummy died.

Perhaps. But remember this, too: freed from the emotional demands of wife and children, I was able to spend my life in the warm embrace of the kitchen.

But back to the rest of the Haji family, none of whom were faring much better. We didn't think anything wrong, at first, when Ammi sang the old Gujarati songs and forgot our names. But then she became obsessed with her teeth, pulling her lips wide as she forced us children to examine her diseased gums, the rotten and bleeding stumps that made us gag. And I'll always remember that horrible night when I came home, opened the front door, only to see Ammi becoming incontinent on her way up the staircase, a river of urine running down her leg.

It was, however, my irritating London-born cousin who first made us aware Ammi was suffering from dementia. Every time the university boy strutted through the General's Hole—lecturing us on macroeconomic this and money-supply that—tiny Ammi could be seen quietly maneuvering herself to his side of the room. He would go on so, and then, midsentence, he would yelp in pain, furiously turning on the tiny crouching figure behind him. The sight of his Indian bum squeezed into a pair of Ralph Lauren slacks simply set her off, and our roars commanding her to stop pinching his bottom only incited her to chase the poor boy through the halls. My cousin got even, however. It was he who spelled out to us in clinical detail how Ammi's mental health was deteriorating.

But she was not alone. A kind of madness was in the air.

Mehtab became unduly preoccupied with her hair, ceaselessly primping for men who never came to take her out. And I myself retreated into the basement haze of hashish and foosball.

* * *

But even in hell there are moments when the light reaches you. One day, plodding to the Southall branch of the Bank of Baroda on an errand for Auntie, a shiny object caught my eye. It was what the English call a "chippie"—a food cart—standing between Ramesh "Tax Free!" Jewelry and a cash-and-carry selling bolts of faux-silk. The chippie had been modified: a silhouette of a train cut from sheet metal was oddly bolted to the front of it. JALEBI JUNCTION, read the sign overhead.

The odd stall, I suddenly realized, was designed to sell the delicious deep-fried dessert that Bappu the cook used to buy for me at Crawford Market. A pang of homesickness and a craving for the old taste suddenly hit with great force, but the unmanned cart was cold and chained to a lamppost. I shuffled forward and read the pink sheet of paper taped to the carriage, fluttering forlornly in the wind: PART TIME HELP WANTED. ENQUIRIES: BATICA CHIPS.

That night I dreamed I was driving a train, joyously blowing its whistle. The caboose rolled through stunning, snow-peaked mountains, taking me through a world rich beyond my wildest imagination, and I was exhilarated at never knowing what new sight lay in store for me through the next alpine tunnel.

I did not know what the dream meant, but the movement of the train spoke to me somehow, and the next morning, like a shot, I was down on the High Street. Batica Chips was one of Southall's two "quality sweet manufacturers," its windows filled with honey and pistachio and coconut shreds. The door tinkled when I entered and the shop itself smelled of dried banana chips. A large woman ahead of me was preordering pounds of galum jamun, fried curd in syrup. When she left I handed in the pink note torn from the Jalebi Junction and timorously announced I'd like the job.

"Not strong enough," said the unshaven baker in his white coat, not even looking at me as he filled a carton with almond crescents.

"I'll work hard. Look. Strong legs."

The sweets merchant shook his head, and I realized my job application was already over, case dismissed. But I stood my ground.

Refused to budge. And eventually the man's wife came over and squeezed my skinny arm. She smelled of flour and curry.

"Ahmed, he'll do," she said. "But pay him the minimum."

And so, not long afterward, I was wheeling the Jalebi Junction down Broadway High Street, in my Batica Chips uniform, selling sticky twists of jalebi to children and their grandparents.

The Jalebi Junction job paid £3.10 an hour, and it consisted of making the house-style runny paste of condensed milk and flour in a cheesecloth, and then squeezing a continuous looping string of the mixture into the boiling oil. Squiggly loops, like pretzels. When done, I scooped the golden dollops of jalebi from the vat of boiling oil, dipped them in syrup, then carefully wrapped the sticky things in wax paper for the outstretched hands, collecting eighty pence.

I can still feel the joy that was triggered by the sound of the simmering oil and my manly voice crying out in the street. By the smell of syrup and the cool feel of wax paper against my hands splattered and scarred by hot fat. Sometimes I'd roll the Junction to a spot in front of the Kwik Fit, or, if the spirit took me, sometimes outside the Harmony Hair Salon. Such a sense of freedom. And I will always be grateful to England for this, for helping me realize my place in the world was nowhere else but standing before a vat of boiling oil, my feet wide apart.

Our departure was as abrupt as our arrival two years earlier.

And I, consciously or unconsciously, was the architect of our hasty exit from Britain.

It was women. Again.

I missed the Napean Sea Road and the restaurant and I missed Mummy. It was in this feverish state of longing, alone sneaking a cigarette in our backyard one evening, that I felt a cool hand on the back of my head.

"What's up, Hassan?"

It was dark and I could not see her face.

But I could smell the patchouli oil.

Cousin Aziza's voice was soft and—I don't know why—but her sweet tone touched me.

I couldn't help it. Tears rolled down my face.

"I miss my old life."

I sniffled and rubbed my nose on my shirtsleeve.

Aziza's fingers softly twisted my hair.

"Poor boy," she whispered, lips against my ear. "Poor thing."

And then we were kissing, hot tongues down each other's throats, groping through the clothes, while all the time I was thinking: Bloody marvelous. Another girl you really feel something for—and this time she is your bloody cousin.

"Aaaaiieee."

We looked up.

Auntie was banging at us from the other side of the glass doors, and her downturned mouth had that famous bitter-lemon look.

"Abbas," Auntie screeched behind the glass.

"Come quick! It's Hassan. And the Toilet Seat."

"Shit," Aziza said.

Two days later Aziza was on a plane to Delhi and relations between Uncle Sami's family and ours were cut. Papa got a bill for work on the house that Uncle Sami claimed to have done. There was great drama, tears—blows, even—and screaming matches in the streets of Southall between Papa and Mummy's relatives. But the uproar finally woke Papa from his deep sleep. He threw off the blanket and for the first time really looked around that Southall house, at what had become of us, and a few days later three second-hand Mercedes stood in front of the house—one red, one white, one black. Just like fishmonger Anwar's phones.

"Come on," he said. "Time to go."

Mukhtar celebrated our exit from England by promptly throwing up creamy prawns and pasta all over the ferry bound for Calais. But then the trip began in earnest: our Mercedes caravan ran through Belgium and Holland, into Germany, then, in rapid succession, Austria, Italy, Switzerland, before winding mountain roads led us back into France.

Harrods Food Hall had profoundly affected Papa. Now acutely aware of his limitations, he decided to expand his knowledge of the world, and in his book that simply meant systematically eating his way across Europe, tasting any local dish that was new and possibly tasty. So, we ate mussels and beer in Belgium bars; roast goose with red cabbage in a dark German *stube.* There was a sweaty dinner of venison in Austria; polenta in the Dolomites; white wine and *Felchen,* a bony lake fish, in Switzerland.

After the bitterness of Southall the early weeks of that trip through Europe were like the first taste of a crème brûlée. In particular I recall our whirlwind trip through Tuscany, in the golden light of late August, when our cars rolled into Cortona and to a mustard-colored *pensione* built into the side of the brushy mountain.

Shortly after we arrived in the medieval hillside town we discovered, much by chance, the locals were in the midst of their annual porcini mushroom festival. As the sun set over the valley and Lake Trasimeno, Papa had us in line at the gates of Cortona's terraced park, the promenade under the cypress trees festively decorated with fairy lights and wooden tables and jam jars of wildflowers.

The fête was in full swing, with a clarinet and snare drum pickety-picketing the tarantella and a couple of aged couples kicking up their heels on a wooden platform. It appeared as if the entire town was out in force, the throngs of children clamoring for cotton candy and roasted almonds, but we still managed to claim an unoccupied wooden table under a chestnut tree. Around us the locals carried on, a swirl of grandparents and baby carriages and laughter and the gesticulations of local chatter.

"*Menu completo trifolato,*" Papa ordered.

"Nah?" said Auntie.

"Quiet."

"What do you mean quiet? Don't tell me to be quiet! Why everyone shushing me all the time? I want to know what you have ordered."

"Must you know everything?" Papa fumed at his sister. "It's mushroom, yaar. Local mushroom."

It certainly was. What came was plate after plate of Pasta ai Porcini and Scaloppine ai Porcini and Contorno di Porcini. One porcini after another porcini, plastic plates streaming out of the tent from across the park, where local women in aprons and dusted with flour dressed mushrooms that looked alarmingly like soggy slivers of liver. And to the tent's side, a giant vat of sizzling oil, the size of a California hot tub, but rather endearingly shaped like a giant frying pan, the handle artfully piping out the fryer's gassy fumes. And around the vat stood three men, fat, in massive toques, dunking the flour-dusted porcini into the sizzling oil while they roared instructions at one another and sipped from paper cups of red wine.

For three days we soaked up the Tuscan heat and swam, gathering every night for dinner on the *pensione* roof terrace as the sun set over the mountains.

"*Cane,*" Papa informed the waiter. "*Cane rosto.*"

"Papa! You just ordered a roast dog."

"No. No. I didn't. He understood."

"You mean *carne. Carne.*"

"Oh, yes. Yes. *Carne rosto.* And *un piatto di Mussolini.*"

The perplexed waiter finally retired once we explained Papa wanted a plate of mussels, not the dictator on a dish. Waves of Tuscan food soon broke over the table as a nighttime musk of lavender and sage and citrus wafted over us from a border of terra-cotta pots. We ate wild asparagus served with *fagiole,* fat slabs of beef perfectly charbroiled on wood fires, walnut biscotti dunked in the patron's own Vin Santo. And laughter, once again laughter.

Heaven on earth, no?

Ten weeks after we started our trip across Europe we were back in our funk. The family had become dead tired of all the driving and Papa's restless rushing to nowhere, these arbitrary scratches in his dog-eared copy of *Le Bottin Gourmand.* And the eating in restaurants, week in, week out, it had become sickening. We would have killed for our own kitchen and a simple potato-and-cauliflower fry-up. But for us, yet another day packed in the cars like in tiffin tins, elbow to elbow, the windows all steamed up.

And on that October day in the lesser mountains of France when it all came to an end, things were particularly bad. Ammi wept silently in the backseat as the rest of us bickered and Father roared at us to be quiet. After a series of sickening turns up a mountainside, we came upon a pass covered in frosty boulders. The place was eerily shrouded in cold fog. The ski lift was closed, as was a shuttered café in cement, and we passed through without comment into another mountainside descent.

Over that ridge, however, on the other side of the mountain, the fog abruptly lifted, a blue sky opened up, and we were suddenly surrounded by sun-dappled pines and clean streams running through the woods and shooting under the road.

Twenty minutes later we came out of the forest into a sloped pasture, the silky grass dotted with white and blue wildflowers. And as we turned at a hairpin in the road, we spied the valley and village below us, a vista of glacier blue trout streams sparkling under a cloudless autumn day in the French Jura.

Our cars, as if intoxicated by the beauty, swayed drunkenly down the meandering road into the valley. Church bells tolled out across the plowed fields; a wild woodcock darted across the sky, disappearing in the russet and gold leaves of a birch-tree clump. Up on the gentler slopes, men carrying baskets on their backs harvested the last grape bunches between rows of vines, and behind them rose the crisp white tops of the granite mountains.

And the air, oh, that air. Crisp and clean. Even Ammi stopped her wailing. Our cars sailed past wooden farmhouses with antlers nailed over barn doors, bell-clanking cowherds, a yellow postal van bobbing across the fields. And in the flat-bottomed valley we crossed a wooden bridge, entering the town of stone.

The Mercedes lurched through the village's narrow eighteenth-century lanes—past cobblestone alleys, past the shoe shop, past watch boutiques. Two chatting mothers pushed baby carriages across the crosswalk to a pâtisserie and tearoom; a portly businessman mounted steps to a corner bank. There was something elegant about the town, as if it had some proud past, and it left a pleasant impression of guild houses and leaded windows, of old church spires and green shutters and World War I memorials carved in stone.

But finally we had circled the town's square—boxes of yellow carnations and a fountain of water-spitting fish at its center—and headed back out of town on the N7, over a roaring river that came down from the Alps. And I distinctly remember looking out the window of the car and seeing a man fishing the river's fast waters with grasshoppers, the entire bank behind him a stunning carpet of bluebells.

"Papa, can't we stop here?" asked Mehtab.

"No. I want to reach Auxonne for lunch. Guidebook says they have very good tongue. With a Madeira sauce."

Not for the first time in my life the outside world seemed to respond to my inner needs.

"Wah dis? Wah dis?"

The car belched black smoke and shuddered. Papa smacked the wheel, but the car wouldn't respond, and he guided us to the side of the road. The younger children screamed with delight as we all piled out of the backseats into the crisp country air.

Our car died on a leafy street of bourgeois limestone houses and potted chimneys and window boxes bursting with geraniums. Behind the houses, apple orchards sloped up hills, and I could just see the tops of headstones jutting up from the local cemetery and church.

My younger brothers and sisters played tag in the street—a terrier yapping at them from behind an old stone wall—as delicious smells of burning wood and hot bread wafted over us from a nearby house.

Father cursed and banged the car hood with his fist. Uncle got out of the second car and gratefully stretched his back before joining Papa over the stalled engine. Auntie and Ammi gathered the hems of their saris and went in search of a bathroom. My oldest brother, alone in the last car, which was overloaded with our valises and bundled luggage, morosely lit a cigarette.

Papa wiped his oily hands on a rag and looked up. I could see he was exhausted, his immense energy finally drained of its reserves. He took a deep breath, rubbed his eyes, and a gust of oxygen-rich air suddenly ruffled his hair. He must have felt the breeze's invigorating presence, for that was when he really looked at the pristine alpine beauty around him for the first time. And as he looked about, breathing effortlessly through his nose for the first time in almost two years, he leaned against a gate, the wooden board next to him wobbling.

The mansion we'd broken down in front of was stately, and even from the road we could see it was beautifully carved from fine stone. On the other side of the self-contained estate, a stable and gatekeeper's lodge stood below linden trees, and a tangle of thick ivy grew along the top of the stone wall encircling the property. "The sign says it's for sale," I said.

A powerful thing, destiny.

You can't run from it. Not in the end.

Lumière, we later discovered, had been a vibrant watchmaking center during the eighteenth century, but the town had shrunk to twenty-five thousand and was now mostly known for a few award-winning wines. The main industries were an aluminum siding factory, located in a modest industrial zone twenty kilometers down toward the mouth of the valley, and three family-run sawmills dotting the foothills. In dairy circles the town had built a minor reputation on a soft cheese, aged with a layer of charcoal in its middle. And the name itself, Lumière, came from the way the early morning light bounced off the Jura granite, suffusing one side of the valley with a pink luminescence.

Papa and Uncle Mayur, unable to revive the car, walked back into the center of town, returning an hour later, not with a garage mechanic, but with a provincial real estate agent sprouting a foulard from his blazer pocket. The three men disappeared inside the house, and we children ran after them, from room to room, our feet clattering over the wooden floors.

The estate agent talked very fast in a sort of Franglais, but we managed to understand a Monsieur Jacques Dufour, a minor eighteenth-century inventor of watch wheels, had built the mansion. We all marveled at the old kitchen, big and airy, with hand-painted pantries and a stone fireplace. Papa broached the idea of a restaurant and the agent thought that most assuredly an Indian restaurant would do well in the area. "You have field to yourself," he said, waving his hands with enthusiasm. "There is no Indian restaurant in this entire section of France."

Besides, the man said gravely, the house was a very good investment. Demand for housing should pick up shortly and push prices up. He had personally heard in the Town Hall that the Printemps Department Store was on the threshold of announcing a 750,000-square meter warehouse in Lumière's industrial zone.

We came out again into the courtyard, the air pink and the top of the Jura Alps sharply white over the mansion's slate roof.

"Wah you say, Mayur?"

Uncle scratched his crotch and mysteriously looked off to the mountains in a noncommittal way. But that's what he always did when asked to make a decision.

"Good, yaar?" continued Papa. "Certainly clear to me. We have new home."

Our Period of Mourning was officially over. It was time for the Haji family to get on with life, to start a new chapter, to finally put behind us our lost years. And at long last we were back where we belonged, back in the restaurant business. For good or for worse, Lumière was the spot of earth where we would dig in our heels.

But of course no family is an island unto itself. It is always part of a larger culture, a community, and we had traded in our familiar Napean Sea Road, even the Asian familiarity of Southall, for a world we knew absolutely nothing about. I suppose that was the point. Papa always wanted to start again fresh, to take us as far away as possible from Mumbai and the tragedy. Well, Lumière certainly was that place. This was, after all, *la France profonde*—deepest France.

It was then—as I stood on the second-floor landing and all around me my shrill brothers and sisters banged doors—I first noticed the building across the street from the Dufour estate.

The building was an equally elegant mansion in the same silver gray stone. A mature willow tree commanded almost the entire front garden, and, like some curtsying Louis XIV courtier, its fluid limbs bowed elegantly over the wooden fence and the town's flag-stone sidewalk. Crisp goose-down duvets hung out for airing from the two top windows, and over their white humps I spotted a green-velvet bedside lampshade, a brass candelabra, dried sprigs of lilac in a translucent vase. A battered-black Citroën was parked on the gravel drive below, before the old stable that served as a garage, and weather-beaten stone steps ran up along the rock garden on the side of the house, up to the polished oak door. And there, swinging ever so slightly in the breeze, a discreet shingle overhead. Le Saule Pleureur—The Weeping Willow—a several-crowned inn.

I can still recall that wondrous first glimpse of Le Saule Pleureur. It was, to me, more stunning than the Taj in Bombay. It wasn't its size, but its perfection: the lichen-covered rock garden, the fluffy white duvets, the old stables with the leaded windows. Everything fit perfectly, the very essence of understated European elegance that was so completely foreign to my own upbringing.

But the more I try and recall that moment when I first set eyes on Le Saule Pleureur, the more certain I am I also saw a white face looking darkly down at me from an attic window.

Lumière

Chapter Five

The old woman staring down at me from the window across the street from so many years ago, that first day we moved into the Dufour estate, that face belonged to Madame Gertrude Mallory. The story I tell is God's truth, even if I did not witness every event firsthand; the fact is many of the details of my own story were revealed to me only years after the fact, when Mallory and the others at long last told me their version of events.

But this you must know: Madame Mallory, across the street from the Dufour estate, was an innkeeper from a long line of distinguished hoteliers, originally from the Loire. She was also very much the culinary nun, a chef who had lived alone in the attic rooms above Le Saule Pleureur for thirty-four years by the time we arrived in Lumière. Just as the Bach family turned out classical musicians, so, too, the Mallorys had reared generation after generation of great French hoteliers, and Gertrude Mallory was no exception.

At the age of seventeen, Mallory was sent to the best hotel school in Geneva to continue her education, and it was there she acquired a taste for the rugged mountain range along the French and Swiss border. An awkward, sharp-tongued young woman with little talent for making friends, Mallory spent her spare time hiking alone through the Alps and the Jura, until one weekend she discovered Lumière. Shortly after her graduation an aunt died and left Mallory an inheritance, and the young chef promptly converted her windfall into a large house in this mountain outpost, remote Lumière perfectly suiting her taste for the austere life of the kitchen.

And there she went to work. Over the next decades Mallory diligently applied her first-rate education and stamina for long hours in the kitchen, building what cognoscenti eventually considered one of France's finest small country hotels—Le Saule Pleureur.

She was a classicist by education and instinct. A rare collection of cookbooks consumed her private attic rooms from floor to ceiling, an archive that grew like a fungus above and around her good pieces of furniture, such as the seventeenth-century gueridon or the Louis XV–style walnut bergère armchair. The book collection was, it must be said, of international renown, built discreetly over thirty years by simply applying her good eye and a modest amount of money to the nation's book bins and country auctions.

Her most valuable book was an early edition of *De Re Coquinaria* by Apicius, the only surviving cookbook of ancient Rome. On her days off Mallory frequently sipped chamomile tea and sat alone in her attic flat with this rare document on her lap, lost in the past, marveling at the sheer range of the Roman kitchen. She so admired Apicius's versatility, how he could handle dormice and flamingos and porcupines just as easily as pork and fish.

Of course, even though most of Apicius's recipes were quite incompatible with modern palates—relying as they did on sickening doses of honey—Mallory did possess an inquisitive mind. And as she also had a taste for testicles, particularly a fighting bull's *criadillas* prepared Basque-style, Madame Mallory inevitably and most memorably re-created for her guests Apicius's recipe for *lumbuli*—*lumbuli* being the Latin for the testicles of young bulls that the Roman chef stuffed with pine nuts and powdered fennel seed, then pan-seared in olive oil and fish pickle before roasting in the oven. Well, that was the kind of chef Mallory was. Classical, but challenging, always challenging. Even of her guests.

The *De Re Coquinaria,* of course, was only the oldest cookbook in her library. The collection rolled right through time, documenting century after century of changing culinary tastes and epochs, ending finally with the handwritten 1907 version of *Margaridou: The Journal of an Auvergne Cook,* and that simple countrywoman's recipe for the classic French onion soup.

But it was precisely this rigorous intellectual approach to cuisine that made Madame Mallory a chef's chef, a master technician much admired by the other leading chefs of France. And it was this reputation among the cognoscenti that one day prompted a national television station to invite Mallory up to Paris for a studio interview.

Lumière was a rather provincial outpost, so it was not surprising Madame Mallory's television debut became a local event, villagers all across the valley tuning in to FR3 to watch their very own Madame Mallory rattle off fascinating culinary facts on air. And as the villagers sipped rough marc in the town's bars or in the comforts of farmhouse parlors, a flickering Mallory up on the box explained how, during the nineteenth century's Franco-Prussian War, starving Parisians survived the long Prussian siege of their capital by eating dogs, cats, and rats. There was an amazed roar when Madame Mallory explained that the 1871 edition of *Larousse Gastronomique,* quite simply the text of classic French cuisine, recommended skinning and gutting rats found in wine cellars—so much more flavorful. It further advised, the chef haughtily informed the television audience, rubbing the rat in olive oil and crushed shallots, grilling it over a wood fire made from smashed wine barrels, and serving it with a Bordelaise sauce, but Curnonsky's recipe, of course. Well, you can imagine. Instantly Madame Mallory was a minor celebrity across all France, not just in little Lumière.

The point is, Mallory never relied on her family connections but had, in her own right, earned her place among France's culinary establishment. And she took seriously the responsibility that came with this elite position, tirelessly writing letters to the papers when it was necessary to safeguard France's culinary traditions from the meddling of the EU bureaucrats in Brussels, so eager to impose their ridiculous standards. In particular it was her *cri du coeur* in defense of French butchering methods—printed in the radical booklet *Vive La Charcuterie Française*—that was so much admired by the nation's opinion makers.

And that was why the space around Mallory's priceless collection of antique cookbooks was stuffed with framed awards and letters of appreciation, from Valéry Giscard d'Estaing and Baron de Rothschild and Bernard Arnault. The flat simply reflected a lifetime of considerable achievement, including a letter from the

Élysée Palace on the occasion of her Chevalier de l'Ordre des Arts et des Lettres.

There was, however, still one small bit of unoccupied wall in her crowded top-floor flat, a bald spot just above her favorite red leather armchair. In this corner of her quarters Mallory hung her most prized possessions, two gilt-framed articles, each clipped from *Le Monde*. The article on the left announced her first Michelin star, in May 1979. The article on the right, dated March 1986, announced her second star. Mallory had reserved an empty space on the wall for the third article. It had not come.

And there we are. Madame Mallory reached her sixty-fifth birthday the day before we arrived in Lumière, and that evening her loyal manager, Monsieur Henri Leblanc, along with the rest of Le Saule Pleureur's staff, gathered in the kitchen at closing to present her with a cake and to sing happy birthday.

Mallory was furious. She sharply told them there was nothing to celebrate and they should stop wasting her time. And before they could grasp what had happened, Mallory was stomping up Le Saule Pleureur's darkened wooden staircase to her private rooms in the attic.

That night, when she passed through her sitting room on her way to bed, Madame Mallory once again saw the empty space on the wall, and a parallel bit of emptiness opened up in her heart. She took this ache into her room, sat on the bed, and involuntarily gasped at the thought that suddenly thrust itself into her head.

She would never get her third star.

Mallory could not move. Finally, however, she undressed silently in the dark, the stiff girdle peeling off her like an avocado skin. She shrugged on her nightgown and passed through to the bathroom for the usual bedtime rituals. She brushed her teeth violently, gargled, and lathered anti-wrinkle creams into her face.

An elderly woman's pale face stared back. The digital clock in her bedroom flipped a minute shingle loudly.

The realization came then, so big and ugly and monstrous she closed her eyes and brought a hand to her mouth. But there it was. Unavoidable.

She was a failure.

Never would she rise above her current station in life. Never would she join that pantheon of three-star chefs. Only death awaited her.

Madame Mallory could not sleep that night. She stalked the attic, wrung her hands, muttered bitterly to herself about the injustices of life. Bats flitted through the night outside her window snatching bugs, while a lonely dog on the other side of the church cemetery howled its anguish, and together the beasts seemed to perfectly articulate her lonely torment. But finally, in the early hours, unable to stand the pain any longer, Madame Mallory did something she had not done in many, many years. She got down on her hands and knees. And she prayed.

"What . . ." she whispered into her clasped hands, "what is the reason for my life?"

The only sound was emptiness. Nothing.

Shortly thereafter the exhausted woman crawled into her bed, at long last entering a kind of unconscious state among the tangle of her sheets.

Le Saule Pleureur was closed for lunch the following day, so the exhausted Madame Mallory uncharacteristically allowed herself to stay in bed later than usual. She thought it was the pigeon cooing on her windowsill that woke her. But it fluttered away and she finally heard the yelling, the strange voices, the commotion rising up from the street, and Mallory rose stiffly from her bed and crossed the room to the little attic window.

And there we were: ragged Indian children hanging from the Dufour estate's windows and turrets.

She couldn't quite comprehend what was going on. What was this she was seeing? Diesel-belching Mercedes. Yellow and pink saris. A ton of tatty luggage and boxes stacked up in the cobblestone courtyard, Mummy's gray Storwel closet still tied to the roof of the last car.

And in the middle of this courtyard, my bearlike father raising his arms and yelling.

Chapter Six

What blissful early days. Lumière was one big adventure—of unexplored cupboards and attics and stables, of lumberyards and pastry shops and trout streams farther afield—and I remember it as a joyous period that helped us forget our many losses. And Papa, too, was finally restored to himself. For restaurant work was his center, and he immediately commandeered a rickety desk just inside the main doors, burying himself in the details of remaking the Dufour estate in his Bombay image. In no time at all the halls were filled with local craftsmen—plumbers and carpenters—with their tapes and tools and hammering noise, and it was once again the fever of Bombay re-created in this tiny corner of provincial France.

My first real sighting of Madame Mallory was perhaps a week or two after we had moved in. I was strolling through the headstones of the neighboring cemetery, furtively smoking a cigarette, when by chance I glanced over at Le Saule Pleureur. I instantly spotted Madame Mallory on her knees, bent over her rock garden, gloves and spade in hand, humming to herself. The damp stones to her left were warming up under the surprisingly strong morning sun, and trails of steam rose from the rocks, disappearing in the air.

Behind the chef stood the glorious granite slabs of the Alps, bottle green pine forests broken by patches of pasture and hardy cows grazing. Madame Mallory pulled her weeds vigorously, as if it were some satisfying form of therapy, and I could hear, even from where I stood, the violent sound of tearing roots. But I also saw, in the softness of her round face, the woman was calm and at peace tending to her corner of earth.

Right then the stable door across the road slammed open with a mighty bang. Papa and a roofer with a ladder suddenly emerged from the door's shadows and they hobbled over to the front of the house. The roofer secured the ladder against the guttering while Papa roared, waddled back and forth across the courtyard in his armpit-stained kurta, and by sheer heckling backseat-drove the poor roofer up the ladder.

"No, no," he yelled. "The gutter over there. Over there. Are you deaf? Yaaar. That one."

The tranquillity of the Jura was shattered. Madame Mallory wrenched her head sideways, her eyes rooted on Papa. She was squinting under the straw garden hat, her liver-colored lips pressed tightly together. I could see she was both horrified and strangely mesmerized by Papa's grotesque size and vulgarity. But the moment passed. Mallory lowered her eyes and pulled off her canvas gloves. Her quiet gardening moment was ruined, and, clutching her basket, she wearily climbed back up the stone steps to the inn.

Her back was to the street when she hesitated after unlocking the front door, just as a particularly virulent burst of Papa's roars rolled across the forecourt. From where I was standing, off to the side, I saw the look on her face as she paused before her door—the lips pursed in utter disgust, the face a mask of icy disdain. It was a look that I would see many times again as I made my way through France in the coming years—a uniquely Gallic look of nuclear contempt for one's inferiors—but I will never forget the first time I saw it.

Then, bang, the slam of the door.

The family discovered the local *pain chemin de fer*—rough and gnarled and tasty—and this "railroad" bread immediately became our new sauce-mopping favorite. Papa and Auntie were constantly asking me to pick up "just a few more" loaves at the *boulangerie,* and on one such foray, cutting back from the town center with the crusty bread wrapped in paper under my arm, through the back alleys where the wealthy watch merchants once kept their horses, I casually glanced over a stone-and-stucco wall.

It was, I quickly realized, the back view of Le Saule Pleureur. The small hotel's garden was quite long and deep, almost a field, and it gently sloped down a hill to where I stood. The verdant property was filled with mature pear and apple trees, and against the far wall there stood a fruit-drying shed made of rough Lumière granite.

The boughs of the trees were bent with heavy brown Bosc pears, ready for the picking, and autumn bees were buzzing drunkenly around the sugar-filled fruit. But there were also tidy rows of boxed herbs under glass next to bow-shaped beds of wildflowers and patches for cabbages and rhubarb and carrots, all neatly embroidered by a flagstone path that ambled through the garden's fertile plots.

Down at the bottom of the garden, a compost heap stood in the moist corner to the left, while an iron-and-copper tap in the shape of a nymph gurgled water into a heavy stone trough off to the right, next to a bench and yet another ancient and majestic willow tree.

I stopped in my tracks. Madame Mallory was again in her garden, this time up at the top of her field, just before it began to roll downhill. She sat upright at a long wooden table, next to who I assumed was one of her sous chefs, for both women wore peacoats over kitchen whites.

I could not, not at first, see their faces because both had their heads down as they worked briskly and professionally at the table filled with bowls and platters and utensils. But I could see there was something in Madame Mallory's hand, which she promptly dropped into a bowl. Then, without pause, she reached down with her other hand into the rough wooden crate sitting on the flagstone between the two of them. From the crate, Mallory pulled what to me looked like a bizarre form of spiky hand grenade. I later discovered it was an artichoke.

I watched the famous chef expertly trim the vegetable's leaves with a pair of scissors, the smart snips of her flashing tool ensuring each ragged leaf of the artichoke was symmetrically aligned and aesthetically pleasing to the eye, like she was tidying up after nature. She then picked up one of the lemons that had been cut in half, and doused each of the artichoke wounds—wherever she had snipped a leaf—with a generous squirt of lemon juice. Artichokes contain an acid, cynarin, and this neat trick, I later learned, prevented the sap-oozing leaves from discoloring the vegetable around its wound.

Next, Madame Mallory used a heavy and sharp knife to cleanly take off the top of the artichoke with a firm downward crunch of the blade. For a few seconds her head was down again, as she plucked some pink, immature leaves from the plant's center. Picking up a new utensil, she cut at the inner artichoke and elegantly scooped out the thicket of thistle fuzz called the choke. You could see the satisfaction in her face when she finally and surgically removed the soft prize of the artichoke's heart and set it aside in a bowl of marinade, already heaped with succulent and mushy cups.

It was a revelation. Never before had I seen a chef take such meticulous artistic care, particularly not with something as ugly as this vegetable.

St. Augustine's bells chimed noon. The crate was almost empty, but the young sous chef at Chef Mallory's side was trailing the older woman, not quite as quick as her *maîtresse*. Madame Mallory, studying her sous chef, abruptly held out the small knife she herself had been using and said, not unkindly, "Margaret, use the grapefruit knife. It's a trick *Maman* taught me. The bent blade makes it much easier to remove the choke."

There was something in Madame Mallory's gravelly voice—not quite maternal, no, but still strongly suggestive of a kind of culinary noblesse oblige and duty to pass the techniques of the kitchen on to the next generation—and it was that inflection that instantly made me sit up.

As it did the young chef, who lifted her head, to gratefully take Madame Mallory's grapefruit knife. "*Merci, madame*," she said, in a voice that, as it wafted down to me with the wind, seemed redolent of fresh red berries and cream.

It was my first good look at Margaret Bonnier, Le Saule Pleureur's quiet sous chef. She was clearly just a few years older than myself, and wore a no-nonsense bob of blond hair, just the right length to tuck behind the ears that were rather modishly studded with silver earrings. Her dark eyes were set deep in pale skin, like pearls inside oyster-sized cheeks red from both the sharp wind and the sturdy Jura stock that was her genetic makeup.

My unabashed staring was interrupted at that moment by Le Saule Pleureur's portly apprentice, Marcel, and Jean-Pierre, its darkly handsome *chef de cuisine,* both emerging from the side of the building and carrying the staff's noontime meal, to be gobbled down before the restaurant opened for lunch less than thirty minutes hence. The platter Jean-Pierre held was steaming in the wind, a flat steel tray of minute steaks and *frites,* while Marcel carried cutlery and a glass salad bowl of butter lettuce and chives.

Chef Mallory instructed the apprentice to take the artichokes and their hearts back into the kitchen, while Margaret expertly set the wooden table with the cutlery and napkins and plates, along with glass tumblers, a *vin rouge,* and a carafe of cold Jura well water. As Jean-Pierre leaned in to place the tray at the table's center, Margaret's tapered hand, elegant like a pianist's but scarred by oven burns, darted forward, her long fingers pinching a yellow-golden fry. She brought the shoestring *frite* up to her lips, her teeth delicately biting off its tip, her face lit by a smile provoked by something Jean-Pierre had just said.

The church clock chimed quarter after noon.

I turned to continue on home and to our family lunch of Madras mutton, but as I walked back to the Dufour estate, my heart was fluttering and filled by what I had just witnessed, a scene that instantly brought forth pictures of Mummy and steaks and *frites* and Café de Paris, Bombay memories all richly coming back to me in the streets of that alpine village.

But then, suddenly, a gust of wind came rushing down the mountain, and in one fell swoop these old memories of Mummy and Mother India were swept away, and in their stead stood an entirely new sensation, tremulous at first, but then growing in intensity with each passing step. What came to me in that wind, so long ago, was an intense yearning triggered by the sights and smells of French food intermingled with the musty aroma of women. Perhaps it was something seeded in childhood, but at that moment it crossed over into something else, something more grown-up.

* * *

A few days later, Papa abruptly ordered the entire family out into our courtyard. Even the timid French boy Papa hired as a waiter was forced out, nervously wiping a wineglass on his apron as he stood among us.

The roofer and Umar, up on ladders above us, yanked at pulleys and swung wrenches around bolts. Suddenly, as we stood open-mouthed at their feet, staring up, a large placard arose over the iron Dufour gates.

"There," yelled Umar, high up on the ladder.

MAISON MUMBAI, written in massive gold letters on an Islamic green background, filled the entire billboard.

Such yelling. Such joy.

Hindustani classical music blared out scratchily over makeshift speakers Uncle Mayur had set up in the garden. And that, or so I was later told, was the final straw. Le Saule Pleureur staff, all the way downstairs in the kitchen, heard the shrieks of disbelief coming from the attic. Monsieur Leblanc hastily put down the phone as Madame Mallory flew past his office on the second floor, and he went to the top of the landing to watch his *maîtresse* below him furiously rummage through the *chinoise* stand for her umbrella. It did not look at all good to Leblanc. A kind of African warrior's shield and spear secured a knot of iron hair to the back of Mallory's head.

"This is too much, Henri," she said, finally wrenching the unwieldy umbrella out of the stand. "Did you see that placard? Hear that plinky-plinky music? *Quelle horreur. Non. Non.* He can't do such a thing. Not on my street. He's destroying the ambience. Our customers. What will they think?" But before Leblanc could reply, Chef Mallory was out the door.

Madame Mallory did not do the decent thing. She did not cross the street and talk directly with Papa, try to reason with him. She never tried in any way to make us feel welcome. No, her first impulse was to crush us under her heel. Like we were bugs.

What precisely happened was this: Madame Mallory marched down to the mayor's office. Of course, everyone in Lumière was afraid of the sharp-tongued chef, so, not surprisingly, Mallory was immediately ushered into the Town Hall's boardroom.

And there we should have met our demise. But clever people were always underestimating Papa. He was sharp, sharp as a filleting knife. Papa assumed politics in a small French town were little different from politics in Bombay—all was greased by the oil of commerce—and so his first move in Lumière was to put the mayor's brother, a solicitor, on a hefty retainer. Nothing so crude as what transpired up on Malabar Hill, but just as effective.

"Tell that man to stop," Mallory imperiously ordered the mayor. "That Indian. Have you seen what he is doing? He's turned that beautiful Dufour mansion into a bistro. An Indian bistro! *Horrible.* I can smell that oily cooking all up and down the street. And that placard? *Mais non.* This is not possible."

The mayor shrugged. "What do you want me to do?"

"Shut him down."

"Monsieur Haji is opening a restaurant in the same zone as you, Gertrude. If I shut him down I have to shut you down as well. And his lawyer won permission from the Planning Committee for the placard. So, you see, my hands are tied. Monsieur Haji has done everything correct."

"*Mais non.* This is not possible."

"But it is," continued the mayor. "I can't close him down without justification. He is acting completely within the law."

Her parting remark, I understand, was singularly unpleasant.

Our first face-to-face with *la grande dame* took place three days later. Mallory arose at six every morning. After she ate a light breakfast of pears and buttered toast and strong coffee, Monsieur Leblanc drove her to Lumière's markets in the beaten-up Citroën. You could set your watch by their ritual. Promptly at six forty-five Monsieur Leblanc retired with the newspaper *Le Jura* to Café Bréguet, where some of the locals were at the bar and already on the day's first *ballon* of wine. Meanwhile, Mallory in her gray flannel poncho and wicker baskets on each arm made her way from market stall to market stall, buying fresh produce for the day's menu.

Mallory was a magnificent sight to behold, pounding the streets like a workhorse, each of her hard breaths exploding in white smoke. The bulk orders—a half dozen rabbits, perhaps, or fifty-kilo sacks of potatoes—were delivered by van to Le Saule Pleureur no later than nine thirty a.m. But the chanterelles and the delicate Belgium endive and perhaps a paper cone of juniper berries, they went into the baskets hanging from Mallory's meaty arms.

On that particular morning, just weeks after we arrived in town, Mallory as usual started her shopping at Iten et Fils, the fishmonger that occupied a white-tiled corner shop on Place Prunelle.

"What's that?"

Monsieur Iten bit the corner of his mustache.

"Eh?"

"Behind you. Move. What's that there?"

Iten stepped aside and Madame Mallory got her first good view of a cardboard box on the counter. It took just a second before she knew the claws waving in the air belonged to crayfish scrabbling over one another.

"Wonderful," said Mallory. "I haven't seen crayfish in months. They look fresh and lively. Are they French?"

"*Non, madame.* Spanish."

"Never mind. I'll take them."

"*Non, madame. Je regrette.*"

"*Pardon?*"

Iten wiped a knife on a tea towel.

"I'm sorry Madame Mallory, but he just came in and . . . and . . . bought them."

"Who?"

"Monsieur Haji. And his son."

Mallory squinted. She couldn't quite comprehend what Monsieur Iten had just said. "That Indian? He bought these?"

"*Oui, madame.*"

"Let me get this straight, Iten. I have come to you—and before you, to your father—for over thirty years, every morning, and bought your best fish. And now you are telling me, at some godforsaken hour, an Indian came in here and bought what you knew I would buy? Is that what you are telling me?"

Monsieur Iten looked down at the floor. "I am sorry. But his manner, you see. He is very . . . charming."

"I see. So what, then, are you going to offer me? Yesterday's *moules*?"

"Ah, *non, madame,* please. Don't be like that. You know you are my most valued customer. I . . . I have here some lovely perch."

Iten scurried over to the cooler and took out a silver tray of striped perch, each the size of a child's palm.

"Very fresh, see? Caught this morning in Lac Vissey. You make such lovely perch *amandine,* Madame Mallory. I thought you would like these."

Madame Mallory decided to teach poor Monsieur Iten a lesson and she blew out of the shop like a winter storm. Still furious, she marched up to the open-air market in the square, her heels grinding into the rubbery carpet of discarded cabbage leaves.

At first Mallory flew through the two rows of vegetable stalls like a bird of prey, her eyes darting about over the shoulders of housewives. The vendors saw her but knew it was unwise to say a word during her first sweep through the market, unless they wanted a vicious tongue-lashing. Her second cruise through, however, one was permitted to engage her, and each farmer did his best to attract the famous chef to his produce.

"*Bonjour, Madame Mallory.* Lovely day. Have you seen my Williams pears?"

"I did, Madame Picard. Not very nice."

The vendor next to Madame Picard guffawed.

"You are wrong," called Madame Picard, sipping a thermos cup of milky coffee. "Wonderful flavor."

Mallory turned back to Madame Picard's stall and the other vendors turned their heads to see what would happen next.

"What's this, Madame Picard?" snapped the chef. Mallory took the top pear off the pyramid and tore off its small sticker proclaiming WILLIAMS QUALITÉ. Under the sticker, a small black hole. Mallory did the same to the next pear, and the next.

"And what's this? And this?"

The other vendors laughed as the red-faced Madame Picard rushed to restack her pears.

"Hiding worm holes under 'quality' stickers. Disgraceful."

Madame Mallory turned her back on the Widow Picard and walked to a stall at the far end of the first row, where a shrunken white-haired couple in matching aprons and looking rather like salt-and-pepper shakers stood behind the counter.

"*Bonjour, Madame Mallory.*"

Mallory grunted a good-morning and pointed to a basket of waxy purple orbs on the floor at the back of the stall.

"I'll take the aubergines. All of them."

"I am sorry, madame, but they are not for sale."

"They've been sold?"

"*Oui, madame.*"

Mallory felt a tightening in her chest. "To the Indian?"

"*Oui, madame.* A half hour ago."

"I'll take the zucchini, then."

The elderly man looked pained. "I am sorry."

For a few moments Mallory was unable to move, to speak even. But suddenly, from the far end of Lumière's markets, a booming voice in accented English rose majestically above the general din.

Mallory's head jerked toward the sound of the voice, and before the elderly farmer couple could recover, Mallory was barging through the early morning market crowd, her baskets bunched in front like a snowplow, forcing the other shoppers out of her way.

Papa and I were at the edges of the market bidding for two dozen red and green Tupperware bowls. The trader—a tough Pole—was holding firm, and Papa's approach to such obstinacy was to roar his price at an ever-louder decibel. The final touch was the menacing pacing back and forth in front of the stall, intimidating other potential customers from coming forward, a tactic I had seen him use to devastating effect in the markets of Bombay.

But in Lumière there was the slight obstacle of language. Papa's only foreign language was English, and it was my job to translate his ravings into my schoolboy French. I did not mind: this was how

I eventually met several girls my age, such as Chantal, the mushroom picker from across the valley, her nails always gritty with dark humus. In this case, however, the Pole across the table could speak no English and just a little French, and that protected him from Papa's full frontal assault. So what we had was a stalemate. The Pole simply crossed his arms across his chest and shook his head.

"What is this?" Papa said, poking a green Tupperware lid. "Just a bit of plastic, no? Anyone can make this."

Madame Mallory deposited herself squarely in front of Papa's path as he paced, and he was suddenly forced to stop short, his great bulk towering over the little woman. I could see this was the last thing he expected—to be stopped by a woman—and he peered down at her with a puzzled expression.

"Wah?"

"I am your neighbor, Madame Mallory, from across the street," she said in excellent English.

Papa gave the woman a dazzling smile, the Pole and the savage Tupperware negotiations instantly forgotten. "Hello," he boomed. "Le Saule Pleureur, nah? I know. You must come over and meet the family. Have tea."

"I don't like what you are doing."

"Wah?"

"To our street. I don't like the music, the placard. It's ugly. So unrefined."

I have not often seen my father at a loss for words, but at this remark he looked as if someone had punched him hard in the stomach.

"It's in very bad taste," Mallory continued, brushing an imaginary thread off her sleeve. "You must take it down. That sort of thing is all right in India, but not here."

She looked him straight in the face, tapped him on the chest with her finger. "And another thing. It is tradition here in Lumière that Madame Mallory has the first choice of the morning's produce. It's been this way for decades. As a foreigner, I appreciate you would have no way of knowing this, but now you do."

She offered Papa a wintry smile.

"It's very important for newcomers to start off on the right foot, don't you agree?"

Papa scowled, his face almost purple, but I who knew him so well could see—in the downturned corners of his eyes—he was not mad but deeply hurt. I moved to his side.

"Who you tink you are?"

"I told you. I am Madame Mallory."

"And I," Papa said, raising his head and slapping his chest, "I am Abbas Haji, Bombay's greatest restaurateur."

"*Pff.* This is France. We are not interested in your curries."

By this time a small crowd had gathered around Madame Mallory and Papa. Monsieur Leblanc pushed his way into the center of the ring. "Gertrude," he said sternly. "Let us go." He pulled at her elbow. "Come, now. Enough."

"Who you tink you are?" repeated Papa, stepping forward. "Wah dis talk in third person like maharani? Who you? God give you right to all best cuts of meat and fish in the Jura? Nah? Oh, then perhaps you own dis town. Yaar? Is that what give you right to the fresh produce every morning? Or perhaps you are some big important memsahib who owns the farmers?"

Papa thrust his enormous belly at Madame Mallory and she had to step back, a look of incredulity slapped across her face.

"How dare you talk to me in this impertinent manner."

"Tell me," he roared at the onlookers, "does this woman own your farms and your livestock and vegetables, or do you sell to highest bidder?" He smacked his palm. "I pay cash. No waiting."

There was a gasp from the crowd. This they understood.

Mallory swiftly turned her back on Papa and shrugged on a pair of black leather gloves.

"*Un chien méchant,*" she said dryly. The assembled crowd laughed.

"What she say?" Papa roared at me. "Wah?"

"I think she called you a mad dog."

What happened then is forever burned in my memory. The crowd parted for Madame Mallory and Monsieur Leblanc as they began to leave, but Papa, agile for a man of his size, quickly ran forward and stuck his face close to the chef's retreating ear.

"Bowwow. Roooff. Rooff."

Mallory jerked her head away. "Stop it."

"Rooff. Rooff."

"Stop it. Stop it you . . . you horrible man."

"Grrrrr. Rooff."

Mallory covered her ears with her hands.

And then she broke into a trot.

The villagers, never before having seen Madame Mallory ridiculed, roared with amazed laughter and Papa turned and joyously joined them, watching the elderly woman and Monsieur Leblanc disappear behind the Banque Nationale de Paris on the corner.

We should have known then what trouble was ahead. "She was jabbering away like a madwoman," Auntie told us when we came home. "Slam car door. Pang." And over the next days, as I glanced across the street, I periodically spotted a pointy nose pressed up against the fogged windowpane.

Maison Mumbai's opening day approached. Lorries backed into the Dufour courtyard: tables came from Lyon, dishware from Chamonix, plastic menu folders from Paris. One day a hip-high wooden elephant, trumpeting, suddenly greeted me as I entered the restaurant's doors. A hookah went into the corner of the lobby, and brass bowls on little tables were filled with plastic roses purchased at the local cash-and-carry.

By now the carpenters had converted the three reception rooms into the restaurant's dining room, and across the teak-paneled walls Papa hung posters of the Ganges, the Taj Mahal, Kerala tea plantations. On one wall he had a local artisan paint a mural of Indian life—of a village woman hauling water from a well, of all things. And all day while we worked speakers on the walls blasted out geets and ghazals, the warbling Urdu ballads and love poems of our heritage.

Papa was Big Abbas again. He worked for days with my oldest brother designing and redesigning an advertisement for the local newspapers. They finally settled their differences in a note-book of inky scratches, driving their design to Le Jura's office in Clairvaux-les-Lacs. A silhouette of a trumpeting elephant, usually between the sports and television listings, filled an entire page of the newspaper. The balloon coming out of the elephant's mouth offered everyone who showed up at Maison Mumbai's opening night a free carafe of wine. The ad ran in Le Jura three weekends in a row. The restaurant's slogan: "Maison Mumbai—la culture indi-enne en Lumière."

And I, at the age of eighteen, finally took up my calling. It was Papa's idea, ordering me into the kitchen. Ammi was simply inca-pable of serving a hundred people at a time, and my aunt was the only woman in all India who could not cook. Not even an onion bhaji. But I choked, suddenly afraid of my destiny. "I am a boy," I yelled. "Make Mehtab do it."

Papa swatted me across the back of my head. "She got other tings to do," he roared. "You spend more time than anyone else in the kitchen with Ammi and Bappu. Don't worry. You're just ner-vous, yaar. We'll help."

And so my days disappeared in belching smoke and the steamy rattle of pots. Tentatively, backed by constant consultations with my sister and Papa, a rough vision of my menu emerged. I rehearsed and rehearsed until I was sure: lamb brain stuffed with green chut-ney, coated with egg and tawa-grilled; chicken cinnamon masala and beef cooked with vinegar-spices. For side dishes I settled on steamed rice crumpets and cottage cheese simmered with fenu-greek. And as a starter, my personal favorite: clear trotters soup.

The wheel of life was turning. Ammi steadily lost control as I steadily gained it. Dementia had her now, full by the throat. The occasional erratic scene we witnessed in London had become com-monplace, and she drifted in and out of this fragile mental state, only rarely again returning to us in moments of lucidity. I recall her looking over my shoulder, giving me useful tips on how to extract the rich flavor from cardamom, very much like she was in the old days on the Napean Sea Road. Moments later, however, she was frothing at the mouth and cursing me as if I were her worst enemy.

It broke my heart. But with the restaurant opening so soon, I could ill afford hand-wringing, and I instead buried myself in the kadais.

But there were scenes. Ammi's obsessions often fixated on the daal, the chickpea staple of Indian cooking I was making in the kitchen, and we frequently argued over the subject. One day, as I was preparing for the grand opening, I simmered an aromatic mix of onions, garlic, and daal. Ammi wandered over and smacked me hard on the arm with a spoon.

"That not how we Hajis make it," she said, grimacing the Indian way. "Do like I said."

"No," I said firmly. "I add a tomato at the end. When it bursts, give a bite to the daal and lovely color."

Ammi scrunched up her face in disgust and again swatted me on the head with the spoon. But Papa nodded at me over the old woman's back, and his support shored up my confidence. I rubbed the back of my skull, still smarting from her smack, and then gently eased her toward the door and out of the kitchen.

"Leave, Ammi, please! Leave until you can control yourself. I must prepare for the opening. You understand?"

It was around this time that I undid my apron and walked into town with Uncle Mayur, just a young man desperate for a break from all the pressures of the opening. It was late morning and Mehtab had sent us out in search of supplies, laundry detergent and steel wool pads to scrub the pots and pans.

It was when we returned from town, arms laden with bags from the local Carrefour, that Uncle Mayur made a face and clicked his tongue, nodding in the direction of Le Saule Pleureur.

A young farmer led a monstrous pig around to the back of the restaurant by a rope tied to the ring through its nose. Must have been five hundred pounds of animal. Mallory, Leblanc, and the rest of the staff were looking very officious as they fussed out back with buckets of water and knives and laid out large planks of wood and scrubbed down the country table standing at the top of the field. The snorting pig clattered onto the planks of wood at the sight of a dish of nettles and potatoes carefully placed in a strategic spot under a sturdy chestnut tree. I noticed a complicated system of pulleys hung from the branches overhead.

St. Augustine's parish priest read from the Bible, sprinkled holy water on the pig, on the ground, on the wooden plank, his lips ceaselessly moving in whispered prayer. The mayor was there, too, standing alongside the local butcher, who was sharpening knives on a whetting stone.

I remember Lumière's mayor respectfully had his hat off, and in the sharp wind his elaborate comb-over unraveled and began to flick foolishly about his head. And I remember this ludicrous picture of the mayor and his dancing hair as the butcher removed a revolver from his apron, walked over, and dispatched the pig with a shot through the head.

A bark, a defecation, and the thud of the pig as its legs buckled and it landed heavily on the wooden planks. Leblanc and three of the other men instantly pulled at the pulleys, hoisting the planks over onto the scrubbed table, even while the pig still twitched madly, its hooves scrabbling and jerking.

"Christians." Uncle Mayur snorted contemptuously. "Come, let us go."

But we couldn't move, not as the pig's throat was slit and blood by the liter pulsed from the gash, the red spray pumping into a large plastic bucket. And I'll always remember the sight of Madame Mallory washing her arms under the outside tap, then whipping the hot blood with her forearms as her sous chef added vinegar to the bucket, to keep the blood from coagulating. The way they later added cooked leeks and apples and parsley, along with fresh cream, to the bucket of fresh blood, before stuffing boudin skins with the thickened paste. And I remember the smells that came to us in the wind, so powerfully of blood and shit and death, and the way they scraped the pig's hooves clean, scattered straw around the carcass, and set it alight to remove the animal's bristles. All this I remember, as the three of them carved the animal up over the rest of the day, the butcher and Mallory and her sous chef periodically sipping from tumblers of white wine as they hacked away at the warm slabs of bloodied meat still steaming in the air. And how this public butchering went on into the next day, almost all through the weekend. How they showered shoulder meat with salt and pepper and then spooned the ground flesh into skins, *saucissons* to dry in Mallory's back shed, where pears and apples and prunes were stacked on wooden shelves according to size.

"Disgusting," hissed Uncle Mayur. "Pig eaters."

And I found myself unable to confess what I was really thinking. That I had seen few things so beautiful. That few things spoke to me so eloquently of the earth and where we come from and where we are heading. How could I tell him, moreover, how could I tell him that I found myself secretly and passionately wanting to be a part of this pig-butchering underworld?

Chapter Seven

Aiee, Abbas. Guess who book a table? The woman from across the road. Table for two."

Auntie sat behind the antique desk at the main entrance taking reservations, carefully entering the seating in a black ledger. Papa yelled, "Nah? You hear that, Hassan? The old woman from across street come try our fantastic concoctions."

And there, clutching the banister, Ammi descending the stairs, so bewildered. Auntie had closed the ledger and was now examining herself in a compact mirror. "Stop looking at yourself, you vain girl," Ammi screeched. "When does Hassan get married? What do I wear? Who has my tings?"

They brought her down to the kitchen and gave her a simple task—that sometimes helped. Of course, Ammi in the kitchen was all I needed; the kitchen on the opening day was already a chaotic mess. I was terribly nervous and had just thrown handfuls of cubed lamb and okra into pots, squeezed in some lemon, dropped in some star seed and cardamom, cinnamon, and crushed grapefruit. Green peas, too. It was a blur of bubbling vats, spicy fumes, nervous yelling.

Mehtab helped, of course, chopping onions in the corner, but she was always somewhere in between tears and uncontrollable giggles. And Papa was driving me mad, nervously pacing back and forth, past the stove, where bubbling sauces spat so hard they spattered the floor.

"Wah?" said grandmother. "Why am I here? What I doing?"

"It's all right, Ammi. You're washing—"

"Doing the washing?"

"No. No. Pears. I want you to wash the pears."

And then the woolly heads of Arash and Mukhtar appeared between the swinging doors. Little bastards. "Hassan is a girl," they chanted. "Hassan is a girl."

"If you little rascals bother your brother again," Papa yelled, "I'll make you sleep in the garage tonight."

Auntie slammed through the doors.

"It's full! It's full! We book every table."

Papa grabbed my shoulders in his big hands and turned me around so I would look into his eyes, eyes brimming with emotion. "Make us proud, Hassan," he said with a quivering voice. "Remember, you are a Haji."

"Yes, Papa."

We were, of course, all thinking of Mother. But there was no time for sentimentality, and I quickly turned back to the pan to sauté vanilla pods with chanterelle mushrooms.

Meanwhile, at Le Saule Pleureur across the street, Madame Mallory stood at her spotless steel kitchen counter examining hors d'oeuvres of pike carpaccio and fricassee of freshwater oysters. Behind her the staff wordlessly, efficiently, prepared the night's fare with a rat-tat-tatting of knives, the hissing of meat seared under a flame grill, the scraping of steel utensils, and the constant back-and-forth thudding of wooden clogs on tile.

Mallory let nothing out into the dining room without her explicit approval, and she checked that the oysters in front of her were hot with the back of her knuckle, dabbing a spoon into the carpaccio's truffle-and-asparagus vinaigrette. Not too salty, not too tart. She nodded her approval and dabbed a tea towel in a bowl of water to her side, carefully wiping the fingerprints and slopped sauce from around the plates' rims.

"Pick up," she cried, "table six."

Mallory needed everything to be clear, transparent, controlled. A waiter stood before the board—on which a miniature plan of the dining room tables outside had been re-created—ticking in blue felt-tip under the first course box, table six. This board on the wall allowed Mallory to know, at a glance, precisely who was at what stage of their meal and where.

"Hurry up. The oysters are getting cold."

"Oui, madame."

The waiter came around to the other side of Madame Mallory's steel counter and slid the dishes onto a tray lined with a linen cloth. He settled a silver dome over the steaming oysters, bent his knees, and suddenly it was all up in his arms and out through the swinging doors in one graceful move.

Madame Mallory spiked the order for table six and checked her gold watch. "Jean-Pierre," she cried over the kitchen din. "Take over. Two orders for duckling. Table eleven."

Mallory untied her apron, examined her hair in the mirror, and then pushed through the swinging doors. Le Comte de Nancy Selière was taking his usual seat near the bay window. The gourmet banker came from Paris every year at this time, for two weeks. A good customer—always Suite 9 and the full meal plan—and Madame Mallory overcame her shyness to greet him warmly and sincerely as he looked up from the menu.

Mallory instantly had the impression the aristocrat was more wistful than normal, saddened by the turmoil of middle age, but perhaps that was because he usually came to Le Saule Pleureur with a much younger woman. This year the gourmet was alone.

Mallory's favorite painting, a nineteenth-century oil of the Marseille fish markets, stood to the side of the count, and she discreetly straightened the painting's light after another guest had brushed against it, knocking it slightly askew as he took his seat. A bread boy in gold buttons and cotton gloves magically appeared at her side, a basket of homemade breads on his shoulder.

"We've just created this spinach-and-carrot semolina," Madame Mallory informed the count, pointing with silver tongs at a two-toned bread roll. "Slightly sweet. Particularly good with tonight's chilled *terrine de foie gras,* served under a white truffle and port *gelée.*"

"Ah, madame," said Le Comte de Nancy, a playful smile on his lips. "What painful decisions you force me to make."

Mallory wished him *bon appétit* and continued across the room, nodding at familiar guests, straightening a drooping stalk in the centerpiece of orchids, stopping briefly to furiously whisper in the ear of the wine steward. The steward's sleeve was stained with wine and she ordered him to change his tunic.

"*Immédiatement,*" she hissed. "I shouldn't have to tell you this."

At the front desk, Monsieur Leblanc and his assistant, Sophie, took the coats of arriving clients, weekenders from Paris, and Mallory waited discreetly to the side until Leblanc was free. "Let's get this over with," she said. "And you, Sophie. The Satie tape is a fraction too loud. Turn it down. It should be very faint, in the background."

The night was as black as a *boudin noir,* and the stars, I recall, appeared to me as clots of blood-pudding fat. The owls too-wooed deep in the branches of linden and chestnut, and the birch trunks under the moon stood out like solid bars of silver in the night.

But not so still, our street. The brightly lit windows of the Dufour mansion, the festive chatter of arriving guests, the comforting smell of birch smoke drifting through the night.

Our restaurant was already half-full and cars from all over the region jammed our street when Madame Mallory and Monsieur Leblanc crossed the short distance between our restaurants, wading through the inky night, standing their turn at Maison Mumbai's door, just behind Monsieur Iten and his family of six.

Papa's massive silhouette appeared in the light-flooded door frame, his immense bulk squeezed into a raw silk kurta, his bosom and hairy nipples pressed unattractively against the shiny tan material. "Good evening," he boomed. "Welcome, Monsieur Iten. And your lovely family. My, what beautiful boys you have, Madame Iten. Come, bring the rascals in. We have a wonderful table for you near the garden. My sister will show you."

Papa stepped forward again once they had passed, to peer down the stone steps at the dimly outlined night shapes. "Aah," Papa said, finally recognizing Mallory and Leblanc. "Our neighbors. Good evening. Good evening. Come."

Without another word Papa turned and slowly waddled in his white slippers across the restaurant. "We're completely booked," he yelled over the din of the crowded restaurant. They passed the plastic roses, the Air India posters, the trumpeting elephant, and Mallory protectively pulled her shawl tighter over her shoulders.

Papa dropped two plastic menus on a table for two. Suresh Wadkar and Hariharan wailed in Urdu from speakers overhead, and the wall visibly vibrated as the sarangi and tabla erupted during a particularly passionate passage.

"Very good table," Papa yelled above the music.

Monsieur Leblanc quickly pulled out Madame Mallory's chair, hoping to head off an acerbic remark. "Yes, Monsieur Haji, I see," he said. "Thank you very much. Congratulations on your opening. We wish you great fortune."

"Thank you. Thank you. You are most welcome."

Madame Mallory closed her eyes in horror as Papa bellowed, "Zainab," so loudly across the room it made several of the guests jump in alarm. My seven-year-old sister dutifully came over to Madame Mallory's table with a clutch of pansies. Zainab wore a simple white dress, and even Madame Mallory had to admit her cinnamon-colored skin looked beautiful in the light, against the clean cotton. Zainab handed Madame Mallory the flowers and shyly looked at the floor. "Welcome to Maison Mumbai," she said softly.

Papa beamed and Mallory leaned over and patted Zainab's head, which had been recently oiled with one of Mehtab's hair tinctures. *"Charmant,"* Mallory said stiffly, wiping her hand under the table on the linen napkin over her knees.

She turned her attention back to Papa. "Help us, Monsieur Haji," she said, pointing at the menu. "We have little understanding of your food. You order for us. Bring us your house specialties."

Papa grunted and plunked a bottle of *vin rouge* down on the table. "On the house," he said. Madame Mallory knew the label well. It was the only truly bad wine in the valley. *"Non,"* she said. *"Merci.* Not for us. What do you drink with your food?"

"Beer," said Papa.

"Beer?"

"Kingfisher beer."

"Bring us two beers, then."

Papa waddled back into the kitchen, as I was cooking ground corn and coriander on the tawa, and he spat out their order. I could tell by his ruddy cheeks his blood pressure was rising, and I raised my finger at him, a warning to stay cool.

"Kill them," he said. "Just kill them."

The restaurant was now roaring with life, and Madame Mallory must have been surprised to see so many of the townsfolk from Lumière helping us celebrate our opening. Madame Picard, the fruitier, with a friend, getting drunk on the house wine; and the mayor, with his entire family, even his brother the lawyer, roaring off-color jokes at each other around the corner table. As she was peering around the room in this way, Uncle Mayur waddled over and opened, with a hiss, Mallory's bottles of beer.

Mukhtar and Arash, my younger brothers, suddenly ran hollering through the tables until my uncle grabbed Arash by his nape and boxed his ears. His howl sliced through the restaurant. And shortly thereafter Ammi wandered out of the kitchen, annoyed at all the people in her house, and she went right to the corner table and pinched the mayor hard. The man was rather surprised—he swore, actually—and Papa rushed over to apologize and explain Ammi's condition.

But it was all right. The first few dishes emerged from the kitchen, dishes rattling in the inexperienced French boy's hands, and there was great oohhing and aahing as the steaming, prattling iron platters passed through the dining room. The mayor recovered his good humor when a stack of prawn samosas and another bottle of wine arrived at his table—on the house. And that was when Madame Mallory abruptly stood and made her way to the back of the restaurant.

There I was, my back to the kitchen door, my hands and forearms discolored by a mixture of chili powder and grease. I shook some garam masala into a vat of mutton. A pot of clarified butter exploded over the counter, and I rather excitedly ordered Mehtab to spoon the runny butter—which had congealed with onion skins, spilled salt, and saffron—into a frying pan.

"Don't waste it. Never mind. Still taste good."

I looked over at the door.

I cannot describe the feeling that made me turn around like that, as if a great force of negative energy was at my back, shoving me forward.

But the glass portico in the door was empty.

Madame Mallory had seen what she wanted to see, and she returned to the dining room to take her seat opposite Leblanc. She sipped her beer and contentedly pictured the scene that was unfolding in her own restaurant across the street.

Stravinsky orchestrations softly playing in the background. The drama of silver domes over delicious dishes lifted simultaneously. The polite sipping of a bouillabaisse. The fecund aroma of orchids and roast suckling pig. Precision, perfection, predictability. "To Le Saule Pleureur," Mallory said, holding up her glass of beer to Monsieur Leblanc.

Our pimply young waiter arrived with their food. Not very experienced, I'm afraid, and he just banged the pots down on the table. There was an urn of Goa fish stew, thick and gooey. Chicken tikka marinated in pink spices and lemon, grilled until the edges were black and curling. A skewer of yogurt-marinated lamb liver, sprinkled with crunchy pine nuts, was barely contained on a chipped dish. Mushrooms that thickened a masala appeared as unidentified lumps under the film of tarka oil floating atop the dish. There was a copper pan of okra and tomatoes, and cauliflower heads in, I admit, an unattractive brown sauce. Yellow rice was fluffily heaped in a ceramic bowl, with pungent bay leaves buried under the kernels of basmati. Then came a confusing array of side dishes—pickled carrots, cool yogurt and cucumber, unleavened bread blistered with black boils and garlic.

"What a lot of food," said Mallory. "I hope it is not too hot. The only other Indian food I've had, in Paris, was awful. Burned for two days."

But the smells of the restaurant had made her hungry, as they had Monsieur Leblanc, and they spooned out the rice and fish and cauliflower and crispy liver onto their plates.

"You won't believe what I saw in the kitchen."

Mallory swallowed a forkful of yogurt and rice and okra and fish. "They'll have the health inspectors in there shortly. The boy spilled—"

But Mallory did not finish the sentence. She looked down at her plate, her brow knitted. She took another forkful, chewing methodically, letting the flavors sensually roll across her tongue. Her fingers leaped across the table and dug into Monsieur Leblanc's forearm.

"What is it, Gertrude? Good God. You look awful. What is it? Too hot?"

Madame Mallory trembled, shook her head in disbelief.

She took another forkful. But now all uncertainty, all shreds of hope, drained away and she was left with the awful truth.

It was there.

Madame Mallory dropped her fork with a clatter. *"Ah, non, non, non,"* she moaned.

"For God's sake, Gertrude, tell me, what is wrong? You're frightening me."

Never before had Monsieur Leblanc seen such a terrifying look. It was, he thought, the picture of someone who had lost her reason for living.

"He has it," she hissed. "He has it."

"What? He has what? Who has what?"

"The boy," she croaked. "The boy has what . . . Oh, the injustice of life."

Mallory brought her napkin up to her lips to muffle the squeaks involuntarily popping out of her mouth.

"Oh. Oh."

Diners at the other tables turned to look at Madame Mallory and she suddenly became aware she was an object of fascination. Gathering all her inner strength, she sat up straight, patted her bun of hair, a frozen smile plastered across her face. Heads slowly went back to their own food.

"Didn't you taste it?" Mallory whispered.

Her eyes were ablaze, as if cayenne pepper and curry had internally set her afire. "Crude, yes, but there. Under all the fire, hidden, brought out by the cool yogurt. There, yes, distinctly there. It's in the point and counterpoint of tastes."

Monsieur Leblanc slapped his napkin down on the table. "What in heaven's name are you talking about, Gertrude? Now, speak clearly."

But Madame Mallory, to his utter amazement, lowered her head and began to weep into her napkin. Never before—never in their thirty-four-year partnership—had he seen her cry. Let alone in public.

"Talent," she said through the muffled clutch of her napkin. "Talent that cannot be learned. That skinny Indian teenager has that mysterious something that comes along in a chef once a generation. Don't you understand? He is one of those rare chefs who is simply born. He is an *artist*. A *great artist*."

Unable to contain herself anymore, Madame Mallory burst into heartfelt sobs, great wracking gasps of pain that filled the restaurant and brought the entire room to a standstill.

Papa ran over. "What? What matter wit' her? Too hot?"

Monsieur Leblanc begged their apologies, paid the bill, pulled the distraught chef up by the elbows, and half dragged the weeping woman back across the street to her restaurant.

The church dog howled.

"Non, non," she wailed. "I can't bear my guests to see me like this."

Leblanc managed to get her up the back stairs of Le Saule Pleureur, up the winding servants' stairway to her attic rooms, where the wretched woman collapsed on to the sofa.

"Leave me—"

"I'll be just downstairs if you need—"

"Get out! Just get out! You don't understand. No one understands."

"As you wish, Gertrude," he said quietly. "Good night."

He gently eased shut her door. But in the darkened room Mallory suddenly missed Leblanc's kind presence, and she turned to the shut door, her mouth agape. But it was too late. Leblanc was gone. And the elderly woman, all alone, threw her face down on the sofa, and sobbed like a teenager.

Mallory slept poorly that fateful night of Maison Mumbai's opening, flopping about her bed all night like a distressed fish. Her sleep was a montage of horrid visions, of giant copper vats in which a mysteriously delicious food simmered. It was, she realized with a gasp, the long-searched-for Soup of Life and she had to have its recipe. But no matter how she circled and circled, how she tried to get a foothold on the pots' smooth sides, she was unable to taste the *potage.* She kept on sliding down and landing in a heap on the floor, a Lilliputian, too small to learn the cauldron's great mystery.

Mallory shook herself awake when it was still dark, when the first sparrows twittered in her beloved willow tree outside her window, the whiplike branches now covered in a seasonal *gelée.*

Mallory rose stiffly and went about her dark room with a stiff-legged determination. She violently brushed her teeth in front of the bathroom mirror without looking at herself—at the jowls of age, the bitterness around the brows. She folded her white bosom into a wire bra, dropped a navy blue wool dress over her head, and gave her hair a couple of violent yanks with a steel brush. In no time she was clattering down the attic stairs and banging on Monsieur Leblanc's door.

"Get up. It's time for the shops."

In his blackened room, under a cocoon of warm duvet, an exhausted Monsieur Leblanc rubbed his face. He turned his creaky neck toward the luminous alarm clock.

"Are you mad?" he yelled through the door. "My God, it's only four thirty. I went to bed just a few hours ago."

"Only four thirty! Only four thirty! Do you think the world waits for us? Get up, Henri. I want to be first at the shops."

Chapter Eight

We arrived in the town bleary-eyed but triumphant at seven thirty that morning, later than usual because the family celebrated the successful opening into the early hours. Our first stop, as always, was Monsieur Iten, the fishmonger's shop smelling tartly of pickled herring. Several customers stood in line before us, and we took our place in line, Papa trying out his pidgin French on the wife of Lumière's sawmill manager.

"*Maison Mumbai. Bon, nah?*"

"*Pardon?*"

It was our turn. "Good morning," bellowed Papa. "What special ting can you offer us today, Monsieur Iten? Everyone loved Hassan's fish curry last night."

Monsieur Iten was a lurid red, as if he had been drinking, and he stood stiff-legged at the back of the shop.

"Monsieur Haji," he slurred. "No fish."

"Ha, ha. I like a little joke."

"No fish."

Papa looked down at the trays of silvery salmon, at the Brittany crabs with their claws rubber-banded together, at the ceramic dish of marinated Norwegian herring.

"Wah dis? Fish, no?"

"Fish, yes. Sold fish."

Papa looked around and the other villagers backed away from him, studying their feet, sticking fingers into string bags.

"What going on here?"

We left the shop—empty-handed—and made our way across the square to the markets. Villagers who had dined at our restaurant just the night before lowered their heads and avoided our looks. Sullen mumbles returned our greetings. At every stall we were met with the same cold response. That particular gourd or that cabbage or that tray of eggs was "with regret" already sold. We stood alone in the center of the market, ignored, ankle-deep in purple tissue and wilted lettuce leaves.

"Haar," Papa exhaled, as he saw the gray loden coat of Madame Mallory suddenly disappear around a corner stall.

I tugged at Papa's elbow and made him look at Madame Picard's wind-seared face, a twisted mask of loathing riveted at the spot where we had just seen the disappearing tail of the town's famous chef.

Widow Picard turned in our direction and gestured with her filthy hand for Papa and me to follow her behind the canvas flap of her stall. "That bitch," she hissed, letting go of the flap. "Mallory. She forbid us to sell to you."

"How?" Papa asked. "How can she stop you from selling us tings?"

"*Pff.*" The Widow Picard waved her hand in the air. "That woman's got her nose in everyone's business. She knows everyone's secrets. I overheard her promising to report Monsieur and Madame Rigault—such a nice elderly couple—to the tax authorities. Just because they might not ring up every centime they sell. Imagine. Such a terrible, terrible woman."

"But why she hate us?" Papa asked.

Madame Picard spat a thick wad of phlegm into a heap of discarded cabbage leaves. "Who knows?" she said, shrugging her shoulders and rubbing her hands together to stay warm. "Probably because you're foreigners. You don't belong here."

Papa stood rigid for a few seconds and then abruptly left. He didn't even say good-bye. Wanting to make up for his rudeness, I profusely thanked Madame Picard for her help. She pressed two bruised pears into my hand. Said she'd like to help more but she couldn't. "She got me, too, you know."

Madame Picard spat again, reminding me of the old crones of Bombay.

"Watch out, boy. She's evil, that one."

I caught up with Papa in the town parking lot, his great weight making the Mercedes sag as he dropped himself into the driver's seat and pensively leaned over the wheel. Papa did not rage, just looked immensely sad as he stared out into the parking lot and the Alps beyond. And that was more upsetting to me than anything else he could have done.

"What, Papa?"

"I am thinking of your mother. These people, we cannot hide from them. Yaar? You agree? These people lived on the Napean Sea Road. And now we find them here in Lumière, too."

"Oh, Papa."

I was afraid the depression of Southall was about to return, but my shaky voice seemed to stir Papa from his melancholy, for he turned toward me with a smile as he started the engine.

"Hassan. Don't worry. We are Hajis."

He placed his immense hand on my knee and squeezed it until I yelped.

"This time we don't run."

His arm was around the back of my seat while he sent the car lurching backward onto the road, the other cars behind us honking furiously. And there was cold steel in his voice, when he put the Mercedes in drive and we roared down to the light.

"This time we fight."

Papa drove us to Clairvaux-les-Lacs, the provincial city seventy kilometers away. We spent the entire day negotiating with suppliers, crossing back and forth across the cobblestone backstreets, and playing one fruit-and-vegetable wholesaler against another.

I never saw Papa so brilliant an operator—so charming, so ruthlessly determined to bend the will of others, and yet so generous in making them feel they had won.

We bought a refrigeration truck, secondhand, and hired a driver. Late morning we called Maison Mumbai and my father ordered my sister to feed the lunch crowd; he said I'd be back in time to take charge of the evening shift. After a consultation at the local branch of Société Générale and wiring funds for the truck, Papa and I loaded the back of our dilapidated Mercedes with haunches of mutton, baskets of shellfish and pike, orange mesh sacks of potato and cauliflower and *mange tout.*

We never missed a beat.

No customer would have even suspected we had had difficulties.

The following morning Madame Mallory flung open the door of her restaurant, breathed deeply, and felt good. She smelled the snow that now dusted the tops of the Jura rock faces overlooking Lumière, and everywhere rhinestone frost, not yet burned off by the morning sun, glittered theatrically back at her. St. Augustine was finishing a peal of late-morning bells as a mature stag suddenly made a dash across a silvery field to the safety of the pine forests. Hunting season. It reminded her to go see Monsieur Berger about her haunch of venison, already hanging in his shed.

It was just as she was basking in this cold-morning beauty that a truck rumbled down the road. She heard the sound of its gears grinding into low, and she turned her head to follow the rattle. The truck mounted the curb into the old Dufour estate, the large gold lettering garishly leaping from its back.

MAISON MUMBAI.

"Ah, non. Non."

Hot-orange-and-pink Urdu poems squiggled across the truck's sides. Strips of black crêpe hung from the fenders. HONK PLEASE, read an English sign attached to the back door. BEWARE, said another, MOTHER'S PRAYERS ARE WITH US.

The driver jumped from a front seat fringed with tassels. He snapped open the back doors, revealing to the world an entire cooler of high-quality lamb and poultry and onion sacks.

Madame Mallory slammed the door shut with such force Monsieur Leblanc jumped, a blotch of ink splattering across the accounts.

"Gertrude—"

"Oh, leave me alone. Why haven't you done those accounts yet? Honestly, it's taking you longer and longer. Maybe we should get a younger man in to keep the books."

The chef did not wait for a response, or, indeed, look to see how her remark had cut Monsieur Leblanc to the quick. Instead, Mallory barreled down the hall, through the dining room, slamming open the kitchen door.

"Where is the terrine, Margaret? Let me taste it."

The sous chef, just twenty-two years old, handed Madame Mallory a fork and gingerly slid over to the master chef the *cassata*-like brick of spinach, langoustine, and pumpkin. The elderly woman concentrated, smacked her lips as she let the flavors dissolve on her tongue.

"How long have you been with me, Margaret? Three years?"

"Six years, Madame."

"Six years. And you still do not know how to make a proper terrine? It's almost unbelievable. This terrine tastes like a baby's bottom. It's tasteless, mushy, horrible." She swept the offending dish off the counter and into the trash.

"Now do it right."

Margaret, choking back tears, dipped below the counter to retrieve another glass dish.

"And you, Jean-Pierre, don't look so shocked. Your daube has become unacceptable. Just unacceptable. The meat should be so tender it shreds with a fork—your daube is bitter, burnt. And look, look how you're doing that. Where did you learn that? Not from me."

In her eagerness to get across the kitchen, Madame Mallory pushed young Marcel out of the way, and the apprentice stumbled, gashing his arm painfully on the sharp edge of the steel stove.

Madame Mallory bore down on Jean-Pierre and the roasting pan, aggressively snapping large tongs. And this unsettled the staff even more, for the tongs were from her personal cooking utensils—kept locked in a leather case under the main counter—and they meant business.

"Guinea fowl need to be turned, turned every seven minutes, so the juices flow through the meat. I've been watching how you work. You manhandle the birds. You're so rough, like a farmer. You have no feel for game. You must be delicate. See? Look how I do it. Can you manage that, you imbecile?"

"Oui, madame."

Madame Mallory stood in the middle of her kitchen, her large bosom heaving, her face mottled with red blotches of rage. And the staff stood frozen in the glare of her majestic fury.

"I want perfection. Perfection. And anyone who doesn't deliver what is expected of him will be terminated." Mallory picked up a terra-cotta dish and smashed it on the floor. "Like that. Like that. Do you understand? Marcel, clean that up."

Madame Mallory blew out of the kitchen, pounding up the wooden stairs to her attic rooms. For a few minutes, as the smoke cleared, the survivors in the kitchen found they were too shocked to speak, too stunned to fully comprehend what had just happened.

Luckily for them, however, Madame Mallory's attention was suddenly focused elsewhere. She pounded furiously back down the stairs and this time shot out the front door. "What are you doing?" she screeched across the forecourt.

The mayor, crossing the street, stopped in his tracks. He turned slowly with his shoulders hunched up about his ears.

"Gertrude, damn it, you scared me!"

"Why are you slinking about like that?"

"I'm not slinking."

"Don't lie to me. You were going into that place for lunch."

"And what of it?"

"And what of it?" she mocked. "Aren't you the mayor of this town? Aren't you meant to preserve our way of life? You shouldn't be encouraging these foreigners. It's a disgrace. Why are you eating there?"

"Because, Gertrude, the food is excellent. A nice change."

My heavens. Like he'd hit her. Madame Mallory let out a horrible squawk, and then turned abruptly, fleeing back to the safety of Le Saule Pleureur.

It was most curious that the very things Madame Mallory hated most about Maison Mumbai—the hysteria, the lack of professionalism—now took root in her own impeccably run restaurant. Chaos overwhelmed the endlessly rehearsed rituals of the two-star inn, and Mallory, although she would never have admitted it, had only herself to blame for this turn of events.

Margaret, the sensitive sous chef, spent the evening kissing the crucifix around her neck and trembling as she went about her duties. Jean-Pierre was still stewing over Mallory's claim he had "no feel for game," and throughout the evening he cursed a blue streak and violently kicked the stove's steel side panels with his wooden clogs. And young Marcel was so rattled he thrice dropped plates when the kitchen's swinging doors suddenly slammed open.

Nor were things much better out front. The wine steward was terrified Madame Mallory might find another stain on his tunic, and that evening he took unusual pains to stay spotless, pouring wine from as great a distance as possible from the table, his bottom unattractively stuck out into the aisle. And when he aerated wine in a glass, he swirled the wine in the crystal with too much nervous energy, sloshing the precious amber out onto the floor, much to the guests' annoyance.

"*Merde*," said Le Comte de Nancy, swiveling in his seat at the latest metallic *boing* coming from the kitchen. "Monsieur Leblanc. Monsieur Leblanc. What the hell is going on in the kitchen? The noise is impossible. The plate smashing in the back. Like some Greek wedding."

That night guests innocently stepped over the threshold of Le Saule Pleureur, expecting, like always, to be whisked away in a soufflé of fine dining. Instead, they were met at the door by a wild-eyed Madame Mallory tugging at their elbow. "Have you been across the street?" she demanded of Madame Corbet, owner of an award-winning vineyard two villages down.

"Across the street?"

"Come on. Come on. You know what I am talking about. The Indians."

"The Indians?"

"I don't want you in my restaurant if you've been across the street. I repeat, have you been across the street?"

Madame Corbet nervously looked around for her husband, but

she couldn't see him, as he and Monsieur Leblanc had walked on ahead into the dining room.

"Madame Mallory," said the elegant vintner. "Are you ill? You seem rather feverish this evening—"

"*Ah, pff.*" Mallory waved the woman away, disgusted. "Take her to the table, Sophie. The Corbets are incapable of telling the truth."

Luckily for Madame Mallory, at that moment a bread boy bumped the aisle-hogging wine steward, and that bump in turn jogged pouring wine all over Le Comte de Nancy's arm. It was the count's roars and curses that prevented Madame Corbet from hearing Mallory's insulting and intemperate remark.

Shortly after ten thirty p.m. Monsieur Leblanc acknowledged to himself the evening was in the toilet. Two guests were so insulted by Madame Mallory's harsh questioning at the door, they immediately turned and left. Other diners picked up on the electrical charge in the air, the stress that crackled through the service, and they complained bitterly to Monsieur Leblanc how they were unsatisfied by the evening's fare.

Enough, Leblanc decided. Enough.

He found Madame Mallory in the kitchen, standing over Jean-Pierre as he prepared a dessert of fennel ice cream and toasted figs with *nougatine*. She had just grabbed the duster of powdered sugar from his hand. "This is one of my specialties," she raged. "You're ruining it. Look, like this. Like this. Not like that—"

"Come," said Leblanc, taking Mallory firmly by the elbow. "Come now. We must talk."

"*Non.*"

"Yes. Now." And Leblanc forced the chef out back, into the fresh night air.

"What, Henri? You see I'm busy."

"What's the matter with you? Can't you see what you are doing?"

"What are you talking about?"

"What are you doing to the staff? Is it this unnatural obsession with the Hajis? You're acting like a madwoman. You've got everyone on edge. You even insulted your own customers, Gertrude. My God. You know better than that. What are you doing?"

Mallory placed a hand on her chest as cats hissed somewhere out in the night. In her eyes nothing was worse than disrupting a customer's dining experience, and she was disgusted with herself. She knew she was out of control. But even so, admitting she was wrong never came easily to Madame Mallory, and the two old culinary comrades stood tensely in the dark glaring at each other until Mallory exhaled, a deep release of breath that told Leblanc everything would be all right.

She slipped a wisp of gray hair under her black velvet hair band.

"You're the only person who could say such a thing," she finally said, tartness still in her voice.

"You mean tell you the truth."

"All right, now. I heard you."

Mallory took the proffered cigarette, and the flame of his lighter flickered in the damp evening air.

"I know I am acting strange. But, *mon Dieu,* every time I think of that revolting man and his boy in the kitchen, I just see—"

"Gertrude, you've got to get ahold of yourself."

"I know. You're right, of course. Yes. I will."

The two smoked silently in the night. An owl hooted in the fields; the sound of a distant train at the other end of the valley rolled out across the evening. It was so serene and calm that for the first time that day Madame Mallory felt herself come back to earth.

Her patch of earth.

At that precise moment, however, Uncle Mayur cranked up the outside speakers of our restaurant, and Lumière's evening filled with twanging sitars and the mesmerizing drumming of a ghazal, punctuated with the tinkling of finger cymbals. Every dog in the neighborhood joined in by baying.

"*Ah, non, non.* Those bastards."

Mallory slipped through Leblanc's grasp, crashed through the back door, and within minutes she was on the phone to the police. Leblanc shook his head.

What could he do?

Mallory quickly discovered a call to the police was not going to take care of her problem. Apparently, the police no longer had jurisdiction over noise; noise complaints were now handled by the brand-new Department of Environment, Traffic, and Ski Lift Maintenance.

The next day—like a shot—Mallory was down at the Town Hall. After a great deal of incomprehensible hemming and hawing, the young man running the new bureaucracy admitted he indeed could, with the proper evidence, launch proceedings against Maison Mumbai. The problem was he didn't have enough financial resources to gather the evidence during a night patrol. The department could only investigate noises between the hours of nine a.m. and four thirty p.m.

You can imagine. Madame Mallory gave the poor man such a tongue-lashing that he instantly agreed to lend Mallory the noise-measuring equipment. She herself, under strict guidelines, could record the nocturnal decibels emerging from our restaurant.

And so, one dark night, Mallory and Leblanc crept out the back of Le Saule Pleureur, lugging the cumbersome equipment across the street into a field that lay adjacent to our restaurant. Monsieur Leblanc fumbled with the battery-operated machinery while he sank up to his ankles in spongy moss. Mallory, meanwhile, was the lookout, peeking through the holly hedge that marked our perimeter, scrutinizing the brilliantly lit windows of Maison Mumbai and the French doors leading out to the garden.

A saggy canvas tarp was strung over the flagstone patio, secured by wires and metal spikes. Diners occupied three garden tables, huddled around large portable heaters spitting flames, fiery cones that looked like the back ends of jet engines. As Uncle Mayur passed through the back door, lit plate warmers, and poured wine, the hissing industrial heaters made his skin glow blue and red in the dark. The two offending speakers hung from the wall, and Kavita Krishnamurthy was singing loudly over the roar of the jet-engine heaters.

"There," said Monsieur Leblanc. "It's running."

The needle ratcheted wildly across the white tape and Mallory, finally, smiled in the dark.

*　*　*

We had no idea what they were up to, buried as we were in hard work and long hours. Mallory's strategy of intimidation was starting to pay off. The heavy traffic that so cheered us on opening night fell off quite rapidly, and by the end of the week we were lucky to fill five tables. Mukhtar was beaten by bullies at the local school and chased down the town's side streets to the taunts of "Curry-head, curry-head, curry-head."

A few village families were kind to us. Marcus, the mayor's son, rang to ask if I would care to go boar hunting with him. I heartily agreed, of course, and that Sunday, the morning of my day off, Marcus swung by the restaurant to pick me up in his open-topped Jeep. He was very chatty, not like so many of the locals.

"We only shoot the mature boar," he yelled above the rushing wind, "the ones around three hundred pounds each. Iron rule. We're a cooperative and we divide the big animals equally so each of us walks away from a kill with a couple of pounds of solid meat. The meat is a little tough and bitter, but that is easily taken care of during the cooking."

Marcus drove us through several valleys, south at first, and then east into the mountains. We went up logging roads and back down dirt tracks, always in the thick of forest, until at last we came across a string of cars lined up in ditches along the side of a mountain. Marcus pulled the Jeep in behind a battered Renault 5 badly parked under a chestnut tree.

You had be a local to know where we were. It was wild, dense, and foreboding, the kind of primitive wood one doesn't commonly see in Europe. Marcus slung his Beretta over his back, and we plunged into the woods, up a muddy path pasted with leaves.

I first smelled the birch smoke before I saw the crackle through the thicket. Some forty men in waxed jackets, corduroy knickerbockers, and woolen socks stood around a fire, their deer rifles and shotguns stacked against the trees behind them. A battered Land Rover, splattered with mud, had made it all the way up to the clearing on an abandoned loggers' track, and behind the vehicle beagles and sad-eyed bloodhounds from the South of France sat in a large dog cage fashioned from a cart.

The unshaven men, I saw, were mostly from Lumière and the valley's surrounding farms, a democratic assembly of bankers and shopkeepers briefly social equals during this late autumn ritual of the boar hunt. They looked up at our arrival—a few called out good-natured greetings—before returning to the roasting of sausages and veal chops on the birch fire.

A rough-looking fellow told a joke about a woman with big breasts and the others roared with laughter as they slapped their sizzling meats between wads of country bread. A bottle of cognac was pulled from a jacket and the flask's smooth glass flashed in the light as it was passed around, spiking plastic cups of steaming coffee.

Feeling awkward, I went off to inspect the caged dogs, as Marcus knelt by the fire and cooked our minute steaks. Monsieur Iten came to stand by my side, quietly whittling a piece of birch as he explained how the best dogs were gored by a boar once a season and had to be sewn up. And as he talked—about how the hunt master had been out since the early hours searching the forest floor for fresh boar tracks and plotting the day's hunt and should be back shortly—I sensed someone new had joined the hunters, for a roar of greetings rose with the hot-air crackle of the bonfire.

When we turned around, Madame Mallory, a cracked shotgun resting in the crook of her arm, was standing directly opposite me on the other side of the fire, her feet solidly and squarely apart. I tensed when I spotted her, that familiar look of imperialism now under a Tyrolean hat, but she was calmly talking with the gentleman to her side. And although she was the only woman among this circle of rough-looking men, she did not at all seem uncomfortable, but laughed alongside the others. It was I who felt ill at ease, for though she must have known I was standing there, she never looked directly at me or acknowledged my presence in any way.

And I remember how the light of the fire suddenly seemed to smooth her skin in a kind of illusory face-lift, and how, for a brief moment, I caught a glimpse of Madame Mallory as she might have been—light of heart, hopeful, butter-skinned. But in that tremulous, insecure light, I also saw how she could so easily go the other way, and a moment later, she did. For the fire's flicker suddenly cast shadows over her, horribly exaggerating the jowls of her face, a slashing and scarring across the eyes, and I saw the cruelty that lurked there, too, all tightly bound under that feathered Tyrolean hat.

The master of the hunt, walkie-talkie squawking in his hand, came suddenly through the woods with the three men who were the "beaters." I'm not sure what transpired then—there was much gesticulating and heated exchanges and veal chops being waved in the air to make a point—but suddenly we were all on the march, through the woods and up the sides of mountains, leaves and rubble cascading down the raked slopes behind us.

A sweaty hour later the hunt master began depositing us on a high ridge deep in the forest, tapping a hunter every thirty yards or so. At his touch, the hunter fell to his belly in the crinkle-leaf carpet, and it appeared to me, as one hunter after another fell off behind us, the hunt master was dropping human pebbles across the forest floor so he might remember his way back to the camp.

We were tapped as the rough track bent back at a turning, and Marcus immediately took off his jacket and quietly loaded his Beretta with a single twelve-bore slug. And he told me, just with his eyes and a nod, to lie down in utter silence. Which I did, turning my head briefly to watch the hunt master continue on his journey, the walkie-talkie connecting him to the beaters now silenced. I followed the silly bobbing of Madame Mallory's hat and feather, until the master tapped her, and she, like us, suddenly disappeared into the forest floor, but higher up the ledge.

And there we sat in monotonous silence, for some time, on our bellies, peering over the ridge at the mountainside dropping below us.

The air suddenly filled with the cry of the beaters down below, the baying of their dogs, together moving up the mountain, driving all forest game before them up to our deadly gauntlet.

Marcus concentrated intensely on a faint track and slight clearing below us, his Beretta at his shoulder. I heard then the faint tinkling of a dog's bell and the patter of its paws across a forest floor layered in dry leaves. And then a different sound, what seemed to me, in my ignorance, the heavy thump of hooves, running in panic.

The red fur stopped abruptly, sensing danger. Marcus, experienced, instantly relaxed and at this movement the fox bolted from the clearing. What we had been waiting for came then from the clear blue sky above—the single blast of a gun rolling through the hills like a small explosion.

And that was it. The master of the hunt let out his familiar cry. The hunt was over.

Back at the camp Madame Mallory stood proudly by her kill and held court. The boar hung by its hind hooves from the branches of an oak tree, its blood periodically tapping the forest floor. And I remember how a feverish Mallory, with each returning hunter, told and retold how she bagged the animal as it came through the woods.

I could not take my eyes from this strange fruit hanging before me, with its neat hole, the size of a dumpling, gaping tidily in the animal's chest. And to this day I remember that little snout-face: the small protruding tusks that forced the top lip to curl up, making the boar appear as if it had been highly amused by a witty remark heard at the moment of death. But mostly I remember the eyes with the long lashes, closed so tightly shut against the world, so prettily dead. And now when I think back on it, perhaps it was the boar's size that so unsettled me, so sickened the young man already well accustomed to the bloody and unsentimental endings of the kitchen. For this boar, hanging undignified from its hindquarters before me, was just a baby, not more than forty pounds in weight.

"I want nothing to do with this," I overheard a furious farmer telling the master of the hunt. "It's a disgrace. A sacrilege."

"I agree, but what do you want me to do?"

"You've got to say something to her. It's not right."

The hunt master took a swig of cognac before stepping forward to censure Madame Mallory for violating the club's rules. "I saw what happened," he said, manfully hitching up his trousers. "It is simply not permissible what you did. Why did you not shoot the mature boars when the colony moved before you?"

Mallory took her time to answer. Someone who didn't know our history might even have thought it was innocent, the way she seemed to nonchalantly glance over the hunt master's shoulder to look directly at me for the first time that day, a faint smile tugging the corners of her lips.

"Because, my friend, the young, I find their flesh so tasty to eat. Don't you agree?"

Chapter Nine

Papa received the registered letter on the following Tuesday. It came as I wandered out of the kitchen to take a look at the reservations for the evening. Auntie was doing her nails in crimson polish, and she used her elbow to shove the ledger around so I could read it. It was bleak. Just three out of thirty-seven tables booked.

Papa sat at the bar, rubbing his bare foot with one hand, the other hand sorting through the mail.

"What this say?"

I slung a kitchen towel over my shoulder and read the letter he was rattling at me. "It says we are in violation of the town's noise code. We must shut down our garden restaurant by eight p.m."

"Wah?"

"If we don't close down the garden restaurant we'll be taken to court and fined ten thousand francs a day."

"It's that woman!"

"Poor Mayur," Auntie said, whirling her wet nails through the air. "He so liked serving in the garden. I must tell him."

The hallway filled with the swish-swish of her yellow silk sari as she went in search of her husband. When I turned back to address Papa, I found he had already slipped from the bar stool. The light was filtering through the stained glass of the hall windows, and the air swirled with silver dust motes. I could hear Papa yelling down the telephone at the back of the house. At his lawyer. And I knew then: No good will come of this.

No good.

Papa's counterstrike took place just days later, when the bureaucrat from Lumière's Department of Environment, Traffic, and Ski

Lift Maintenance parked an official Renault van in front of Le Saule Pleureur. It was a poetic justice of sorts, for this was the very same official who had closed down our garden restaurant and made us take down the outdoor stereo speakers.

"Abbas, come, come," Auntie screeched, and the entire family, in great anticipation, poured through the front door to stand on the gravel drive and watch the goings-on across the street.

Two men emerged from the Renault van. They held chain saws. Filterless cigarettes hung from their mouths as they spat the local patois at each other. Papa smacked his lips with satisfaction, as if he had just popped a samosa into his mouth.

Madame Mallory opened the front door of her restaurant, a cardigan draped over her shoulders. The environmental officer stood on her path, squinting up at her as he cleaned his spectacles with a white handkerchief.

"Why are you here? And these men?"

The official took a letter from his front shirt pocket and handed it over to Madame Mallory. She read it in silence, her head moving back and forth.

"You can't. I won't permit it." Mallory smartly tore up the letter.

The young man exhaled slowly. "I am sorry, Madame Mallory, but it is quite clear. You are in violation of code 234bh. It's got to come down. Or at least the—"

But Mallory had moved over to her ancient weeping willow, its high branches swooping so elegantly down over the front fence and the town pavement. *"Non,"* she said acidly. *"Non. Absolument pas."*

Mallory wrapped her arms around the trunk and straddled it lewdly with her knees. "You will have to kill me first. This tree is a Lumière landmark, my restaurant's trademark, everything—"

"That's not the point, madame. Please step back. Local ordnance clearly prohibits trees from hanging over the pavement. It's dangerous. A branch could break—such an old tree—and hurt a child or an elderly person walking by below. And we've had complaints—"

"That's ridiculous. Who could have complained?" But even as she posed her question, Mallory knew the answer, and she turned to look hatefully at us across the street.

Papa gave her a big smile and a wave.

It was exactly what the two workmen were waiting for. The moment Mallory shifted her focus to us across the street, the two burly men grabbed her wrists and adroitly peeled her off the tree. I remember the scream, like an enraged monkey, heard all the way down the street, and the dramatic way Mallory fell to her knees. Her cries, however, they were not to be heard, drowned as they were by the rip-cord roar of the buzz saw.

Several curious villagers had by now gathered in the street, and we were all riveted to the spot by the violent sound of the working saws. Limbs clunked to the ground. And then, as suddenly as it had begun, it was over. There was a hushed, shocked silence as the small crowd took in the results. Mallory, still on her knees, her face cupped in her hands, was finally unable to stand the silence any longer and she raised her head.

A third of the gracious willow's limbs, brutally amputated, sat twisted and oozing sap over the pavement. Her once-elegant tree—a tree that stood for all she had accomplished in life—was now a grotesque, stubby parody of its former self.

"It is very unfortunate," said the town bureaucrat, clearly shocked by his own accomplishments. "But it had to be done. Code 234bh—"

Mallory gave the official such a look of loathing that he stopped in midsentence and scurried back to the safety of the van, gesturing at the men to quickly clean up.

Monsieur Leblanc came rushing down the front path. "Oh, dear, what a tragedy," he said, wringing his hands. "Terrible. But please, Gertrude, get up. Please. I'll pour you a brandy. For the shock."

Madame Mallory was not listening to him. She got off her knees and stared across the street at Papa, at our family gathered on the stone steps. Papa looked back at her, coldly now, and they stood locked like that for several moments before Papa told us all to go back inside. There was work to be done, he said.

Mallory took back her arm from Monsieur Leblanc's fussing grasp, brushed herself off. And then she marched across the street after us, banging on our door. Auntie opened the door slightly, to see who it was, and was instantly slammed backward as Le Saule Pleureur's chef pushed through and strode across the dining room floor.

"Abbas," Auntie shrieked. "Abbas. She here."

Papa and I were back in the kitchen and we did not hear the warning. I was standing over the gas ring, whipping up shahi korma for lunch. Papa sat at the kitchen counter reading the *Times of India,* dated copies sent to him by a newsdealer in London. I turned the flames up full, to sear the lamb in the kadai, when Mallory slammed her way through the kitchen doors.

"There you are. You bastard!"

Papa looked up from his paper, but otherwise stayed seated and calm.

"You are on private property," he said.

"Who do you think you are?"

"Abbas Haji," he said quietly, and the threat in his voice made the hairs on my neck shimmer.

"I will drive you out," she hissed. "You will lose."

Papa stood now, his great bulk towering above the woman. "I have met people like you before," he said in a sudden rush of heat, "and I know what you are. You are uncivilized. Yaar. Underneath your cultural airs, just a barbarian."

Madame Mallory had never before been called "uncivilized." Quite the contrary, she was, in most circles, considered the very essence of refined French culture. So to be called a barbarian, and by this Indian, to boot, was just too much for her and she smashed Papa on the chest with her fist.

"How dare you? HOW—DARE—YOU?"

Although Papa was big, Madame Mallory's passion was great, and the impact of her clenched fist on his bosom made him take a step back in surprise. He tried to take hold of her wrists, but she flurried them through the air like a boxer working a bag.

And now Auntie, disheveled, slammed through the door.

"Aiieee," she screamed. "Aiieee. Mayur. Mayur, come quick."

"You animal," Papa fumed. "Look at you. You're nothing but a savage. Only the weak are . . . Madame, will you stop!"

But Mallory's fists and curses kept on flying unabated.

"You are scum," she screamed back. "Filth. You have—"

Papa was forced to take another step back, and now he was panting from his attempts to grab her arms. "Get out of my house," he bellowed.

"*Non,*" Mallory yelled back. "You get out. Get out of my country, you . . . you dirty foreigner."

And with that, Madame Mallory gave Papa a mighty shove.

It was the push that changed my life, for when Papa staggered back two steps, he hit me with his great bulk, and I in turn slammed full force into the stove. There was a scream and flurrying arms, and only days later did I realize that the yellow I witnessed was the sight of my tunic going up in flames.

Chapter Ten

I remember the wail of the ambulance siren, the swaying of the drip overhead, and my father's worried face looming over me. The next few days were lost in a haze—an unreliable, drug-addled ride through this world and that. It was an odd mix of sensations: the metallic dry mouth and cracked lips of the anesthesia coupled with the aural assault of my grandmother and auntie and sisters carrying on at my bedside. Then another squeaky stretcher ride to the operating room for yet another skin graft.

But soon a kind of hospital monotony took over. The pain eased somewhat and the trays of samosas from the Haji camp outside my door were much appreciated. And there, always, my father in the corner of my room, a looming, tight-lipped mountain of man, little Zainab on his lap as he kept his black eyes on me.

Then, one day, it was just the two of us in the room. He was sitting flush against the bed, and we were playing backgammon on my tray, sipping tea like we did ages ago on the Napean Sea Road, in a life that now seemed so far away.

"Who's doing the cooking?"

"Don't worry about dat. Everyone's helping. All covered."

"I had an idea for a new dish—"

Papa shook his massive head.

"What?"

"We are going back to London."

I threw down my dice and looked out the window. The hospital was in a valley one mountain range over from Lumière, but I had a backside view of the Jura Alps that I could also see from my attic room at Maison Mumbai.

It was winter. The pine forests were dusted with snow, and icicles dangled like daggers from the eaves overlooking the hospital window. It all looked so beautiful, pristine and pure, and tears, inexplicably, rolled down my face.

"What? What you crying for? We are better off going back to London. They won't make any room for us here. I was foolish to think they would. Look at you. Look what my pighead has done to you—"

But Papa's outburst was cut short by a knock on the door. I wiped my eyes while Papa yelled "Hold on" at whoever was knocking. He came over and kissed the undamaged skin of my forehead. "You are my brave boy," he whispered. "You are a Haji."

When Papa opened the door, his massive build filled the frame, but I could still see over his arm. Monsieur Leblanc and Madame Mallory stood before him. Le Saule Pleureur's chef was wearing a chocolate brown wool suit, a bouquet of roses sticking out of the cane basket hanging from her arm. Behind her, Auntie and Uncle Mayur and Zainab sat in the hospital corridor, silently staring. Their silence was deadly, and it seemed to drown out the general cacophony of the working hospital.

"How can you come here?" an incredulous Papa finally asked.

"We came to see how he is."

"Don't bother," he said, his lips curled with disgust. "You have won. We are leaving Lumière. Now go. Don't insult us with your presence."

Papa slammed shut the door. But he was like a beast in a cage, spinning around to pace across my hospital room floor, walloping his hands together like he had when Mummy died.

"Imagine the nerve of dat woman. Imagine."

Mallory was momentarily flustered. She tried to give Zainab the roses, the packet of pastries, but Auntie hissed at the little girl and Zainab scuttled back to her aunt's knees.

"We are sorry to have upset you further," Monsieur Leblanc told an expressionless Uncle Mayur. "You are quite right. It is too late for flowers."

And so they returned to the Citroën in the hospital parking lot.

They did not exchange a word as Leblanc fired up the car, or when he pulled out onto the A708 back to Lumière. Each was lost in thought.

"Well," Mallory finally said. "I tried. It's not my fault—"

But Mallory would have been wise to keep her mouth shut. To Monsieur Leblanc's ears, her protestation was just too much, simply one insensitive remark too far. Leblanc slammed on the brakes and the car came to a skidding halt on the side of the road.

He turned his crimson face to Madame Mallory, and the chef put a defensive hand to her chest, for she could see that even the tips of his ears were a throbbing red.

"What, Henri? Drive."

Leblanc leaned over and popped open her door. "Out. You can walk."

"Henri! Are you mad?"

"Look, look what you have accomplished with your life," he hissed, cold with fury. "You have such fortune. And what have you given back to the world but selfishness?"

"I think—"

"That's the problem, Gertrude. You think far too much—about yourself. I am ashamed for you. Now out. I simply can't stand the sight of you right now."

Monsieur Leblanc had never before talked to her in this manner. Never. She was in total shock. No longer recognized him.

But before she could process this incredible turn of events, Leblanc was around the side of the car, pulling her out onto the shoulder of the road. He jumped into the car's backseat and this time emerged with Mallory's basket, roughly shoving it at the startled chef. "You can walk home," he said tersely.

And then the Citroën was roaring down the country road in a blast of blue exhaust smoke.

"How dare he leave me here like this?" Mallory stamped her feet on the ice. "How dare he talk to me like that?"

Just snowy silence.

"Has he gone mad?"

And she stood fuming like that, incredulous, for quite some time.

Finally, however, reality began to sink in and she looked around the wintry landscape to get her bearings. Mallory was at the foot of a frozen field, the iced-over mountains staring coldly down at her with their tops knotted in dark clouds. Along the valley's floor a thin gray mist hovered, but at the far end she could just make out two chalets, some barns, cones of smoke rising from wood-shingled roofs.

Ah, she thought, Monsieur Berger's farm. Not so bad. She'd use the opportunity to check on her haunch of venison and have the old farmer drive her back to Lumière.

Madame Mallory started her march across the valley. A caw-ing raven scratched at the frozen stubble in the field. And the far-ther she walked along the back roads to Monsieur Berger's farm, the more the brittle, icy vista about her began to invade her mood. What if he leaves me? she suddenly thought. What will I do with-out Henri?

Mallory stumbled on in her ankle boots through the ice and snow, never seeming to get closer to the two farms at the far end of the valley. She crossed a black stream slicing through a snowdrift; she passed an old army depot once used for tank maneuvers and a forlorn clump of leafless silver birch alone in a dead field.

When the old track circled around a hill, she came across a roadside chapel. It was small and its paint was flaking. Mallory had been walking hard for almost forty minutes at this point, and she stopped to catch her breath, steadying herself with a hand on the gate. The chapel, she realized, would have a bench inside for her to sit on.

No one knows for sure what happened in that chapel and it is likely not even Madame Mallory rightly understands. But for many years I have wondered about what occurred in that roadside house of worship, imagined it, and perhaps the picture that I have in mind is not all that far off from the truth.

I imagine Madame Mallory primly sitting for some time on the chapel's only pew, the cane basket on her lap, staring up at the washed-out mural of Christ's Last Supper covering the opposite wall. Disciples, faded into a dull wash, break bread. The figures are shrouded in the gloom, mere smudges in the dark, but she can just make out, on the set table, a bowl of olives, a jug of wine, a loaf of bread.

The air itself is leaden with a cold and musty rot. The chapel's wooden crucifix stands stiffly and mechanically erect, and the unlit oil lamp to the side of the stone altar is caught up in a dewy net of cobwebs. Not a flower. Not a melted candle or even a burned matchstick. No sign of human life.

It is then Madame Mallory realizes the chapel has died, that long ago all religious meaning had slipped from the neglected room. And as Mallory sits stiffly on that pew, clutching that basket on her lap, her soul fills with a horrific thought: How cold this chamber. Dear God. How cold this chamber.

The feeling is unbearable and, being who she is, she tries to fight against the discomfort. She rummages in her basket for a match-book, lights a match, leans forward to bring some life to the altar lamp. In this small gesture everything changes, for when the flaring match head meets the oil lamp's wick, the chapel convulses violently in new light and new shadows. The crucifix leaps out across the room, an emaciated and tortured man imploring her with outstretched arms. The cobwebs twitch, like a fisherman's net full of fish thrashing about for dear life, and a humping mouse scurries behind the altar.

Mallory wonders if she might be going mad, for she suddenly hears a voice, the angry voice of her father, of years ago, taking a little girl to task. Her forehead beads with sweat but she is too frightened to move. She musters all her strength and lifts her eyes to the ceiling, desperately in search of relief.

The Last Supper has been transformed by the lamp's light. Christ and the disciples are in their familiar poses, their garments now glinting with threads of silver and gold paint caught in the light. But it is not the weak-chinned Christ gazing wanly out over the horizon that catches her attention, but the table itself, not sparsely decked with olives and bread as she had first surmised, but groaning under a feast.

Figs in port. A white clump of sheep's cheese. A leg of roast mutton and a dish of herbs. And over there. A peeled onion. A boar's head on a plate.

It is the eyes of that boar that lock on to her, a decapitated head curiously full of life, and a trembling Mallory, always brave, she forces herself to look resolutely back at the animal. And in the depths of those glinting little eyes she sees the balance sheet of her life, an endless list of credits and debits, of accomplishments and failures, small acts of kindness and real acts of cruelty. And the tears finally come as she looks away, unable to see this thing to the very end, for she knows without looking of the terrible imbalance, how long ago the credits stopped while the debits of vanity and selfishness run on and on. And her involuntary cry for mercy, it rings out into the chapel, witnessed only by a painted boar with a puckish, tusk-toothed smile.

Chapter Eleven

It was sometime after dinner when Madame Mallory slipped into my hospital room. I was resting my eyes, and she spent several undetected minutes quietly studying my chest, my arms, my neck, all painfully wrapped in bandages. And most of all, she studied my hands.

At long last I sensed her great force in the room, like I had when I was cooking on opening night, and I snapped open my eyes.

"I am sorry," she said. "I didn't want it to come to this."

It began to rain outside.

Mallory was partly in shadow, but I could see the outline of her bun, the muscular arms, the trademark wicker basket from earlier in the day. This was, I realized, the first time we had ever talked with one another.

"Why do you hate us?"

I heard the sharp intake of her breath. But she did not reply. Instead, she moved over to the window and looked out into the dark. Sheets of water poured down the black glass.

"Your hands are all right. They were not damaged."

"No."

"You'll still have the same sensitivity in your hands. You can still cook."

I didn't say anything. My emotions were too jumbled and in my throat. I was grateful that I could still cook, yes, but all my family's troubles were because of this woman, and I could not forgive her. At least not yet.

Madame Mallory pulled a package out of her basket, almond and apricot pastries. "Please, try one of my pastries," she said. I sat up and she leaned over to fluff the pillows behind my back. "Tell me," she said, turning her back on me and again looking out the window, "what do you taste?"

"Apricot and almond filling."

"Anything else?"

"Well, there's also a thin layer of nutmeg and pistachio paste, and the glaze is a lacquer made from egg yolks and honey. And you've—let me think—is it almond? No. I know. It's vanilla. You've crushed vanilla pods and worked the powder right into the puff pastry."

Madame Mallory could not find words. She continued to look out the window, rain pouring down the pane as if some goddess up above were weeping with a broken heart.

And when she did turn around, her eyes glistened like Spanish olives, a single eyebrow arched up, and she stared fiercely at me like that in the dusk until I realized, for the first time, I had the culinary equivalent of perfect pitch.

Mallory finally placed the wax paper and pastries on the portable hospital tray. "Good night," she said. "I wish you well."

A few moments later she was out the door again, and I immediately let out a sigh, as the air rushed from the room. Only after she was well and truly gone did I realize how incredibly tense and *sur mes gardes* I had been in her presence.

But she was gone, a great weight was lifted, and I sank back into my bed and closed my eyes.

Well, that's that, I thought.

The dining room was full when Mallory arrived back at Le Saule Pleureur late that night. Monsieur Leblanc stood at his spot at the reception desk, greeting the guests and taking them to their tables. The white jackets of the junior waiters quickly flashed by the window, silver domes glinting as they were borne aloft among the maze of starched linen tables.

Mallory saw all this from outside, as she stood up to her ankles in snow and looked in silently through the brightly lit windows above her rock garden. She saw the wine steward warming a brandy while Le Comte de Nancy Selière laughed, his gold-capped tooth sparkling in the light. And she watched the count as he lifted a piece of pineapple spice bread to his lips, his aging face suddenly filled with a hedonistic pleasure.

Mallory brought a hand to her throat, moved beyond words at the sight of her life's work elegantly, effortlessly turning over in the night. And she stood like that in the cold dark for some time, silently observing her staff devoting themselves to the restaurant and its customers, until the exhausting events of the day at long last settled into her weary joints. It was shortly before St. Augustine chimed midnight that Mallory took the back stairs to her attic, finally surrendering body and soul to the rhythms of the night.

"You had me worried," Monsieur Leblanc scolded the next morning. "We couldn't find you. I thought, My God, what have I done? What have I done?"

"Ah, cher Henri."

But that was all the emotion Mallory could express, and she busied herself with the buttons on her cardigan. "You have done nothing wrong," she said lightly. "Come, let us get back to work. Christmas will be on us soon. It's time we collected the foie gras."

Madame Degeneret, the Weeping Willow's foie gras supplier, lived on the slopes above Clairvaux-les-Lacs. Degeneret was a feisty old woman in her eighties who kept her dilapidated farm ticking over with the income she earned force-feeding a hundred Moulard ducks. And as Leblanc pulled the Citroën into the pot-holed drive of the old farm, brown ducks, heads held high and quacking, waddled briskly back and forth across the courtyard.

Old Degeneret, in her gray wool tights and tatty sweaters, barely acknowledged their arrival while she fussed over a bag of feed, and Mallory was relieved to see the gnarled old woman still standing, still in hot pursuit of her ducks. Mallory impulsively told Leblanc he should pick the foie gras while she waited outside with Madame Degeneret.

This, of course, was highly unusual. Mallory always insisted on judging the livers herself, as no one else was ever competent enough. But before Leblanc could object, Mallory had taken a milking stool and was sitting alongside Madame Degeneret, watching the old woman's arthritic, knobby hands gently slide a feeding funnel down a duck's gullet. So—what else was there to say?—Leblanc disappeared into the barn, where the young work hand was plucking and bleeding a dozen ducks before removing the prized foie gras and the *magret*.

"Are you well, Madame Degeneret?" Mallory asked, pulling a tissue from under her cardigan sleeve and discreetly wiping her nose.

"Can't complain."

The old woman pulled the funnel out of the duck's crop and grabbed another squawking bird. But she suddenly stopped, looked at the mark on the bird's leg, and let the bird go.

"Not you. Shoo. Get away."

The bird flapped across the courtyard and a half-dozen ducklings waddled energetically after her. Mallory's hands were calmly clasped on her lap, and the wintry sun felt good upon her face.

"Why not that one?" she asked mildly.

"Can't."

"But why?"

"A few weeks ago," Degeneret said with a snort of contempt, "a no-brains tourist drove into the farm too quickly and killed the mother of those six ducklings. Usually that's the end for the little ones. The others peck them to death. But that old bird took care of the motherless chicks. Let them join her brood."

"Oh, I see."

"*Non, non, madame.* That duck will live a full life. I will not kill her. For what? A liver? I wouldn't be able to sleep at night. Imagine. A duck showing more kindness than a human being. I can't have that."

Just then Leblanc emerged from the barn with two plastic bags of foie gras, and Madame Mallory rose from her stool, unable to utter a word.

Papa picked me up from the hospital in the Maison Mumbai van, and before long we were pulling into the open gates of the Dufour estate, the crêpe-lined banners stretched across the courtyard wel-coming me home. A crowd of well-wishers, not just my family but some fifty citizens of Lumière, stood under the banners and broke into raucous clapping and roars and piercing whistles at our arrival. And I, getting into the mood of it all, quite liking all this attention, opened the van door and waved like a returning war hero.

It was such a lovely homecoming. There was Monsieur Iten and his wife. And Madame Picard. And there, too, the mayor and his son, my new friend, Marcus.

And Madame Mallory.

She had come directly from Madame Degeneret's farm, with urgent purpose.

Papa and I spotted her at the same moment, loitering as she was in the back of the crowd, and you could feel the mood of the homecoming change instantly. Papa was furious and he scowled, the crowd turning their heads to see what he was staring at. There were gasps. Whispers.

But Madame Mallory ignored them all and stepped forward, the crowd parting to let her pass.

"You are not welcome," Papa roared from the van. "Leave."

"Monsieur Haji," Mallory called back, stepping to the front. "I came to ask for your forgiveness. Please. I beg you. Don't leave Lumière."

A murmur of excitement rippled through the crowd.

Papa stood magnificently on the running board of the van, above everyone, not looking at Mallory, but like a politician appealing directly to the crowd. "Now she want us to stay, yaar?" he bellowed. "But the time for that has passed. It is too late."

"*Mais non*, it is not too late," she said. He still wouldn't look at her, although she now stood at his feet. "Please, I want you to stay. And I want Hassan to come work in my kitchen. I will teach him French cooking. I will give him a proper education."

My heart skipped. It was, however, this request for me to come work for her that finally got Papa to look down at the famous chef.

"You are utterly mad. No. Worse. You are sick. Who you tink you are?"

"*Ah, merde,* don't be so pigheaded—"

But Mallory stopped herself, visibly trying to stay in control of her temper. She took a deep breath and tried again. "Listen, you, listen to what I am saying. This is a chance for your son to become a truly great French chef, a man of taste, a proper artist, not just some curry cook working in an Indian bistro."

"Aaaarrgh. You just don't get it."

Papa stepped down from the van, his great belly aggressively thrust forward.

"What is it with you?" he yelled, forcing her back through the crowd, step by step, back to the gates. "Can't you hear what I am saying? Nah? We can't stand you, you barren old woman. We want nothing to do with you." And by the time he had finished his tirade, she was back in the cobblestone street.

Alone.

We in the courtyard, we were jeering.

Mallory smiled softly, pulled some stray hairs behind her ear, and walked back alone toward her restaurant. We turned our backs, too, and went inside. But I would not be telling you the truth if I did not also admit to a small lump of regret sitting in the pit of my stomach, as we turned from Mallory's incredible offer to the fussing festivities of my homecoming.

But Madame Mallory was not alone, for Monsieur Leblanc had seen everything from behind the curtains of the restaurant, and he rushed forward to greet her at the door, tenderly taking her hand. And anyone who would have seen his tipped, balding head would have recognized his tender hand-kiss expressed nothing but the deepest respect and affection.

And in the instant when those lips brushed the back of her hand, Madame Mallory understood how deep was Leblanc's love and devotion, and she caught her breath, a girlish hand on her chest. For Mallory finally understood her great fortune, understood how lucky she was to have such a good and decent friend at her side, and it was this, Leblanc's tender support, that gave her the feeling she could suffer through anything in the name of justice.

So none of us noticed, cavorting as we were under flashing disco lights within the restaurant, the quiet turn of events taking place outside the front door of Maison Mumbai. But batty old Ammi did. She wandered out from the garage, talking to herself about goodness knows what, and almost walked straight into Madame Mallory.

Ammi circled, as the chef calmly placed a wooden seat in the middle of our cobblestone courtyard.

As three large bottles of Evian went under the chair.

As Mallory sat down and crossed her arms over her bosom, a tartan blanket on her lap. The sun was setting behind the Alps.

"Wah?" said Ammi, puffing on her pipe. "Wah you doin' here?"

"Sitting."

"Haar," said Ammi, "good place," and continued on her walkabout. But perhaps something did get through her muddled brain, for Ammi eventually made her way into the party, through the gyrating bodies, and tugged at Papa's kurta.

"Visitor."

"Wah you mean, visitor?"

"Outside. Visitor."

Papa swung open the front door and a chilly wind rattled through the hall.

His roar, I tell you, stopped the party in its tracks.

"Are you deaf? Are you mad? I told you to get out."

We all piled out onto the icy steps to see what was going on.

Madame Mallory stared straight ahead as if she had all the time in the world. "I will not move," she said calmly. "I will not move until you let Hassan come work for me."

Papa laughed, and many on the steps joined in his mocking laughter.

But not I. Not this time.

"Crazy woman," Papa sneered. "Never will that happen. But do what you want. You are welcome to stay there. Until you rot. Bye-bye."

He shut the door and we returned to our festivities.

In the early evening the party disbanded. Our guests left

through the front door, chatting to themselves, startled to discover Madame Mallory still sitting in the middle of the courtyard.

"*Bonsoir, Madame Mallory.*"

"*Bonsoir, Monsieur Iten.*"

The excitement of the homecoming was too much, and I mounted the steps to my room while the rest of the family went about their duties for the evening meal. I was so pleased to finally be with my things again in my room up in the turret—my cricket bat and Che Guevara poster and my CDs. But the world could wait, and I lay down on the bed, too tired even to get under the duvet.

It was late evening when I awoke and the downstairs dining room was in full roar. I went to my window; water dripped from the roof's gutter.

There she was, down below, bundled up in a heavy overcoat. Someone had since plied her with blankets, and she was buried under them like an ice fisherman, patiently waiting in the night. Her head was wrapped in a flannel scarf, and I remember how a column of steam roared from her face with each breath. Guests arrived at the restaurant, uncertain of the etiquette required in such an unusual situation, and stopped nervously to chat with her, moved on, wished her well again as they left near midnight.

"Is she still there?"

I turned. It was little Zainab in her pajamas, rubbing her eyes. I took her carefully in my arms and we sat on the windowsill, staring down at the forlorn figure in our courtyard. We sat there for some time, almost in a trance, until we heard an odd noise different from the restaurant din. It was an unpleasant sort of chattering. Ammi, we figured, having one of her dialogues with the past, and we went into the hallway to help her snap out of it.

Papa.

He was peeking out from the upper corridor window, hiding behind the curtains. "What am I to do, Tahira?" we heard him mutter. "What am I to do?"

"Papa."

He jumped, dropped the corners of the curtain.

"Wah? Why you sneak up on me like dat?"

Zainab and I looked at each other, and Papa barreled past us down the stairs.

Madame Mallory sat on the chair all that night and all the next day.

The news spread and her hunger strike became the talk of the valley. By noon a three-deep crowd had gathered at the gates of Maison Mumbai; by four in the afternoon a local reporter from *Le Jura* was at the gates, his long lens stuck between the bars, snapping away at the squat figure resolutely sitting in the middle of our courtyard.

When Papa saw this—saw this from the upstairs corridor window—he went absolutely mad. We could hear him roar all the way through the house, heard him pounding down the central staircase and out the front door. "Get away," he yelled. "Go. Shoo."

But the townspeople wouldn't budge from the other side of the gate.

"We're not on your property. We can stay here."

Local boys jeered him, chanted, "Haji is a tyrant. Haji is a tyrant."

"Monsieur Haji," the reporter called out. "Why do you treat her so shabbily?"

Papa's face trembled with disbelief. "Me treat her shabbily? She try to ruin my business. She almost kill my son!"

"It was an accident." It was Madame Picard.

"You, too?" he asked incredulously.

"Forgive her."

"She is just a foolish old woman," said someone else.

Papa scowled at the mob.

He turned around and marched up to Madame Mallory.

"Stop it! Stop it now. You will fall ill. You are too old for this nonsense."

And it was true. The elderly woman was now quite stiff, and when she turned her head her whole torso had to twist with her.

"Let Hassan come work for me."

"Go freeze to death. Please. Be my guest."

* * *

I remember that night, before turning in, sitting again with my little sister Zainab at my turret window. We watched, in the moonlight, the elderly Frenchwoman in the courtyard, her arms folded, not budging. The moonlight and swirling clouds above were caught at her feet, reflected back up to us from the puddles of the uneven cobblestone court.

"What will happen to her?" Zainab asked. "What will happen to us?"

I stroked her hair. "I don't know, little one. I don't know."

But that was when I crossed sides and secretly began rooting for the elderly woman. And I think little Zainab must have sensed this, for I remember she squeezed my hand and nodded, like she alone understood what had to be done.

P apa tossed and turned in his bed that night, thrice got up to look out the window. The thing that most galled him was the idea that Mallory was using passive resistance to get what she wanted. Of course, this was the very same method with which Gandhi had created modern India, and it was intolerable, so infuriating, that she would use the same methods against us. Papa, I tell you, he was the picture of a man in turmoil during this time, and all through the night he slid eerily in and out of consciousness, muttering to himself in broken sleep.

Around four in the morning the hallway filled with creaking.

I, in my room, Papa in his, woke instantly at the noise and we clambered out of bed to see what was going on. "You hear it, too?" he whispered as we crept down the corridor, our nightshirts rippling in the frigid air.

"Yes."

Luminous figures hovered on the stairs.

"What are you doing?" Papa bellowed, snapping on the overhead chandelier.

Auntie and Ammi screamed and dropped a plate. It smashed on the steps and three pieces of naan and a bottle of Evian rolled to the bottom of the staircase. We looked back at the two offenders. Ammi clutched a chamber pot.

"Who dat for? Who dat for?"

"You're an animal, Abbas," yelled Auntie. "The poor woman. She is starving. You will kill her."

Papa roughly grabbed Ammi and Auntie by the elbows and hauled them back upstairs. "Everyone go back to bed," he roared. "Tomorrow I will have that woman removed. Finish. I will not have this. She is an insult to the memory of Gandhi, using these techniques on us."

Of course, no one slept a wink after that and we were all up early, watching Papa pace back and forth in front of the telephone. Finally, the slow-dragging watch hands pointed at the allotted time and Papa rang his lawyer at the office, demanding the police cart Mallory away for trespassing.

A funk had settled on the entire family, and we morosely shoveled our potato breakfast back and forth across the plate as Papa talked and talked and talked into the phone. Only Ammi ate well.

But Zainab, we learned that morning, Zainab was cut from the same cloth as Papa. My little sister walked over to Papa as he bellowed into the phone, and she tugged his kurta, utterly fearless.

"Stop it, Papa. I don't like this."

The look on his face, my God, it was horrible.

I stepped forward and took her hand. "Yes, Papa. It's time to stop this. Now."

I'll always remember that moment. His mouth hung open, his torso frozen in an odd twist, half-talking on the phone, half-turned toward his two children. Zainab and I stood resolutely like that for some time, waiting for the bellow or the slap, but he turned back to the phone and told his lawyer he'd call him back.

"What you say? I don't tink I heard you right."

"Papa, if Hassan becomes a French chef, that means we stay here and make this home. Well, good. I am tired of moving, Papa. I don't want to go back to drizzly old England. I like it here."

"Mummy would want us to stop running," I added. "Can't you hear her, Papa?"

Papa stared at us coldly, as if we had betrayed him, but gradually the hardness in Papa's face dissolved, and it was something quietly miraculous, like watching a chilled lump of goose fat warming in a hot pan.

The mountain air was crisp and clean, just like that first day when we arrived in Lumière those three months ago, and the region's famous morning light was busy washing the mountains in pinks, mauves, and mild browns.

"Madame Mallory," Papa called out gruffly across the courtyard. "Come and have breakfast with us."

But the chef no longer had the strength to turn her head. Her skin was a deathly white, and her nose, I recall, was bitter red and sore, with beads of mucus hanging from its tip. "Promise," she croaked in a weak voice, still staring straight ahead through a small opening among the layers of blankets. "Promise Hassan come work for me."

Papa's face darkened at the woman's obstinacy, and he was again at the threshold of blowing his top. But little Zainab, his conscience, she was in his hands and at his side, tugging her warnings. Papa took a deep breath and released his terrible sigh.

"What you think, Hassan? You want to study French cooking? You wanna work for dis woman?"

"I want nothing more in this world."

I think he was physically struck by the fervency of my answer, that irrefutable call of destiny that spoke through me, and for a few moments he could do nothing but stare intently at the cracks of the cobblestones beneath his feet, holding on to little Zainab for strength. But when enough time had passed, he raised his head. He was a good man, my Papa.

"You have my word, Madame Mallory. Hassan, you must work in Le Saule Pleureur's kitchen."

The joy I felt, like that incredible explosion of cream when you bite into a *religieuse* pastry. But Mallory did not have the arrogant smile of the winner on her lips, but something humble, something that expressed relief and somber thanks and somehow acknowledged my father's sacrifice. And I think Papa appreciated this, for Papa planted his feet solidly before her, for balance, and offered her his outstretched hands.

And I remember, so well, that moment when she clapped her hands in his and Papa pulled her to her feet with a grunt, the way my *maîtresse* slowly and creakily rose from her courtyard chair. This, too, I remember.

And so, next day, Auntie and Mehtab helped me pack my bag and I crossed the street. A lot of emotion went into that hundred-foot journey, cardboard suitcase in hand, from one side of Lumière's boulevard to the other. Before me the sugar-dusted willow tree, the leaded windows and the lace curtains, the elegant inn where even the warped wooden steps were soaked in great French traditions. And there, standing on Le Saule Pleureur's stone steps, in white aprons, the taciturn Madame Mallory and kind Monsieur Leblanc, an elderly couple waiting with outstretched hands for their newly adopted son.

I went to them and my adopted home and the growing I had yet to do—as a student of French cuisine, as a servant of the kitchen. But at my back was the world from where I had come: little Zainab and watery-eyed Ammi, pomfret tikka and Kingfisher beer, the wailing of Hariharan, the hot kadai spitting oil and peas and ginger and chili.

And as I passed Papa at the iron gates, as each new generation is meant to do, he wept unabashedly and wiped his grief-stricken face with a white handkerchief. And I remember, as if it were yesterday, his words as I passed.

"Remember, sweet boy, you are a Haji. Always remember. A Haji."

It was such a small journey, in feet, but it felt as if I were striding from one end of the universe to the other, the light of the Alps illuminating my way.

Chapter Twelve

My room at Le Saule Pleureur was at the top of the house, down the narrow hall from Madame Mallory's flat. In winter, my monk's cell was intensely cold; in summer, it was unbearably hot and stuffy. The bathroom was down a half flight of stairs at the end of the hall.

That day when I moved to Le Saule Pleureur, I found myself standing alone, for the first time, in the attic room that was to be my home for the years to come. It smelled of old people and a long-ago-sprayed bug treatment. A gaunt Christ on a crucifix was gushing blood from his wounds, and the emaciated figure hung, with a small mirror, on the wall directly above my bed. A dark-wood closet, with two ancient cedar hangers hanging inside, seemed to glower malevolently from the corner of the room, opposite the narrow cot. There was hardly enough space to turn around in; a portico high up on the wall looked out on the gabled roof outside but did little to alleviate the close space.

I set my suitcase down. What had I done?

I was—I don't mind admitting it—completely rattled by the austere room, so Catholic and foreign to my upbringing, and a voice in my head, half-hysterical, urged me to dash back to the safety and comfort of my cheerful bedroom in Maison Mumbai.

But a book on the bedside table caught my eye and I stepped forward to examine it. It was a fat tome with yellowed pages and ornate illustrations depicting different butchering cuts on every kind of livestock from cattle to rabbit.

An unsealed envelope was slipped inside its pages.

The handwritten note, from Madame Mallory, was a formal welcome to Le Saule Pleureur and stated, in her old-fashioned penmanship, how much she looked forward to having me as a student in her kitchen. She urged me to work hard and absorb as much as possible in the coming years; she was there for me and would help me any way she could. To start our adventure, she said, I should study this Lyon butcher's treatise with utmost care.

Her letter hit just the right note, and a manly voice inside my head suddenly and roughly said, *Get on with it and stop acting the damn fool.* So I made sure Madame Mallory and Leblanc had closed the door firmly behind them, before locking it tight. Reassured I couldn't possibly be disturbed, I stood on the cot and took down the frightening crucifix, hiding it deep in the back of the closet, totally out of sight. And then, finally, I unpacked my bag.

There was a dream that repeatedly visited me during those early days of my apprenticeship, which now, looking back, seems quite significant. In this dream I was walking alongside a large body of water when suddenly an ugly, primordial fish from the water's deep, flat and round with a bull head, crawled up the beach using its fins as primitive feet, pushing itself with a great deal of effort out of the water and onto dry land. And there, exhausted by the Herculean effort, the fish rested, its tail still in the water, its head on the dry sand, gills opening and closing like fire bellows, shocked and pumping and gasping in this new amphibian state, half-in and half-out of the two vastly different worlds.

But truth be told, there was no time to concern myself with such things, or even the niceties of boudoir décor, because from that first afternoon forward, I was hardly ever in my room, but to put my head down and pass out.

My alarm went off at 5:40 every morning. Twenty minutes later I was having breakfast with Madame Mallory in her attic flat. Bombarding me with questions on what I had studied during the previous twenty-four hours, Madame Mallory used these early morning sessions to lay the intellectual groundwork for the real lessons held down in the kitchen later in the day.

Verbal interrogations completed, we promptly headed off to the markets in furtherance of my education, before returning to the inn with our purchases, where the day's work began in earnest. The first six months of my apprenticeship Madame Mallory rotated me through every low-level job: At first I did nothing but wash dishes, mop the kitchen floors, and scrub and prepare *les légumes;* the next month I was out front, in the restaurant, a bread-boy in tunic and white cotton gloves, instructed to closely study the ballet of service unfolding around me, or ordered in off-hours to set the dining room, Madame Mallory personally following me from table to table and clicking her tongue in consternation every time I positioned a silver spoon not perfectly aligned with the other cutlery's military order.

No sooner had I found my footing there, than I was marched back to the kitchen, this time to spend my days plucking and cleaning wild pigeons, quail, and pheasant for hours on end, until I thought my arms might drop off. Chef de Cuisine Jean-Pierre barked at me continuously during this period, and by the end of the day I was barely able to stand, for the stiffness of my back. This assignment was followed, then, by a stint alongside Monsieur Leblanc, at the front desk, taking reservations and learning the skill of properly seating a restaurant and the delicate politics of not offending repeat customers.

But still no hand at cooking.

I worked this way every day until three thirty, when we were given the midafternoon break hoteliers call "room hour," and I crawled back to my attic cell for a nap that bordered on a coma. Early evening, I tumbled bleary-eyed down the stairs again, to engage in my next lesson: thirty minutes of wine tasting and cor-responding lecture, under the tutelage of Le Saule Pleureur's som-melier, before taking up my regular work shift until midnight. The alarm would go off at the unforgiving hour of 5:40 the next morn-ing, and the tyranny of the workday started all over again.

Monday was my day off, and all I had the energy for was to stag-ger back across the boulevard, to the Dufour estate, to collapse on our old couch.

"They make you eat pig?"

"Arash, stop it with the stupid questions. Leave your brother alone."

"But did they, Hassan? You eaten pig?"

"You are looking so thin. I tink dat woman starve you."

"Try this, Hassan. I made it just for you. Malai peda. With golden blossom honey."

I lay stretched out on the couch like a Mughal prince, Auntie and Mehtab feeding me sweetmeats and milky tea, Uncle Mayur and Ammi and Zainab and my brothers dragging chairs over to listen spellbound to the morsels of information I passed on from the inner sanctum of Le Saule Pleureur across the street.

"The special tomorrow will be *palombe,* wood pigeon. I tell you, I have been plucking and cleaning pigeon for two days. Very difficult work. Mehtab, please, massage the shoulders. See how tense, from all the work? We are serving *salmis de palombes,* which is pigeon pie, very succulent, in a Merlot and shallot sauce. It is best served with . . ."

Papa behaved very curiously during this period. Warmly roaring his greetings at the door and throwing his arms around me when I first entered, he would then drift off, oddly distant, allowing the rest of the family to swarm in. For some reason, Papa never partook in the family's ritual interrogation about my work, but hovered at the back of the room, pretending to fuss over some task at the partner's desk, like slitting open bills with an ivory letter opener, but clearly listening to every word that was being said, even though he never asked a question himself.

"All week I have been learning about the Languedoc-Roussillon, the wine region around Marseille. Makes a huge quantity of wine but, you know, it produces only ten percent of the nation's Appellation Contrôlée." Seeing how wide-eyed they were, at my every pronouncement, I couldn't resist adding, with an affected wave of the hand, "I recommend the Fitou and Minervois. The Corbières is rather disappointing, particularly the vintages of the more recent years."

They oohed and aahed quite agreeably.

"What a ting," said Uncle Mayur. "Imagine dat. Our Hassan. Knows French wines."

"And what is Mallory like? She beat you?"

"No. Never. She doesn't have to. Just one eyebrow up and we are all dashing about like nervous chickens. Everyone is scared of her. But Jean-Pierre, her number two. He yells and swats my head. Quite a lot."

Slit. Slit. From the back of the room.

It was only later in the day, when I was stuffed with our food and coddled and suitably stroked by the family, ready at long last to return to Le Saule Pleureur with renewed determination, that Papa would formally summon me for a private talk, gesture at me to sit down at his desk, his fingers in a steeple and his voice laden with gravitas.

"Tell me, Hassan, has she showed you how to make the tongue? With the Madeira sauce?"

"Not yet, Papa."

His face fell in disappointment.

"No? Hmm. Not very impressive. Perhaps she not as good as we tink."

"No, Papa. She a great chef."

"And that scoundrel Jean-Pierre. Does he know you are from an important family? Nah! Do I need to teach this fellow a lesson or two?"

"No, Papa. Thank you. I will manage."

In short, I never let on to Papa how difficult the transition was during those first few months, how I missed him and the rest of the family dearly, and how frustrated I was by the work during those early days at Le Saule Pleureur.

For I desperately wanted to get my hands dirty with the cooking, but Madame Mallory wouldn't let me near a stove, and my frustrations finally came to a head late one morning when I was climbing Le Saule Pleureur's back stairs, on Jean-Pierre's order, to fetch lightbulbs from the supply closet on the third floor.

Madame Mallory was at that moment descending the stairs, fresh as could be, on her way out to the driveway where Monsieur Leblanc was waiting in the idling Citroën, ready to take her to a social function in town.

Chef Mallory was shrugging on brown leather gloves and

wore a heavy wool wrap thrown around her shoulders. The narrow wooden stairway in which we stood filled with her Guerlain perfume, and I respectfully pressed myself against the wall to let her pass. But she stopped, two stairs above me, and peered down through the artificial gloaming of the staircase.

I undoubtedly looked wan and weak and possibly at rope's end. "Hassan, tell me, do you regret your decision? To come here?"

"Non, madame."

"The hours are very difficult. But you'll see. One day you'll wake up, and, *voilà*, you will have a second wind. The body adjusts."

"Yes. Thank you, Chef."

She continued down the stairs, and I upward, and I don't know what possessed me, to be so impertinent, but I blurted out, "But when can I start cooking? Will I only be peeling carrots here?"

She stopped on a lower step, in the dusk, but never turned her head. "You will start cooking when the time is right."

"But when will that be?"

"Patience, Hassan. We will know when the moment has arrived."

"Now focus. In what waters do the *Ostrea lurida* grow?"

"Umm. Off Brittany?"

"Wrong. Completely wrong, young man."

Madame Mallory stared at me with her most imperious look, one eyebrow raised. It was six fifteen in the morning and we sat as usual under her turret window, sipping coffee from delicate Limoges porcelain. I was stupid with sleep.

"The *Ostrea edulis* is the oyster that grows off Brittany. Hassan, honestly, you should know this. We learnt about the *Ostrea lurida* two weeks ago. Here is the book on shellfish again. Study it. Properly this time."

"Oui, madame . . . Oh, I remember now. The *lurida* is the tiny oyster that grows only in a few bays off the northwest coast of the United States. In Puget Sound."

"Correct. I've never tried them myself, but I understand they have a very fine taste of seaweed, iodine, and hazelnut. Considered among the world's finest. Hard to believe, that they should be better than a good Brittany oyster, but that is some people's opinion. It is a matter of taste."

Madame Mallory leaned forward to attack the bowl of fruit salad sitting at the center of the table. Her early morning appetite, the amount of fuel she took on board for her rigorous schedule of the day, was quite astounding. She had far more in common with Papa than either cared to admit.

"Now, European markets have been infested by a foreign import. What is the name of this invasive oyster, and tell me its history, briefly."

I sighed. Glimpsed at my watch. "Will you be stuffing the veal breast today?"

Madame Mallory delicately spat out the pit of a stewed prune into a silver spoon and deposited it on the side of her bowl.

"*Ah, non.* Do not change the subject, Hassan. It won't work."

She put her bowl down. And stared.

"*Crassostrea gigas,* a Japanese oyster, commonly called the Pacific oyster, became dominant in Europe during the 1970s."

It was a tad wintry, true, but it was still a smile.

Later that day, however, I caught my first glimpse of what lay ahead, when down in Le Saule Pleureur's cold kitchen, leaning over the sink, Madame Mallory spontaneously reached out and patted my cheek after I correctly identified a specific type of *les creuses de Bretagne* oyster solely by sipping a teaspoon of its briny juice.

It was essentially a kind gesture meant to convey affection and approval, but in all honesty that tap-tap at my cheek, with her dry hand, so stiff, made my toes curl. And the incredible awkwardness of the moment was compounded by the fact she had ordered her *chef de cuisine* to demonstrate a certain oyster dish for us, and Jean-Pierre was at that moment standing at the stove glowering at me over Madame Mallory's shoulder.

I knew then there was trouble ahead. But powerless to shape events, I avoided Jean-Pierre's red face and instead focused intently on his hands, how he prepared the *Sauternes sabayon* sauce for the oysters, swiftly and expertly combining ingredients in the shuffling hot pan, as Madame Mallory droned on, explaining in minute detail the magical transformations happening in the searing heat, entirely oblivious to the emotions she had unleashed in her *chef de cuisine.*

I was slave to Le Saule Pleureur's rhythms but still clinging to Maison Mumbai's doorknob, and this weird transitional phase all comes vividly back to me when I remember that time, a month or two after I moved, when Madame Mallory and I went into town to the markets for our early-morning purchases and lessons.

Madame Mallory had spent the first part of the morning tour making me smell and taste various cabbages—the savoy, chubby little cancan dancers luridly fanning their ruffled green petticoats so we could get a sneak peek at their delicately pale and parting leaves inside, and the giant red cabbage, deep in color, like a bon vivant soused in a ruby red port wine before showing up merrily on the stall's counter.

"The thing you need to understand, Hassan, is that kohlrabi is the bridge between the cabbage and the turnip, and it melds the flavors of both vegetables. Remember that. It's a subtle but important distinction that will help you decide when one vegetable is an ideal side dish, but not the other."

Wicker baskets on both arms, leaning over to listen to my small voice in the boisterous market, Madame Mallory was, I must tell you, the very essence of patience on those trips, prepared to answer any of my questions, no matter how puerile and basic.

"We have a preference, in this region of France, for the Early White Vienna and the Early Purple Vienna kohlrabi varieties. Now, the *navet de Suede* is, in contrast, a robust turnip that grew wild up in the Baltic region, before Celts brought the nutritious root south and it began proper cultivation in France. This was thousands of years ago, of course, but it is my opinion the Swedish turnip today surpasses all other turnips, because of its sweetness, a characteristic bred into the vegetable over time. We should be able to find the yellow and black *navet* varieties at Madame Picard's—"

We both looked up, to orient ourselves in the market and locate Madame Picard's stall, and found, much to our surprise, Papa standing in front of the French widow's operation. His feet were planted firmly apart, one hand on his hip, the other thrashing the air. He was talking with a great deal of animation, and I suspect I must have imagined it, at that distance, but I distinctly recall spittle flying like fireworks from his face.

Meanwhile, rough-looking Madame Picard, in her army boots and the usual layers of black skirts and sweaters, and that wispy hair, she had her head back and was lustily roaring with laughter at Papa's story, so taken with mirth she had one hand out, to steady herself on Papa's forearm.

I cringed when I saw the two of them like that, and immediately wanted to turn away, but Madame Mallory, perhaps sensing my instinct to bolt, put her hand on my elbow and marched us forward.

"*Bonjour, Madame Picard. Bonjour, Monsieur Haji.*"

Papa and Madame Picard had not seen us approach, were in fact still laughing, but their amusement instantly withered at the sound of that familiar voice. Papa in fact turned in a slightly defensive crouch, until he saw me, and then there was this flicker of insecurity behind the eyelids, as if he was unsure of how he should behave. But we were all like that—me in the markets accompanying Madame Mallory, and Papa with Picard on the "other side," it was head-bending.

"Hello, Chef Mallory," Papa said awkwardly. "Beautiful day. And I see you have brought your most talented student with you."

"Hello, Papa. *Bonjour, Madame Picard.*"

The Widow Picard looked me up and down in that French way. "Don't you look the part, Hassan. *Le petit chef.*"

"So, how is my boy doing? Ready to take your place yet?"

"Certainly not," Madame Mallory said stiffly. "But he is a quick learner, I will grant him that."

We all stood, awkwardly, at a loss on how to proceed, until Madame Mallory pointed at a basket in the back of the stall and said, "Look there, Hassan, as I told you. But they are the white *navet de Suede,* not the yellow or black I was hoping to find." She leaned forward, ignoring Papa, and said, "Do you, Madame Picard, by any chance have some of the other, less common varieties hiding somewhere?"

There was a strange look on Papa's face—not angry, more startled, like someone who'd just had his eyes opened as to how things would be from now on. And I will always remember how Papa, after blinking slowly a few times, taking it all in, put a hand on my shoulder, squeezed his good-bye, and then withdrew from the market without another word.

Six months after I started my apprenticeship, after a luncheon sitting, Marcel and I were in the kitchen mopping the floor spotless as Madame Mallory insisted, finishing our duties before we could crawl back to our respective rooms for our "room hour" rest.

There was a rap at the back door and I went to see who it was.

It was Monsieur Iten with a box.

"*Bonjour, Hassan. Ça va?*"

After the ritualistic exchanges about the state of health of various members of our respective families, Monsieur Iten informed me he had just received a special delivery of *Bretagne* oysters, and he brought them immediately by Le Saule Pleureur because he knew Madame Mallory would want to serve such fresh oysters during the evening's sitting, if she knew they were available.

But she wasn't at the restaurant. Neither was Jean-Pierre, Margaret, or even Monsieur Leblanc. No one of authority was around. It was just Marcel and me mopping up.

"What do you think, Marcel?"

Marcel shook his head vehemently, his chubby cheeks shuddering in horror at the notion we might make so crucial a decision. "Don't do it, Hassan. She will kill us."

I peered into the box. "How many, Monsieur Iten?"

"Eight dozen."

I poked around in the box.

"Okay. I'll sign for them. But subtract four."

"*Pourquoi?*"

"Because these four are *Crassostrea gigas*. You know perfectly well, Monsieur Iten, Chef Mallory would never serve them to her

143

guests. How did they get in here? She would be furious with you if she saw you trying to pass Pacific oysters off as *huîtres Portuguaises Sauvages*. And, besides, it's all a jumble. The rest are all Breton oysters, true, but I see at least another six that are not the very fine *La Cancale pousses en claires* from around Mont Saint-Michel. Look, *La Cancale* have a pale beige mantle and toothed shells, like this. I would guess these ones over here are *La Croisicaise,* from the Grand and Petit Traict channels in the south. See, here, the signature pale yellow in the shell? And look at the varying sizes. These here are number fours, but these must be number twos. *Non?* There is no mention of this on your bill, Monsieur Iten. So I am sorry, but you will have to adjust the bill accordingly if you want me to accept delivery."

Monsieur Iten removed the four offending oysters, made a note on the bill about the other details on size and quality I had noticed, before saying, "Forgive me, Hassan. An oversight. I will not let it happen again."

It was only when Madame Mallory promoted me to *commis* the next day, to personally assist her in the kitchen, that I realized the box of oysters had been a test quietly prearranged with the fishmonger. Of course, neither of them ever owned up to the fact.

But that's the way Chef Mallory was.

Challenging, always challenging.

Particularly of her staff.

It was a busy Saturday in deepest winter. The world outside was crystalline and white, with fat icicles hanging from Le Saule Pleureur's copper gutters like hams curing in a shed. Inside, the steamy kitchen was in full roar, pot lids rattling, flames flaring, and in this culinary fervor I was tasked with making the day's soufflés, a lunchtime favorite made from goat cheese and pistachios.

I pulled a set of ceramic molds from the chilly storage room in the back of the kitchen and, as was normal, lathered their white walls with soft butter, before sprinkling the dishes' bottoms with cornmeal and finely chopped pistachios. The soufflé's base was also executed by the book: unripened goat cheese, egg yolks, finely minced garlic, thyme, salt, and white pepper, all heated and folded, before adding, to lighten the base, a liberal dose of beaten egg whites and cream of tartar—that crusty acid scraped off the sides of wine barrels and pulverized, after purification, into the white powder that miraculously stabilizes egg whites. The final touch was, of course, the top layer of whipped egg whites, elegantly smoothed with a knife and given just a suggestion of an artistic swirl. Preparation finally complete, I put the molds in a water bath and placed the pan in the center of the oven to bake.

A half hour later, while I was making the veal stock, Jean-Pierre cried, "Hassan! Over here!" and I dashed to his side of the range to help lift the heavy pork roasts from the ovens for the ritualistic basting in lemon juice and cognac.

Madame Mallory, on the next counter, smothering *daurade* in herbs and lime, every now and then looked over at us impatiently, to see if I had gone back to my own station.

"Hassan, keep your eye on the soufflés!" she barked.

"Watch it! You almost dropped the pan, you idiot!"

Margaret, the quiet sous chef, looked up from her corner in the cold kitchen—where she was making a blancmange—and we locked eyes over the hissing flames.

Margaret's sympathetic look, it made my heart flutter, but I could not linger, and I dashed back to my ovens to retrieve the soufflés. "Not to worry, Chef," I called out. "Trust me. All under control." I banged open the oven door, extracted the hot tray of soufflés, and lifted it onto the countertop above.

All shriveled, like a biology experiment gone bad.

"Ah, non, merde."

"Hassan!"

"No. But look. I don't understand. I have done this a dozen times before. The soufflés. They died."

They all came over to look.

"Pff," said Jean-Pierre. "Utter disaster. The boy, he's incompetent."

Madame Mallory shook her head in disgust. Like I was hopeless.

"Margaret, *vite,* take over for Hassan. Do the soufflés again. And you, Hassan, prepare the day's pasta. You will do less harm there."

I slinked off to the corner of the kitchen to lick my wounds.

Twenty minutes later Margaret came by my station, ostensibly to take down a dish, and as I reached up to the shelf to help her lift down the large platter, the backs of our hands touched and a jolt of electricity shot up my arm.

"Don't let them bully you, Hassan," she whispered. "I made the exact same mistake once. In deep winter, the outer wall in the storage room gets intensely cold, chilling the molds on the shelves of that wall. So, when you make soufflés in winter, you must first bring the dishes out into the main kitchen at least thirty minutes earlier, so the molds have time to reach room temperature before you pour in the egg whites."

She smiled sweetly, turned away, and I was in love.

This thing between Margaret and me, it all came to a head a few weeks later, when we found ourselves in the same aisle of the kitchen. Madame Mallory and Jean-Pierre were on either side of us, banging pots and yelling at the front-room staff for a pickup. Margaret and I self-consciously ignored each other, until, that is, she bent down to retrieve some tarts from the oven, and I bent down to retrieve a pan immediately adjacent to her, and our legs inadvertently touched.

There was a shock of fire up my leg, right into my groin, and I gently leaned into it. Much to my delight, I felt her lean in from her side, and a few exquisite moments later, when I came up again with my pan, I was gasping for air and holding the pan strategically before my midriff.

"Come see me at my flat during the break," she whispered.

Well, I tell you, no sooner had we finished the lunchtime service than I had my whites off and was pushing my way down Le Saule Pleureur's raked garden and piles of snow. Finally through the stucco-and-stone wall, I broke into a run, slip-sliding down the icy back alleys to Margaret's flat, just above the local pastry shop in the center of town.

Margaret met me in front of her building, and we exchanged knowing glances, but still did not say a word to each other. I looked nonchalantly up and down the cobblestone street, to see if we were being observed; her hand was shaking as she put the key into her building's frosted front door. An elderly couple entered the Bata Shoe Store down the lane; a young mother and baby carriage exited the pâtisserie; a florist was shoveling snow outside his shop. No one looked our way.

The door swung open and we were inside, past the apartment mailboxes and radiator, taking the stone stairs two by two, laughing, charging up to her studio on the third floor. Through that door, at long last in the privacy of her flat, we were all frantic hands and open mouths and dropping garments wherever they fell.

That afternoon I took lessons on the French interpretation of *la lingua franca,* and after a hot shower involving lots of giggling and large quantities of soap, we reluctantly made our way back to Le Saule Pleureur, separately, far too relaxed and carefree for the rigors of the evening's mealtime duty.

"Focus, Hassan. Where is your mind today?" snapped Madame Mallory.

That's how it started. But our growing intimacy was not without its obstacles. Sleeping in a monk's cell, next to the ever-watchful and austere Madame Mallory, was not exactly conducive to a romantic relationship. So these snatched afternoon encounters—as stimulating as they were—they were always hurried and gasping, with no chance for Margaret and me to ever spend languid time together.

One late afternoon, while I was dashing out the door and literally lashing tight my belt buckle as she stood in her kimono holding the door open, Margaret quietly said, "I am sorry you cannot spend more time, Hassan. Sometimes I get the impression you don't want to know me better. *C'est triste.*"

Margaret then gently eased shut the door of her flat, leaving me to flounder on the apartment building staircase like a fish hooked and hoisted onto a boat's deck. She was like Mother. Didn't say a lot, but when she did, my heavens, it would hit you harder than any of Papa's tirades.

That walk home I discovered, for the first time in my life, I didn't want to run away when a woman I liked opened the door to something deeper. Quite the opposite; I wanted to plunge through Margaret's open gate headfirst. So, walking back to Le Saule Pleureur that afternoon through the back alleys, I muttered loudly to myself, determined to make more time available for Margaret, particularly on our one day off from work.

This meant I had to inform the family I would no longer be regularly coming by the Dufour estate for our weekly feasts. This was, of course, as dangerous and diplomatically fraught as any Middle East negotiation, but the following Monday, knowing what was at stake, I manfully marched the short distance between the two restaurants, bristling with purpose.

My purpose evaporated the moment I crossed Maison Mumbai's threshold. Auntie made me sit in the family's most honored armchair, before fussing and plumping the pillow behind my back. Mehtab had, since my departure, taken over the kitchen at Maison Mumbai, and she emerged from the back of the house with a smile and a puffball pouch of crab-and-prawn paste, plus a few papri chaat, savory biscuits with curd.

"Just to tide you over, Hassan," my sister said. "Lunch will be ready in an hour. I made your favorite lamb trotters soup. Just for you. Now put your feet up. You must rest, poor boy."

I knew how much work had gone into making these delicacies, and my stomach churned with guilt. Mukhtar was on the couch opposite me, absentmindedly picking his nose while reading the newspaper comics jointly with Uncle Mayur.

"Thank you, Mehtab. Umm . . . sorry. But I can't stay for lunch today."

The room froze.

Mukhtar and Uncle Mayur looked up from their newspaper.

"What are you saying? Your sister and aunt have been slaving in the kitchen for you all morning."

This remark was of course predictable, but not from laid-back Uncle Mayur, who always outsourced such acid remarks to his wife. It underlined how serious my trespass was, and his attack shook me.

"Umm . . . I am sorry. . . . Sorry. But I have other plans."

"What do you mean, other plans?" snapped Auntie. "With whom? Madame Mallory?"

"No. With some of the restaurant's other staff," I said vaguely. "I should have told you earlier. Sorry. But it was decided just this morning."

Mehtab did not say a word. She just lifted her head high, like a great begum who had been deeply offended in her own home, and solemnly retreated to the kitchen. Auntie was furious and shook her finger at me.

"Look how you have hurt your sister, you ungrateful beast!"

To make matters worse, Papa's great bulk suddenly loomed in the doorway, and his deep voice rumbled over us like a tank battalion.

"What this I hear? Not eating with us today?"

"No, Papa. I have plans."

He crooked his finger for me to follow him.

Mukhtar sniggered. "Now you're in for it."

I looked daggers at my brother before following Papa and the ominous sandpaper rasp of his slippers slapping across the floor. When we were out of earshot, deep in the darkened hallway, Papa turned to look at me imperiously from his great height, but I looked right back up at him, ready to hold my ground.

"It's a girl, isn't it?"

"Yes."

"Go. Don't worry about them."

I must have looked confused.

He wobbled his head, the Indian way, and before I knew what was happening, he was leading me farther down the hallway, the slap-slosh of Papa's slippers turning right, down the half staircase, down to the Dufour mansion's side door and the gravel drive. Papa took out his jangling keys, unlocked the door used for deliveries, and held it open.

He smiled kindly and gestured with his head.

"Go. You are working very hard, Hassan. You deserve some fun. I will take care of Mehtab and your aunt, don't you worry. The ting about agitated hens, you throw some corn, you cluck over them a bit, and in no time they settle down. So go. I will take care of them. Not to worry."

"Listen up, all of you."

Madame Mallory and Monsieur Leblanc stood in the doorway of Le Saule Pleureur's kitchen in heavy overcoats and hats.

"Henri and I will be gone for most of the day. We have some errands to run in Clairvaux-les-Lacs. So you will collectively assume the day's responsibilities in my absence, and I will review your work when we return at eighteen hundred hours."

It was a couple of years into my apprenticeship, and not, in itself, entirely unheard-of as Monsieur Leblanc and Madame Mallory occasionally took time off together, a morning here, an afternoon there, for errands or a little relaxation. We were never entirely sure about the true nature of their relationship, whether discreet Monsieur Leblanc and intensely private Mallory indulged in some form of amour when away from the restaurant and its staff; there was much speculation in the kitchen on this point. Margaret and I, perhaps influenced by our own secret, were convinced the elderly couple were lovers, but Jean-Pierre and Marcel took the opposite view.

On such days when the two went on an outing, Madame Mallory divvied up the day's preparations for the evening meal among all of us. I, of course, was always given the least complicated of the assignments. On this blustery fall day, however, Madame Mallory had the devil in her, and she decided to mix things up, to keep us on our toes. Jean-Pierre, *chef de cuisine,* master of the meats, was tasked with making dainty desserts. Margaret, so skilled with sweets and pastry, was ordered to get her hands dirty with the fish. And I, the novice, was expected to prepare and precook the evening's main meat dishes, which included, among other things, six wild hare, the same amount of pigeons, a gigot, and a pork joint.

Most were perennials on the menu and were simple executions of well-known Mallory recipes. They did not worry me.

The hare, however, they were a *surprise.*

"Chef, is there any particular way you want me to cook the hare?"

"Yes. I want you to astonish me," she said, and without further instruction, she and Monsieur Leblanc were out the door.

Well, you can imagine, no sooner had they left than the three of us went to work, lips pursed, brows beaded with sweat, keenly aware we had each been given an exam to determine how flexible we were in the kitchen. Jean-Pierre was soon dusted in flour, whipping up mille-feuille with preserved citrus cream made from Menton lemons, while Margaret, stern-faced with concentration, made a crayfish-and-sherry saffron sauce to accompany meaty chunks of pike grilled perfectly on metal skewers.

If I am honest, most of the day is lost to me in a blur of relentless hard work conducted at a furious pace. I do remember that after I butchered the hares, I marinated the pieces in white wine, bay leaf, crushed garlic, malted vinegar, sweet German mustard, and a few crushed and dried juniper berries, for that slightly pungent and piney aftertaste. Suitably softened, the hare then spent several hours cooking slowly in a cast-iron pot. It was nothing grand. It was simply my take on an old-fashioned country recipe, fleetingly glanced at during a study session up in Madame Mallory's attic library, but it just seemed right for a chilly and windy autumn night.

The side dishes I prepared were a mint-infused couscous, rather than the traditional butter noodles, and a cucumber-and-sour-cream salad dashed with a handful of lingonberries. I thought together they would make soothing and light counterpoints to the heavy mustard tang of the stewed hare. Of course, now, looking back, I realize the cucumber and cream was, conscious or not, inspired by raita, the yogurt-and-cucumber condiment of my homeland.

Madame Mallory and Monsieur Leblanc returned in the early evening, as promised, and we watched anxiously as the chef silently took off her overcoat, donned her whites, and made the rounds, inspecting what each of us had prepared. I recall that she actually had fairly kind words to say about all of our efforts, for her, albeit she never missed an opportunity to point out how each of us could have improved our dishes, with this adjustment or another.

Jean-Pierre's red fruit tarts, for example, had a very respectable crust, firm, and the lip-puckering crème de cassis filling also had just the right balance of fruity sweetness and tart acidity. But when everything came together it all lacked somewhat in originality, she sniffed. A little grated nutmeg on the crème fraîche would have elevated the dessert into something special, as would have a few wild strawberries from the woods, sprinkled around the rim of the plate.

Margaret, meanwhile, had, besides the grilled pike, made rouget stuffed with asparagus and simmered in a grapefruit bouillon, before wrapping the fish in a filo jacket that was lightly baked in the oven. "Very unusual, I grant you, Margaret. But the pastry ruins it, for me. It's a nervous tick with you, always wrapping everything in pastry dough. You must be more confident and leave your comfort zone. Such strong flavors—rouget and asparagus and grapefruit—they do not need a pie crust slapped on top."

By now she had wandered over to my station, where I stood nervously, a greasy tea towel hanging from my shoulder. Madame Mallory inspected the gigot—the spring lamb, its skin perforated with garlic slivers, dusted in cumin and *herbes de Provence,* all ready to enter the oven—but didn't comment. The pork joint was already roasting in the oven, but was still too raw for a tasting, and the *pigeon avec petits pois* simply received a head nod.

Madame Mallory was, however, drawn to the cast-iron pot bubbling on the stove, pulsing and filling the air with a vinegary steam. She lifted the heavy lid and peered inside at the game stew. She sniffed, took a fork to a joint of hare, and the meat broke off easily. Chef Mallory then snapped her fingers, and Marcel rushed over with a little plate and a spoon. She tried the hare with some of the mustard gravy spooned over the minty couscous and the accompanying sour-cream-cucumber salad.

"A bit heavy-handed with the juniper berries, I would say. You only need three or four to feel their presence. Otherwise, the taste, it's too German. But, really, other than that, very well done, particularly the untraditional side dishes. Simple but effective. I must say, Hassan, you have the right feel for game."

The explosion was immediate.

"C'est merde. Complètement merde."

Mallory's public compliment, highly unusual, was just too much for Jean-Pierre. Unable to contain his fury any longer, Jean-Pierre snapped his foot hard, which in turn sent his clog shooting forward like a missile at the startled-looking Marcel on the far side of the kitchen. But the apprentice showed immense grace and speed for a boy his size, for he dropped to the floor like a felled stag at the crucial moment. The footwear continued on its trajectory and hit the kitchen's far wall with a loud crack, taking down on its descent a jug sitting on a shelf, which crashed loudly to the floor in a shower of shattering pottery shards.

Stunned silence.

We braced ourselves for Madame Mallory's inevitable explosion, but to our astonishment it never occurred. Instead, Jean-Pierre, still red-faced with anger, hobbled forward, one clog on and one clog off, and stood before Madame Mallory, shaking his fist at her.

"How can you do this to us?" he fumed. "C'est incroyable. We, who have been so loyal, have put up with your tyranny for so long, have devoted ourselves to your kitchen, cast aside for this little shit? Who is this boy, your plaything here? Where is your decency?"

Madame Mallory was the color of Asiago cheese.

Remarkable as it sounds, until that point she'd had absolutely no idea that by singling me out, by taking me under her wing, by making me so obviously her "chosen" one, she had deeply offended her devoted *chef de cuisine*. But when in that moment she realized what she had done, that as a result of her insensitivity poor Jean-Pierre was tortured with jealousy, her emotions were visibly stirred.

You could see it in her face. For if there was one human condition that Madame Mallory understood, it was jealousy, the intense pain of realizing there are those in the world who simply are greater than we are, surpassing us, in some profound way, in all our accomplishments. She did not show outward signs, of course, for that was not her way, but you could see the strong emotions trembling just behind her eyes. And the pain she felt, it was not for herself, of this I am sure, but for her *chef de cuisine,* long-suffering like her in the dark shadows of Le Saule Pleureur's kitchen.

But Jean-Pierre was off on a tear, strutting back and forth in front of the range, peeling off his whites and theatrically throwing them on the kitchen floor. "I can't work here any longer. I've had enough. You impossible woman!" he yelled.

At that remark, however, Monsieur Leblanc stepped forward, to protectively shield Madame Mallory from Jean-Pierre's anger.

"Now stop that, you ungrateful bastard. You have crossed the line."

But Mallory stepped forward, too, and, much to our amazement, took Jean-Pierre's shaking fist in her hand and brought it up to her lips so she could kiss his raw and red knuckles.

"*Cher* Jean-Pierre. You are entirely right. Forgive me."

Jean-Pierre came to a screeching halt. He was unnerved, maybe even frightened, by this strange Madame Mallory before him, and he looked to me like a child who had just seen a parent act entirely out of character because of something he had done. So now Jean-Pierre fell over himself trying to apologize, but Madame Mallory put a finger to his lips and sternly said, "Hush. Stop there. There is no need."

She held his hands to her and said, with her usual authority, "Jean-Pierre, please, you must understand. Hassan, he is not like you and me. He is different. Lumière and Le Saule Pleureur, they can't hold him. You'll see. He has much farther to travel. He will not be with us long."

Madame Mallory then made Jean-Pierre sit on a stool, which he did, hanging his head in shame. She asked Marcel to fetch him some water, which the boy brought, two hands holding the glass, because he was trembling so. After Jean-Pierre gulped the water down and he seemed calmer, Chef Mallory made him look up at her again.

"You and I, this place is in our blood, and we will both live and die here, in the kitchen of Le Saule Pleureur. Hassan, he has the makings of a great chef, it is true, and he has talent beyond anything you and I possess. But he is like a visitor from another planet, and in some ways he is to be pitied, for the distance he has yet to travel, the hardships he has yet to endure. Believe me. He is not my favorite. You are."

The air, it was electric. But Chef Mallory simply looked over at Monsieur Leblanc and said matter-of-factly, "Henri. Take a note. We must call the solicitor tomorrow. It must be made clear, once and for all, that when I am gone, Jean-Pierre will inherit Le Saule Pleureur."

And she was right. Three years after I began my apprenticeship at Le Saule Pleureur, I was ready to move on. An offer from a top restaurant in Paris, on the Right Bank, behind the Élysée Palace, stoked my ambition and lured me north. Madame Mallory said she thought the offer of sous chef, at a very busy restaurant in Paris, and with the possibility of promotion to premier sous chef, it was exactly what I needed. "I've taught you what I can," she said. "Now you need to season. This job will do that."

So it was, in essence, decided, and a kind of bittersweet mixture of sadness and excitement was heavy in the air. And the ambivalence of this period is crystallized for me in that day when Margaret and I drove to the gorge at the end of Lumière's valley, on our day off, for a walk along the local Oudon River running around the base of the ragged-edged Le Massif.

Our outing started in town, when we first went by the local cash-and-carry to pick up lunch, some Cantal and Morbier cheese and a few apples. Margaret and I drifted through the shop's narrow aisles, past the hazelnuts in red mesh sacks and the clouded Corsican olive oils. Margaret was just ahead of me, passing along the section of the aisles devoted to chocolates and biscuits, when a knot of men in their early twenties, Lumière's handball team, came boisterously down the other side of the aisle, looking to purchase some snacks and beer for their sports club. I remember they had ruddy faces and were immensely fit and their hair was wet from having just come from the showers.

Margaret's face lit up when she saw them, they had all been through the local school together, and she turned and said, "Go pay. I will catch up with you in a minute." So I turned around and crossed over into the next aisle on my way to the cashier. But a pot of imported lemon curd caught my eye, which I wanted to have with the local cheeses, a kind of ersatz chutney, and I popped the jar into the wire basket on my arm before continuing down the aisle.

It was when I was directly on the other side of the stack containing the chocolates and biscuits that I heard a male voice asking what had happened to her *"nègre blanc,"* followed by all the other men laughing. I remember pausing—listening intently—but I never heard Margaret challenge the remark. She just ignored it, pretended it never happened, and then joined their laughter as they continued with their provincial palaver and teasing on some other subject. And there was a moment of disappointment, I must confess, when I held my breath and waited for her response, but I also knew Margaret was anything but a racist, so I pushed on and paid the bill and she joined me shortly thereafter.

We stashed our goodies in her Renault 5 and then drove to the end of the valley, parking in the state forest's sanctioned parking lot, where fall's yellow and orange leaves created a kind of natural papier-mâché carpet under our feet. There we laced on good walking boots and shrugged on our kit, and slammed the car trunk shut, finally setting off at a brisk pace, hands intertwined, across the seventeenth-century stone bridge that spanned the river.

It was a sparkling fall day but summer was dying and a slight melancholia fluttered down on us each time a yellowed leaf fell to the ground. The river below the bridge was as clear and sharp as Sapphire gin, the water gushing and gurgling around fat rocks. Small brook trout flitted about the pools, sucking in flies, or working their fins as they sulked in eddies. A picture-perfect stone cottage stood in the hollow on the far side of the river, and a state employee, a *forestier,* lived in the cottage with his new wife and baby, and at that moment when we crossed the bridge birch smoke was rising from its chimney.

Margaret and I followed the forest trail downstream, the river to our right, the sheer rock face of Le Massif, the snowcapped Jura mountain, rising majestically to our left. I recall that the forest air was cool and damp and mossy, filled with a water spray that fell finely from the mountain's granite face soaring high above us.

Slowly, our hands swinging, we started talking about the offer from Paris, delicately, neither of us really discussing the great underlying question, as to what might happen to us. A stream fell suddenly down the mountain to our left, tumbling and cascading, its lace of white water leaving a trail of mossy carpet on shiny veins of feldspar. I remember, like it was yesterday, the way Margaret looked that morning, the faded blue jeans, the light blue fleece, the day's wind naturally raising color on her cheeks.

"It's a good offer, Hassan. Well deserved. You must take it."

"Yes. It is. And yet . . ."

Something was holding me back, an oppressive knot sitting inside my rib cage, and I didn't really understand, at that point, what it was all about. But the main river, the fast-running Oudon to our right, took a bend at that point, creating a long deep pool and a forest flat at its banks. It was the perfect setting for lunch, and I deposited our rucksack on a lichen-covered boulder, under the immensely ancient pines, lindens, and horse chestnuts, the icy river in sight just beyond their trunks.

We stretched ourselves flat across a rock and languidly ate our lunch, the apples and cheese and the thick-crusted bread Margaret herself had made, which we slathered in lemon curd. I am not sure at what stage we heard the voices, but I remember the way they came to us through the woods, distant at first, but then ever louder as the figures moved across the forest floor, hunched, like crabs scuttling across a seabed. Margaret and I lay still, dozy with contentment, watching in silence as the figures approached.

It was mushroom season and this damp part of the state forest was locally known for prize cèpes and chanterelles. Madame

Picard's family had for years controlled the mushroom-picking license for this patch of the forest, and the widow was the first to come into view. Swathed in her trademark black sweater and skirt, under a billowing rain slicker, Madame Picard jumped from forest clump to forest clump like a mountain goat, kicking rotten birch tree stumps with her army boots, to reveal hidden clusters of *pieds-de-mouton* under the rotting cover.

Suddenly a squawk of excitement, as Madame Picard stood upright, clutching in her grimy hand *trompettes-de-la-mort,* the coal black and prized chanterelle that indeed does look like a trumpet of death but is actually very tasty and safe to eat. She turned to her lumbering companion behind her, a large man panting heavily and lugging two large baskets that were filling rapidly with their musty finds.

"Be careful with these *trompettes*. Leave them on the top. So they won't get crushed."

"Yes, bossy madame."

Papa stood there like a bear in the forest, still in his favorite tan kurta, but buried now under a massive waxed coat that perhaps had once belonged to the late Monsieur Picard. On his feet, he, too, wore army boots, but in his case they were untied, the tongues pulled this way and that, the laces unraveled and wet and dragging behind him in the forest, making him appear, of all things, like a rapper from Paris's suburbs.

Margaret was just about to call out, to wave them over, but, I don't know why, I put my hand on her forearm and shook my head.

"I tink it is time we rested. And ate. I am rather hungry."

"You will drive me crazy, Abbas! We just got started. At least one full basket before lunch."

Papa sighed.

But when Madame Picard turned, to bend down with her stubby knife and cut another mushroom out from the forest floor, Papa saw something that was of great interest. For he tiptoed forward, reached in between Madame Picard's legs for a grab, and yelled, "I found a truffle!" Madame Picard instantly screamed and almost fell forward on her face. But when she found her balance and stood again, the two of them were roaring with laughter. Clearly, she had rather enjoyed Papa's goose.

I was horrified. My head instantly filled with images of my mother and Papa, walking together along Juhu Beach, from so long ago. I felt a heart pang. She was so elegant and understated, my Mummy, unlike this crude woman before me. But after a few moments I finally saw Papa as he truly was, just a man snatching a few of life's simple pleasures.

He was not at that moment thinking about the responsibilities of the restaurant, or of the family, all of which consumed his waking hours day in and day out. He was just an aging man, with a few decades more of life, enjoying his brief time on earth. I was suddenly ashamed of myself. Papa, who shouldered so much for so many, he, of all people, deserved this carefree and joyous moment without my brow furrowed in distaste. And the more I watched Madame Picard and Papa carrying on like randy teenagers—both slightly bent, both hustlers—the more I realized this was entirely right.

It came to me then: it was not my family that was having trouble letting me go to Paris, it was me not wanting to let go of them. This, I would say, was the moment when I finally grew up, because it was in that wet forest that I was able to say to myself, *Good-bye, Papa! I am off to see the world!*

So the hardest good-bye, those final days, was in the end not with the family, or with Madame Mallory, but with Margaret herself. That talented and decent sous chef was just five years older than I, but the affair we had while we both worked at Le Saule Pleureur, it made me a man.

But our relationship reached its logical conclusion during those closing days in Lumière one morning while I was at her tiny flat in town, just above the village's pâtisserie. It was our day off and we were having a late-morning breakfast at the little table under the tall window of her kitchen.

Lumière's famous light was pouring in through the old panes, where a few dried wildflowers—oxlip and yellow gentian—stood in a glass jar on the sill. We were wordlessly having café au lait and brioche and a quince jam her mother had made, each in our own world.

I was sitting at the table in my underpants and a T-shirt, looking out the window, when skinny Monsieur Iten and his plump wife walked hand in hand down Rue Rollin. They suddenly stopped in their tracks and gave each other lusciously wet kisses, before parting company, he to get into their Lancia, she to enter the local branch of Société Générale.

Margaret was naked under her kimono, reading the local paper next to me, and I am not sure why, but I stretched my hand across the table and spontaneously said, "Come."

My voice was shaking as I held out my hand, hoping the woman across the table would grasp the fingers blindly searching contact in the air.

"Come with me to Paris. Please."

Margaret slowly put down the paper and told me—I still remember that horrible feeling in the pit of my stomach—that Lumière was where she was born, where her parents and siblings lived, where her grandparents were buried, up on the hill. She appreciated the offer, loved me for it, but she could not—she was sorry—she could not leave the Jura.

So I took back my hand and we went our separate ways.

Paris

Chapter Thirteen

If I am honest, my rise in Paris over the next twenty years, it was not as difficult as one would suspect. It was as if some unseen spirit were clearing obstacles and helping me take the path that I believe was always destined for me. For I was, as promised, promoted after just two years to the position of premier sous chef, at La Gavroche, that one-star restaurant behind the Élysée Palace.

But here is the great mystery, which I suspect I will never unravel: Was Madame Mallory somehow involved in my steady rise over the following years? Or did I imagine it?

During my time in Paris, my former *maîtresse* and I would exchange seasonal greeting cards, or talk on the phone, maybe once or twice a year. And I would, of course, pay my respects when I returned to see the family in Lumière. But for all intents and purposes, she was no longer actively involved in my education or career, at least not officially.

But I have always wondered whether she did not help me—a discreet call here and there—to help things along at key moments. And if she did, I have often asked myself, how was she able to ensure I never found out about her role?

Pierre Berri was, for example, the bighearted chef who enticed me north to his restaurant La Gavroche, but what I learned, after I got to Paris, was that he was married to a distant relative of Madame Mallory, a second cousin once removed. Naturally, with this connection, I quietly suspected there was a whispered word from Mallory that had elicited this offer from Paris. Chef Berri flatly denied it, of course, but I was never entirely convinced by his denials.

When I was back in Lumière to see the family that first winter after my move north, I crossed the snowy street to have tea with

Madame Mallory in her attic flat. The steam radiators were clanking loudly, infusing the apartment with a cozy heat, and we settled into the old armchairs, drinking coffee and nibbling scalloped madeleines still warm from Le Saule Pleureur's oven. I remember she wanted to know all about the tapas-style restaurant that Chef Pascal had just opened in Paris, which was then creating quite a stir in the capital, and a new craze for smart bistros where the food supported the wine, not the wine the food. It was during the course of our shop talk, however, that I nonchalantly slipped in a thank-you for orchestrating the offer from Chef Berri.

"Don't be ridiculous, Hassan," she said, refreshing our coffee with the same Limoges pot she had deployed during my apprenticeship. "I have far better things to do with my time than to call distant relatives on your behalf. Besides, I haven't seen that particular cousin for thirty years—and I never liked her then. That side of the family is from Paris, you know, and they always thought they were superior to those family members who, like us, remained in the Loire Valley. Why in heaven's name would I ask a favor from her? It would kill me. So I will hear no more of your nonsense. Now, tell me, is it possible for you to talk with your wholesalers in Paris and locate for me a few *Ostrea lurida*? Before I die, I want to try that American oyster. Just inconceivable to me that some French gourmands consider it superior to our Breton oysters."

I returned to La Gavroche, worked hard, and five years after I arrived in Paris I was offered another opportunity and a big jump in responsibility. There was no opening expected to show up at La Gavroche for many years to come, so I handed in my resignation and instead became *chef de cuisine* at La Belle Cluny, a small and elegant restaurant in the 7th arrondissement, where I stayed for a total of four years.

I was very happy working alongside white-haired Marc Rossier, an elderly chef who, to put it politely, had his own ways. Chef Rossier made us dress completely in black, rather than the traditional whites, right down to the clogs, and he used to shuffle around us with his own billowing black pants tucked inside his socks, like a seventeenth-century Dutch pirate, all day singing raucous tunes from his youthful days in the French navy. But it was precisely this eccentricity that made Chef Rossier such a delight to work for. He liked to have fun.

He was, for example, amazingly open to new ideas, despite his advanced age, and so very unlike most other patrons. That meant I had, as his right hand, a great deal of room to try out my own new creations, such as a roast kid with lemons sewn into its stomach cavity. This creative freedom paid off, I think, and within two years of my arrival, La Belle Cluny was elevated from one to two Michelin stars.

This rewarding work at La Belle Cluny whet my appetite, and at the age of thirty I returned to Lumière to have an earnest talk with Papa. I desperately wanted to open my own restaurant, to finally become patron in my own house, but I needed capital. That Haji ambition, it was burning. So I sat in the chair opposite Papa's desk in the old Dufour mansion and pleaded my case. Not five minutes into my fevered pitch, my cash-flow projections spread out across his table, Papa held up his hand.

"Stop! My God. You are giving me a headache."

Spreadsheets with return-on-investment analysis, that was never how Papa worked; with him, it was always through the gut. "Of course I will help you! What did you tink?" he demanded crossly.

Papa took from his drawer a thick sheaf of communications. "I have long been expecting this," he said, opening the file. "I am not some sleepy wallah picking at his toes all day. Nah? I long ago asked the lawyers and bankers to start arranging matters. It is all taken care of. Each of you children will get one-seventh of the family estate. You will get your share now. Why wait until I am dead, yaar? I would much rather see you launched and happy and making me proud. . . . But please. Don't start sending me these computer printouts. I cannot stand such things. Always left accounting to your mother."

I had to blink a few times, to cover up my emotion.

"Thank you, Papa."

He waved his hand dismissively.

"Now. Here is the ting I am worried about. Your share, it will come to roughly eight hundred thousand euros. Is that enough?"

No. It was not. My Parisian accountant and I had figured the cost of securing a long-term lease on a top restaurant location in Paris, the space's complete refurbishment, including a state-of-the-art kitchen, then hiring a team of top-rate staff—in short, all the initial start-up costs of launching an elegant restaurant targeted at the most sophisticated clientele—it would require close to two million euros in initial capital, to safely get off the ground.

"That's what I thought," said Papa. "So I have a proposal for you."

"Yes?"

"Your sister Mehtab. She is troubling me. I cannot find a man in this little mountain town who will have her, and every day she is becoming more and more like your aunt. Cross all the time. She needs a bigger pond to catch her fish. Do you agree? So I tink you should consider taking her in as a partner in your fancy Parisian restaurant. Nah? She will be a great help to you, Hassan, and of course, she brings her own share of the capital to invest. It will also be a great relief to me, to know you are looking after her."

This is the Indian way, of course, and so it was settled. Mehtab moved to Paris with me. But I must confess my one regret of this period: my parting from Chef Rossier, who was so good to me, it was not as I would have liked. Not at all. For when I told Rossier I was going to open my own restaurant, the elderly chef went quite red in the face and threw a pan, two plates, and a pepper-crusted salami. But life perpetually moves forward, not backward, so I dodged the flying projectiles and headed, for the last time, out the restaurant's back door. For some time thereafter, however, Chef Rossier's unusually creative maritime curses continued to ring in my ear.

But onward. Our path forward entirely clear, Mehtab and I embarked on our new mission to open our own restaurant in Paris. It was shortly thereafter, sitting in the bathtub, drinking a tea spiked with garam masala and dripping with sweat, all the while thinking of my father, that the name of the new restaurant suddenly came to me.

Le Chien Méchant.

Perfect. No?

Our first objective was to find the right space, of course, and Mehtab and I tramped through Paris for several months looking for a prime location. Real estate agents seemed to show us either cavernous warehouses in obscure side streets of the unfashionable 13th or 16th arrondissement, or else cramped shop fronts not much bigger than a doll's house in the better streets down toward the Seine. Nothing suitable. But we pressed on, with great determination, in the knowledge the right location could make or break our fledgling restaurant.

After one such hot and fruitless search, back in the flat, Mehtab kicked off her sandals and began examining her bunions, groaning each time she touched upon a tender spot. "My God," she said, "this is worse than finding a flat in Mumbai." She was just about to summon me over to examine her feet, but I was spared by the phone ringing, which I jumped to pick up.

"Am I speaking with Chef Haji?"

It was an elderly-sounding man at the end of phone, and I could hear, somewhere in the background, a dog barking.

"Yes. This is Hassan Haji."

"Chef, I met you many years ago, when you were a young man just starting out. In Lumière. My name is Le Comte de Nancy Selière."

"*Oui, Monsieur Le Comte.* I remember you well. You came every year to Le Saule Pleureur."

"I hear you are looking for space. To open a restaurant."

"Yes, I am. Quite right. How did you know?"

"Aah, Chef. You should know this by now. Paris, it's a village. Gossip spreads with utmost efficiency through the markets, particularly when it involves haute cuisine. Or politics."

I laughed.

"Yes. I suppose you are right."

"Are you free? Perhaps you'd like to come visit me. Number Seven Rue Valette. I might have just the thing you are looking for."

* * *

Le Comte de Nancy Selière owned a *maison particulière*, complete with turrets, up at the top of the Montagne Sainte-Geneviève hill. He was just a half block from Le Panthéon, the basilica and elegant square where France's great men, from Voltaire to Malraux, are buried in its chilly crypt. Mehtab and I, we were awed by the count's imposing home, and we stood meekly out on the street, nervously ringing the bell, fully expecting to be met by a severe butler ordering us to the servants' entrance in the back. But it was, much to our surprise, the count himself who opened the door, tousle-haired, in corduroys and leather slippers.

"Come. It's two doors down," he said, after curtly shaking our hands.

Without waiting for our response, Le Comte de Nancy headed down the raked Rue Valette, still in his house slippers, a large set of keys on a ring jangling from his liver-spotted hand.

I will always remember the first moment I set eyes on Rue Valette's ivy-clad No. 11. The sun was setting over the city's rooftops as I looked down the hill, and a glorious haze of pollution had created a kind of pink halo around the limestone building, reminding me of the lighting in Lumière.

No. 11 was half the size of the count's imposing home, and it appeared rather plump and jolly, the wooden shutters and the ivy encircling the bottom floor giving it a relaxed air of informality. More country, in short, and less the hard elegance so common in Paris.

The entrance hall was quite dark, covered as it was in heavy wood paneling, but through the second set of doors we discovered a series of linked and airy living rooms and anterooms, each in itself not large, but flowing gently from one to the other. I stood in the main salon for several moments, under the crystal chandelier, imagining the possibilities, and it was not at all hard to picture an elegant dining room. Folds of heavy velvet sealed off the tall windows looking out onto the street, and we pulled the drapes back. Even in those weak shafts of dusty sunset, we could see how fine the wood pleating was in the parquet floors.

There was, in the back, a very large room and bathroom, ideal for a kitchen conversion, and it led out to a small courtyard for deliveries. The light-filled floor above we could rent as offices, because there was an internal spiral staircase installed in the 1970s connecting the two floors. The three higher floors in the building had their own side entrance, but the count said he did not rent them out; that was where he stored old furniture and paintings inherited from his family. So a restaurant in the bottom two floors would not be a noise problem for other tenants. Mehtab and I, we tramped between the two floors, up and down the spiral stairs, not believing our eyes and trying not to give too much away.

My heart fluttered.

For the first time in a very long time, I felt like I was home.

"What do you think?"

"Fantastic," Mehtab whispered. "But can we afford it?"

Just at that moment, from downstairs we heard the count impatiently jangle his keys. "Come, now, you two," he yelled. "I can't stand here all day waiting for you to make up your mind. I have work to do. You must leave now."

Back on Rue Valette, I looked at the neighborhood with fresh interest, as Le Comte de Nancy locked the building's door again. Down the hill, Place Maubert, the Saturday farmers' market, and the subway station. Up the hill, the elegant Panthéon. It would take me at most ten minutes to walk to work from my flat over by the Institut Musulman.

And directly across the street, just down from the Collège Sainte-Barbe of the Sorbonne, stood one of the finest addresses of the Left Bank: the elegant Monte Carlo, a brass-plated apartment building where the mistress of the late president of France, a fiery Socialist, was known to be kept in magnificent ancien régime style in a third-floor flat. Two potted palm trees and a uniformed doorman now stood sentinel before the Monte Carlo's carved doors.

No question. It was a fantastic location.

"Well, young man? Are you interested?"

"*Bien sû-sûr*," I stammered. "It's lovely. But I don't know if I can afford it."

"*Pff,*" said the count, waving his hand. "Mere details of finance. We'll work something out. The point is, I want a good tenant, reliable, and a restaurant of quality, well, it rather suits my particular tastes and interests. And you, I believe, you need a good address to make your mark. So we have a common purpose. Terribly important for a partnership. Don't you agree?"

"Yes. I do."

"So there we have it."

He held out his arthritic hand.

"Thank you, Monsieur Le Comte! Thank you! I will not let you regret your decision. I promise."

I shook his hand, rather vigorously, and for the first time the aristocrat smiled, with little yellow teeth. "I am sure of it," he said. "You are a young chef of talent and that is why I am backing you. Remember that in the days ahead. Now do not worry. I will have my lawyer contact you very shortly with the details."

Le Comte de Nancy Selière became not just my landlord but also my best customer. Le Chien Méchant was his "local," as he often said. But even that description does not really do his role justice in what later became of me, for the count was in fact a kind of protective spirit, always looking out for my interests.

The rent we settled on was fifty percent below market rates for the first two years, but even over the subsequent years the count only increased the rent very gradually, and usually prompted by some increased insurance cost of his or to keep up with a wave of inflation. Fact is, throughout the next years the count helped me in a hundred different ways, including, right from the beginning, a line of credit on very good terms from his own bank, for the four hundred thousand euros I still needed to borrow in order to complete my two-million-euro vision.

But more than that, I liked the fellow. Le Comte de Nancy was a surly curmudgeon, that is true, but he was also very decent, to anyone who gave him a chance, and really quite amusing. When, for example, one of my junior staff had the temerity to ask the count if he had room for dessert, he looked at the fellow as if he were a dolt before replying, "My dear man, a gourmand is a gentleman with the talent and fortitude to continue eating even when he is not hungry."

But on that first day, the moment the count expelled his breath with that particular *"Pff"* after I had asked about the property's costs, I knew in my gut what had just happened. For that noise, so arrogant and dismissive, it was very familiar to me, and while I had no proof, indeed never got it, I knew in that instant the arrival of Le Comte de Nancy Selière and his property, it was all somehow the work of Madame Mallory's invisible hand.

For how else can anyone explain how the best customer of Le Saule Pleureur suddenly became both my landlord and my best client in Paris, as if a baton were being passed from one restaurant to another?

"You are alarming me, Hassan," Madame Mallory said into the phone, in a rather clipped and icy tone, when I brought up Le Comte de Nancy. "I am starting to think you are taking drugs, the way you keep running to me with these paranoid fantasies. Honestly, have you ever known me to encourage any of my cus-tomers to go spend money at a competitor? The very idea is preposterous."

Paint fumes, yelling, phone ringing, shopping cart sweeps through stores, interviews, order forms, heated negotiations— what followed were long hours and backbreaking work. Mehtab dealt with the workmen, bossing them about, remodeling No. 11 in the image of my detailed illustrations and vision. I, in turn, when I wasn't being called over to rule on a molding or color, was working on, most important, the hiring of the restaurant's key staff. After hundreds of hours of interviews, for *chef de cuisine* I settled on Serge Poutron, shaped like an extremely large turnip, originally from Toulouse and quite rough, a fellow whom I'd met while working at La Gavroche. Difficult, sometimes even quite brutal to underlings, Serge nonetheless ran a very disciplined kitchen, and I knew he would consistently produce for me, night in and night out, beautifully executed dishes. And in the front room, Jacques, my maître d'hôtel, a veteran of the three-star L'Ambroisie, so elegant and slight, like an upper-class version of Charles Aznavour, always ready to charm the guests.

The first restaurant review we received, shortly after we opened Le Chien Méchant, was in *Le Monde,* and I don't mind admitting that I became very emotional when I saw my name and restaurant politely applauded in that august newspaper, which sits at the center of France's opinion-making establishment. The article brought attention to the restaurant, as did the ever-growing word of mouth passed on by diners, most notably the one-man public relations machine that was Le Comte de Nancy Selière, who, naturally, was granted his regular table at the restaurant. And it is in this early period, the day after I earned my first Michelin star, but well before my second, that a man who would become so instrumental in my life and what followed sat down in a booth at the restaurant.

I was in the kitchen preparing *daurade aux citrons confits* when Jacques came into the kitchen to pass on two new table orders. Without looking up from his task of slotting order chits into the conveyor rack, Jacques tersely informed me I was wanted in the dining room, at table eight. My maître d' looked uncharacteristically austere and harried as he turned and marched smartly back out through the swinging doors again, so I assumed it was someone of considerable importance not happy with the evening's fare.

"Serge, take over. I must go out front," I said over the metallic clatter of pans and clomping clogs, as the kitchen staff dashed back and forth along the steel ranges and across the tiled floor. Serge grunted that he heard me, before yelling, "Pickup"; a *commis* made me shrug off my fat-splattered whites, helping me into a freshly laundered version.

Le Chien Méchant was full that night, and, past the kitchen doors, I nodded at one or two regulars as I passed through the anterooms. Table number eight, in the center room, was one of the better tables, and I knew only a celebrity of some sort would be sitting there.

The half-bald man at table number eight was sitting alone, a ring of silver hair around the back of his neck ending in bushy white sideburns that consumed most of his face, a style much favored in an earlier era. The fellow was brawny and muscular, with a gold chain around his neck and chunky gold rings on his coarse hands, jewelry that would not have been out of place on a member of the Corsican Mafia. But he also wore a beautiful charcoal gray silk suit of considerable taste, and he exuded an aura of quiet authority. I glanced down at his plate—this always tells me a lot about a person—and registered that he was eating a starter of smoked eel with fresh horseradish cream.

"Chef Haji," he said, extending a big hand. "I've been meaning to meet you for some time. I was very upset to learn from my staff you've been to my restaurant twice and never announced yourself to me. I am quite hurt."

Chef Paul Verdun. One of the nation's greatest talents.

I was momentarily starstruck. I knew Chef Verdun well, from a distance, as his story was endlessly repeated in the French press. Over the last thirty-five years, Paul Verdun had transformed a modest country butcher shop into a world-renowned three-star restaurant, his immense talent attracting gourmands from across the globe to the second roundabout in Courgains, a tiny Normandy village where the gold brick Le Coq d'Or occupied a corner *maison*.

Chef Verdun was a master of that lard-heavy school of French cuisine that was just starting, at that time, to fall from favor, overtaken by the molecular cooking established by the fast-rising Chef Mafitte down in Aix-en-Provence. Chef Verdun was famous for his spit-roasted squab stuffed with sweetbreads, duck liver, and scallions; his hare cooked in port wine inside a calf's bladder; and, perhaps most famously, his *"poularde Alexandre Dumas,"* a simple chicken studded with a decadent amount of black truffles.

I was delighted to make Chef Verdun's acquaintance, and I slid into his booth, the two of us talking for a good thirty minutes before I reluctantly returned to the duties of my kitchen. But in that first chat we had the breakthrough moment that forever became the basis of our friendship. Chef Verdun talked a great deal about himself, with great exuberance, and so I wasn't entirely surprised when he finally said, "Tell me, Hassan. Of the dishes you had at Le Coq d'Or, which was your favorite?"

While I was at his restaurant, waiting for the main course, I had impulsively tried the starter omelet with codfish cheeks and caviar. It was deceptively simple, but to my mind the pinnacle of French cooking, so refined and yet also so forceful. I later discovered, through my own research, the dish was originally created in the seventeenth century by Cardinal de Richelieu's chef, served to the controversial cardinal at lunch every Friday until his death, this delicious omelet entirely disappearing from menus until Chef Verdun magnificently reinvented it for modern palates.

"That's easy. The omelet. With codfish cheeks."

Chef Verdun's fork was on his way to his lips, but he paused perceptively at that moment. "I agree with you," he said. "Almost everyone prefers the *poularde Alexandre Dumas*. But I think it is a bit much. Too *opera buffa*. The omelet, so simple, has always been my personal favorite. You and I, Hassan, we are the only two people who agree on this."

In the ensuing years, Chef Verdun and I saw each other periodically. I don't want to exaggerate our closeness; I don't suspect anyone, not even his own wife, ever cracked the high-octane energy of that man. He was an enigma, always slipping away from our grasp. But over the following years, Verdun and I definitely established a deep and abiding professional respect for each other, even, I would say, one of real affection. And that friendship comes to life for me when I think about the time, the day after I won my second Michelin star, when Chef Verdun showed up unexpectedly at Le Chien Méchant.

It was late afternoon and unbeknown to me he had arranged with Serge and the rest of the staff—rather impertinently, when I think about it, but that was Paul—to hijack me for the evening, leaving the evening's fare in Serge's capable hands.

Spluttering with indignation and insisting I was needed in my own restaurant, Paul merely said, *"Oui. Oui,"* like he was humoring an unruly child, before forcibly pushing me down into the passenger seat of his Mercedes.

My staff waved good-bye from the restaurant's doorway, disappearing in a blur when Paul's foot hit the gas pedal and we shot off at an alarming speed in the direction of Orly Airport. He always drove like a madman.

A private plane was waiting for us on the tarmac, and only once airborne did Paul finally inform me that he had decided a proper celebration of my second star was in order, and that meant, naturally, a dash down to Marseille for a good fish dinner. He had bullied an investment banker friend in London into lending us his Gulfstream.

That night Paul and I dined at Chez Pierre, that Old World restaurant sitting on the cliffs above Marseille's harbor. Our table was against the large bay window. When we arrived, the sun was setting, like a mango sorbet dripping over the horizon; the platinum rolls of the Mediterranean produced the soothing sound of waves thudding the cliff rocks below us.

Chez Pierre was old-school, dressed simply with sturdy tables under white tablecloths and heavy silver flatware. The aged waiter with pomade in his hair hauled a dented silver wine bucket to the side of our table. Paul and the elderly man bantered like they were friends from long ago, before Paul ordered a bottle of 1928 Krug champagne.

We sat in reverence as the ancient vintage was opened, as the golden-colored foam rushed to the glass rim and revealed its great age. But the real surprise came when we brought the flutes to our lips. The champagne, it was as fresh and sparkly as a blushing bride, and revealed no sign at all it was near retirement age. Quite the opposite. It made me want to sing, dance, fall in love. Rather dangerous, I thought.

We started, of course, with a teacup of Marseille fish soup, before moving on to a delicate dish of tiny clams, no bigger than babies' fingernails, the translucent shellfish grown in the restaurant's own grotto under the pounding cliff face. As a main course, *loup de mer,* grilled on fennel stalks and then bathed in warm Pernod before the waiter, towel over his forearm, dramatically flambéed the sea bass at our table, using a long matchstick, the fennel stalks and lemon wedges around the fish still smoldering as the plate was placed before us.

We laughed and talked deep into the night, until the sea outside seemed pumped full of squid ink. Sardine and mackerel fishing boats, their masts bejeweled with lights, headed out from the city's harbor for a nighttime haul; far out, an oil tanker flat against the sea, a sugar cube of lights in the inkiest part of the blackening water.

That night I learned Paul's father used to read him *The Fencing Master* and *The Count of Monte Cristo,* the reason why Paul had named his most famous dish after Alexandre Dumas. It was also partly why we were there. Château d'If, the island prison fortress that was the setting for *The Count of Monte Cristo,* was that magical night sitting outside our window in the Bay of Marseille, gray rock and fortress walls looking oddly elegant under a string of fairy lights.

The champagne loosened our tongues, and *in vino veritas* I finally glimpsed a few other interior facts behind the famously extroverted Paul Verdun. It was toward the end of our meal, as we ate a light almond tort, alongside sinus-clearing snorts of cognac, that Paul quietly asked me if I had ever eaten at Maison Dada in Aix-en-Provence, the minimalist restaurant of the up-and-coming Chef Mafitte. The insecurity in his voice, even with so much drink sloshing about his insides, was quite distinct.

Charles Mafitte was at the time emerging clearly as the artistic leader of the postmodern movement deconstructing food. He used nitrous oxide cans, an unusual kitchen utensil to say the least, to create his trademark "crystallized foam"—a hard froth he made from sea urchin eggs, kiwi, and fennel—or a bowl of delicious "pasta" made entirely out of Gruyère cheese and *reine des reinettes* apples. Mafitte's technique involved the total reduction of ingredients, almost to a molecular level, before reassembling an odd mixture of fused foodstuffs into entirely new creations.

I confessed to Paul I had indeed had a memorable meal at Maison Dada, a few years ago, with my then-girlfriend, the thick-thighed Marie, who smelled of mushrooms. Where should I start? Chef Mafitte pulverized Fisherman's Friend throat lozenges, and used this bizarre ingredient as the basis for his "lobster lollipops," a stunning dish served with "truffle ice cream." Even the classic frogs' legs, really the archetypal dish of French country fare, had been unrecognizably transformed by Chef Mafitte's artistry: he deboned and "caramelized" the legs in fig juice and dry vermouth, and then served them alongside a polenta "bomb" studded with foie gras and pomegranates. Not even a hint of the classic frogs' legs ingredients of garlic, butter, or parsley. When I asked Marie what she thought of the dinner, she replied, *"Zinzin"*—Parisian street slang for "Crazy"—and I must confess my inarticulate shop-girl had rather accurately summed up our dining experience, even before that notorious womanizer manhandled her under the table.

All this I told Paul, and as I spoke, he became more and more morose, as if he somehow intuited from my animated chatter that this fast-rising chef from the south would one day become his nemesis, relegating Paul's muscular embrace of classic French cuisine, which he loved with all his being and would defend to his death, as completely and utterly passé.

But he caught himself.

"Enough of this. We are here to celebrate your second star, Hassan. Now drink up. We are off to the discos."

Paul downed his brandy before saying, "Get up, d'Artagnan. Get up. Time for us to sample the justly famous Marseille tarts."

I don't know how much Paul dropped on our celebration that night, but it turned out to be one of the most memorable and enjoyable nights of my life.

A year later, in Normandy to see a supplier, I dropped by Paul's house in Courgains. His wife, Anna Verdun, greeted me stiffly at the door; she was well known to be rather dismissive of Paul's common friends, preferring instead to expend her energy on his most famous clients and hangers-on. After her distinctly cool reception, however, Madame Verdun did have a young woman escort me to Paul's lair in the back of the house.

As I followed the young maid through the halls of their nineteenth-century bourgeois house, the walls all dedicated to framed photos and press clips documenting Paul's steady rise in the world of haute cuisine, I caught sight of a red-wax scrawl, the slant of the letters instantly striking me as faintly familiar.

The framed property in question was a pamphlet from the late 1970s and the firm handwriting scrawled underneath stated, "For Paul, my dear friend, the great butcher of Courgains, a man who will one day astound the world. Keep up the good fight. *Vive La Charcuterie Française!*"

It was signed, simply, "Gertrude Mallory."

And so, finally, we come to the key period in question. I was thirty-five years old when Le Chien Méchant earned its second star, and for several years afterward I hit a creative impasse. I worked hard but made no headway, as the freshness and zeal with which I'd started my work at Le Chien Méchant was institutionalized through constant repetition.

We received a few mediocre reviews during this period, I admit. But the old fires, they still burned deep somewhere, and it was when I turned forty, that a dangerous restlessness set in, an urge to kick things up a notch.

I wished—even willed—for some dramatic change to happen.

They found Papa dead on the kitchen floor, in his bathrobe, surrounded by shards of broken plates and glass bowls. Auntie and his local doctor had stupidly forced Papa, at the age of seventy-two, to go on a strict diet; he was having none of it. Awakened by his loudly rumbling stomach, Papa descended to the kitchen in the middle of the night for a little sustenance. He threw open the refrigerator door and stuck his head inside; according to the medical examiner, he was gobbling the leftovers so fast that a chunk of chicken leg got lodged in his throat.

Frightened by the clump of cold chicken blocking his air passage, he reeled around the kitchen in a panic, until finally felled by a massive heart attack. Mercifully, Papa was dead even before he hit the floor.

We all thought Papa would live forever, and his funeral in Lumière remains to this day bleak and out of focus. The entire family was mad with grief, but I personally was so brokenhearted, my eyes so blurry from the constant flow of tears, that I never noticed how feeble Madame Mallory was looking, as she leaned heavily on

Monsieur Leblanc's arm and stood unsteadily at the back of the cemetery. All I could see was that the cemetery was filled with local residents, thousands of them from as far away as Clairvaux-les-Lacs, their hats off and heads bent in respectful mourning.

He won them over in the end, my Papa.

Two months later, on her way down from the attic, Madame Mallory tripped and tumbled down the stairs, breaking several ribs and both legs on the descent. She died a few weeks later, from pneumonia, confined to a bed in the same hospital that had treated my burns two decades earlier.

It is my great shame and sadness that I never made it back to the Jura to properly say good-bye to my *maîtresse,* but I couldn't, for simply too much was happening in Paris. Life always brings unpredictable surprises, and after all my good fortune, it was apparently time again for an Indian-style hullabaloo.

The world we had known for so long, it abruptly ended in some profound way, when the television screens suddenly filled with the shocking news that stock markets around the world were collapsing.

Economists have their own explanation as to what happened during this dark period, but I like to think the universe at large was itself reacting to the news that Abbas Haji and Gertrude Mallory were no more a part of this life, but had finally been summoned to the abattoir.

Depression, on a global scale, it was the only appropriate response.

Chapter Fourteen

It was Saturday, twenty years after I came to Paris, when I was at the Place Maubert farmers' market acquiring a handsome pair of imported mangoes wrapped in purple tissue and carefully packed like rare orchids in a wooden box, that my sister rang my cell phone and informed me that Paul Verdun had died in a car crash.

Mehtab called just as I was handing over my money to the cashier under the stall's awning, so I was unable to respond to her typically brutal delivery, but my sister chattered on in a voice pitched with excitement.

"They found him at the bottom of a cliff, just outside Courgains. Dead. Just like that. Car, flat as nan. Nah, Hassan? Are you there?"

The *vendeuse* behind the fruit stall handed me my change.

"I cannot talk now," I said, and disconnected the phone.

For quite some time I stood stupid with shock, wondering what should become of us. The world seemed to be coming to an end, and a meaningless and monotonous phrase—*an era is over*—incessantly went around in my head.

But Paris cannot in fact be stopped and the Place Maubert market continued its brisk trade without pause. It was early May and couples lugging string bags stuffed with leeks and joints of spring lamb banged into me. A Vespa beeped with irritation at my statuary immobility before carefully negotiating around my back.

Odd details still stick in my mind: the policemen on in-line skates eating cheese pastries, flakes of dough falling on their blue shirts; the golden charcuterie chickens turning in the rotisserie with windows yellowed from grease. The very air of the market smelled, I remember, of ripe Comté cheese, and a wicker hamper filled with wine bottles from Argentina's Mendoza vineyards stood on the sidewalk opposite me. Not even the North Africans hawking cocaine-like vials of Turkish and Iranian saffron, normally a great personal weakness, could budge me from my spot in the center of the street, where I was rooted like thistle to a rock.

But there it was, inescapable: an important branch of classic French cuisine had just died alongside Chef Verdun, one of its last true defenders.

It was at that moment a cantankerous old woman with a fig face knocked into me, deliberately I am sure, and, without warning I was furious. I pushed back, hard, and she scuttled away yelling, *"Sale Arabe."*

The woman's curse—"You dirty Arab"—brought me abruptly back to the Rue des Carmes, and for the first time I really looked around at the Parisian indifference surrounding me in the market, so typically offhand, as if nothing of true significance had actually occurred.

I was deeply offended. Paul was a national treasure and even I, a foreigner, knew the bells of Le Panthéon up the hill should have been ringing out the country's great sorrow. And yet his departure from this world was greeted by nothing more than a Gallic shrug of the shoulders; but perhaps I should have seen it coming. Just weeks before, *Gault Millau* had demoted Paul from nineteen to fifteen points out of a possible twenty, a brutal reminder that today's critics and customers were obsessed with the culinary cubism of Chef Charles Mafitte.

It was logical, with my heritage, that I would be drawn to Chef Mafitte's "world cuisine," which seemed to revel in combining the most bizarre ingredients from the most exotic corners of the earth, but if I leaned in any direction, it was toward Paul's French classicism. Charles Mafitte's "laboratory" creations were highly original, creative, and even at times breathtaking, but I could not help coming to the conclusion his culinary contrivances were, in the end, a triumph of style over substance. And yet it was undeniably his "chemical" cooking that had struck a chord with the critics and public alike these last several years, and, like it or not, Paul's classically ornate fare was passé and seemed, in comparison, hopelessly outdated. But Paul was all honest blood and bones and meaty substance, and I, for one, was going to miss him deeply.

But it was all over. And thick-headed as I was, I realized, standing in that Saturday morning market, there was nothing left for me to do but to return home and call Paul's widow to express my condolences. So, mangoes under arm and full of this admittedly abstract sense of loss, I headed back to Le Chien Méchant, up at the top of Rue Valette.

As I trudged up the hill, past the flat-faced apartment buildings on Rue des Carmes, marking the postwar rise of French socialism, I walked under a string of children's underpants hung from a clothesline stretched across two balconies. Right then a woman in the ground-floor flat of the working-class building threw open a window in her kitchen, and I was instantly engulfed in a steamy cloud of *tripes à la mode de Caen,* billowing out from the cast-iron pot on her stove.

It was this earthy smell of tripe and onions that finally pulled up from my depths a stew of memories, and in that moment my friend Paul—not the three-star Chef Verdun—was restored to me.

For I remembered that time when, a few years ago, eager not to take the trip alone, Paul convinced me to join him for a produce tour of the Alsace, on the border with Germany. Paul drove his silver Mercedes at a reckless tempo through the countryside, and it was too much, the manic way he pushed us through our tasks. Until, that is, the afternoon arrived when—after countless trudgings up and down muddy lanes to remote farmhouses, where we sampled yet another Gewürztraminer or thyme-infused honey or smoked sausage—I had a fit.

"Enough," I yelled. I would not continue to one more farm, I told Paul in an ice-cold voice, unless he first agreed to stop for a quiet and unhurried meal. Paul, shocked by my uncharacteristic show of steel, quickly agreed to my terms, and we pulled into a sleepy village I can no longer remember the name of.

But I do remember the bistro we ate in was smoke-filled and dark-paneled and along the zinc bar there were a couple of locals huddled morosely over *ballons* of wine. I recall that the place smelled of rotten wood and spilled pastis, and we took the table in the back, under a mottled mirror. A bored young man, a Gitane hanging from his lips, came over and took our order, as an aged woman in a soiled housedress shuffled in and out of the back kitchen.

Paul and I both ordered the day's special, tripe, which was served in chipped bowls and plonked unceremoniously down in front of us. We ate in silence, dunking crusty cuts of country bread into the stew and washing it all down with a local Pinot Gris, slurped noisily from the glass tumblers standing like squat peasants at our elbows.

Paul pushed back his empty bowl and sighed with content-ment. A bit of tripe sauce dotted his chin like a culinary beauty mark, and I noticed immediately the pressures that had been leav-ing deep creases across his face had miraculously disappeared for the moment.

"Never, in all the three-star restaurants of France, will you taste anything finer," he said. "We toil and toil, until we are exhausted, and nothing we do, if we are honest, will ever be as good as this, a simple bowl of tripe. Am I right, Hassan?"

"You are right, Paul."

It was only when I recalled this memory, on the sad day of his car crash, that I finally had the decency to let in the enormity of my friend's death, to really feel the loss of this incredible tragedy.

Paul was no more.

And so it was, halfway up the Rue Valette, that my palate inde-pendently demanded its own homage to Chef Verdun, and I found myself tasting on the broad back of my tongue the rich flavors and textures of his crayfish, a masterpiece of paper-thin slivers of grilled goose liver layered delicately between the pudenda-pink meat of freshwater crustaceans.

Starlings chattering near my window woke me the next morning, but when I swung my legs over to the floor, it felt as if I had been hit with a hammer. All the recent departures, the collapse of the old economic order that we were seeing in the news every day, it was as if all this death and destruction had physically settled in the marrow of my bones. I was profoundly exhausted, dragging my feet, and when I left my flat I found I had to stop off at my local watering hole, La Contrescarpe, on the Rue Lacépède, for a second cup of coffee, before I could continue on to the restaurant.

Marc Bressier, an acquaintance who was the front-room manager at the three-star Arpège, was already at our regular table under the brasserie's green awning, eating an omelet, and he nodded when I pulled out a chair.

At that time in the morning, Place de la Contrescarpe was free of tourists, and when the waiter came by, I ordered a double and a brioche. A street sweeper was driving his whirring green truck around the square's fountain, hosing down the cobblestones with pressurized water and sending dog shit and cigarette butts rolling into the gutter. A *clochard* was asleep on the far pavement under a bush, his grizzled gray head resting on his extended arm, totally oblivious to the spray steadily heading his way.

André Piquot, *chef-patron* at Montparnasse, pulled up a chair as shutters above the bar on the other side of the square suddenly clattered open, the noise sending a flock of pigeons soaring over the houses.

"Salut, Hassan. *Ça va, Marc?*"

"Salut, André."

Paul was all we could talk about, and André expertly jabbed at his cell phone applications with his stubby fingers to read us the latest press accounts. There were unresolved questions about Paul's accident. The absence of tire tread marks on the road suggested there had been no braking of the car before it sailed over the ledge, and the car itself had just been serviced at a garage, so no technical malfunction could have explained the loss of control on a road that Paul knew like the back of his hand. Furthermore, a witness, a farmer across the road, said the car appeared to be accelerating, not braking, as it headed straight for the cliff and disappeared over its edge. Investigations were continuing.

"I still can't believe it. He seemed so full of life."

"What do you think, Hassan? He was your friend."

I shrugged, the French way. "He was as much a mystery to me as he was to you."

We moved on to the upcoming demonstration against the restaurant industry's special value-added tax, a subject then much consuming our world.

"You will be there, Hassan," Piquot said. "Please. As a director of the Syndicat Commerce de l'épicerie et gastronomie, I must deliver bodies for the protest. Please. Bring your staff."

"We must stand together," added Bressier.

"All right. I will be there. Promise."

It was time to go. I shook their hands, crossed the square, and noticed another two shops, a *parfumerie* and a sandwich shop, had permanently closed their doors. But as I descended the raked Rue Descartes, I had to negotiate around a delivery of tarp-covered paintings to the Rive Gauche Gallery, all conducted with much yelling and theater, and it made me recall the time when Paul and I had spent an afternoon at the Musée D'Orsay, to hunt, as he said, *"pour la source d'inspiration."*

He was in good shape that day, at his charming best, and it was a very agreeable afternoon we spent together, even though we moved through the museum at vastly different tempos. I would regularly turn the corner of a room only to see the back of Paul's silver head rushing ahead into yet another of the museum's chambers.

At one point, I sat alone before Gauguin's *The Meal,* painted shortly after the great painter arrived in Tahiti. Not one of his best, according to the experts, but I recall the painting's extreme simplicity—the three locals, the bananas, the bowls on the table. The painting stunned me, for it made me realize only a true master could strip away all obvious artistry and drama, to leave only the simplest and purest ingredients on the plate.

Paul inevitably came back to find me, full of enthusiasm, like a child, to say "you must see" the painting by so-and-so in the next room, and he left again only once I had promised to do so. There was a period, however, when Paul disappeared entirely and there was no sign of him until I finally reached the third floor of the museum.

He was standing stock-still before a painting stuck in the far left-hand corner of the grand parlor. I am not sure how long he had been standing there, but he did not move as I came to stand by his side, but continued to stare blank-faced at the image that seemed to have a fierce hold on his imagination.

The painting wasn't particularly good, I thought then, but now, looking back, the image does come back to me quite vividly. The painting was of a bearded king, sitting on his throne, his wife clinging to his side. They were both deep in shock, each separately wondering what would become of them. A huge and empty gray wall stretched seemingly forever behind them, a ceremonial church candle bluntly extinguished and abandoned on the floor in front of the distraught couple. The painting, by Jean-Paul Laurens, was titled, simply, *The Excommunication of Robert the Pious.*

When after several minutes he never acknowledged me in any way, not even when I shifted my weight and cleared my throat, I said, "Paul?"

He blinked twice and turned in my direction.

"Ready? My God, it's like touring with an old lady, you are so slow. Now, how about we have a drink at a little bar I know not too far from here?"

When I slipped through the front door of Le Chien Méchant, I found my maître d'hôtel, Jacques, at the table in the foyer, busy stacking the silver peaches that had just arrived from Seville. The spotlit table was the first thing guests saw when entering the restaurant's darkened hall, and every day we seductively set it anew with fresh figs, pineapples, and mangoes, colorful pots filled with berries. Among the heaps of lush fruit, we frequently placed a plate of smoke-blackened sausages, or delicate and flaky pastries of the day stacked under a smooth glass dome, all to create a mouth-watering contrast of hues and textures. The only permanent fixtures were a preserved and mounted pheasant—with two glittering glass eyes and a long tail that majestically swept across the table's polished pear-wood planks—and two strategically placed antique copper pots with lids of hammered silver.

Jacques, dressed in a tailored blue suit, stacked the last peach and turned his head in my direction as I eased shut the front door.

"*Chef!* You won't believe it. I cracked it. I know who they are."

Again I was visited by that overwhelming sense of weariness.

"It's a young couple. I am sure of it."

Jacques made me come over to the podium and his leather-bound volume of research to pore over his reams of hastily snapped photographs.

"See? It's all here. Look."

Normally a man of great elegance and reserve, Jacques lost all sense of proportion when it came to restaurant critics. He loathed them. In fact, his great ambition in life was to unmask the anonymous *Guide Michelin* inspectors who secretly reviewed restaurants and doled out Michelin's coveted stars. His strategy, these last several years, was to photograph guests he thought could be the Michelin critics, in the foyer, as they left our restaurant. He would then take his rogue's gallery of photos to Bib Gourmand–designated restaurants, modest-priced brasseries and bistros that were the Michelin inspectors' personal favorites, according to the guides' own definition, and where they took their own families on their days off.

For years now, Jacques systematically dined in his free time at the unpretentious Bib Gourmand restaurants, comparing his portfolio of snapshots with the room full of diners. It was *complètement fou,* of course, like looking for a needle in a haystack, and this was the first time he had ever found a match.

"Look. It's the same young couple. They dined here on the fourth. And then here they are again, four days later, over at Chez Géraud in the 16th arrondisement. I am sure they are Michelin inspectors. He has a rather sneering look about him. Don't you think?"

"Yes. Possibly. But—"

"Well, I am sure of it."

"Actually, that's the son and daughter-in-law of Chef Dubonet from Toulouse. They were here in Paris that week on a research mission. They're opening a bistro. I personally sent the young couple to Chez Géraud."

Jacques looked crestfallen.

I tried to smile sympathetically, but it was halfhearted, and I moved on quickly before he could engage me further in his bizarre obsession.

The center room's jasmine arrangements, faintly perfuming the salon, were from Chez Antoine over in the 6th arrondissement, and were strategically placed among the sea of tables to create a permanently soft and scented air. Le Chien Méchant's china was made to my design at Christian Le Page; the heavy silver flatware, it, too, was stamped under my instructions at a family-run factory in Sheffield, England. The stemware, Moser crystal, was hand-blown in northern Bohemia. The dining room linen, crisp and white, was not machine-made in Normandy, but from Madagascar, hand-stitched by Antananarivo women. And everything the guest came in contact with—from the wineglasses right down to the Caran d'Ache pen to sign the bill—was etched with Le Chien Méchant's insignia, a tiny barking bulldog. Mallory had taught me that details make the restaurant, and no one could say I didn't learn my lessons well, for I even twinned each table with a mahogany footstool, on which the women could rest their precious handbags.

My front-room staff was crisply snapping linen, draping it over the tables; the faint piano tinkling of Duke Ellington's "What Am I Here For?" drifted out from the hidden speakers. An apprentice at the sideboard, wiping down crystal, he saw me surveying the dining room from the darkened wing of the restaurant, and he nodded respectfully in my direction as the cut glass in his hand flashed sharply in the light.

"*Bonjour, Chef,*" cried several waiters as I passed through the salon.

I waved and pushed through the kitchen doors in the back.

Chef de Cuisine Serge was at the gas rings holding a heavy cast-iron pan handle with two hands, a towel across the grip, pouring hot goose fat into a ceramic bowl. The kitchen smelled sharply of just-cut shallots and simmering fish stock. Jean-Luc, a sixteen-year-old apprentice from a farm in Normandy, was standing by, looking on, until Serge barked, "Go put on a glove and help me!" The apprentice, startled by this unexpected command, turned in a panic, but Lucas, my *commis*, was ready at his side, helpfully handing him a glove.

No sooner had the earnest boy thrust his hand deep inside the mitten than he screamed and shook his wrist, sending the glove and a bit of sheep's intestine flying across the kitchen. The entire staff instantly burst out laughing, none more so than the ruddy-faced Serge, who was laughing so hard his entire body jiggled and he had to hold on to the side of the cooking range to steady himself. The apprentice tried to smile and look game, but in fact looked a sickly white, but for his protruding ears, which were a purplish red. Pranks and boxed ears—that was how Serge broke in the young staff.

I had no patience for Serge's antics at that moment, so I backed out of the kitchen and headed to the spiral staircase, to my office and the accounting department up on the second floor.

Maxine, one of my accountants, her hair in a twist atop her head, smiled warmly as I clunked up the stairs, and I think she was going to say something sweet and coquettish from behind her computer terminal, but at that moment Mehtab, sitting at the desk in the back of the room, said, "Have you not finished with last month's accounts? My God, Maxine, hurry up."

Maxine turned toward my sister and snapped, "You gave it to me two days ago, Mehtab. Don't hand me the data late and then get like that. It's not fair. I am finishing them as fast as I can."

I ducked my head down and waved vaguely at the two of them as I quickly crossed the room to my office and shut the door.

Finally alone, I collapsed on the swivel chair behind my desk.

For some minutes I took in Madame Mallory's floor-to-ceiling collection of antique cookbooks, the valuable archive she had bequeathed to me and which occupied half my office. I took in Auguste Escoffier's notes, the great chef's rough ideas for an 1893 Savoy dinner that I had purchased at Christie's, neatly framed on my desk. I looked at the amusing handwritten note of thanks from President Sarkozy, hanging by the door, cheek by jowl with my honorary degree from the École hôtelière de Lausanne. I looked at all these precious artifacts, always a source of great personal joy, and still I could not avoid the facts.

My hands were shaking.

I was not well.

Chapter Fifteen

I am furious. Just furious."

Madame Verdun, shocked by her own vehemence, quickly turned her attention back to the coffee table to pour us a smoky tea from china that had once belonged to her grandmother. She sat at the edge of the white silk couch exquisitely embroidered with birds-of-paradise, and the image I have now is of an angry woman sitting stiff-backed and erect in a cloud of black chiffon, her hair an intricate cocoon of finely spun strands, translucent in the light, as if a chef had taken a blowtorch to sugar and woven threads of the candied filaments through her hair.

Through the French doors behind the widow, the garden was a riot of color—camellias and wood sage and flowering bilberry— and I tried not to let my attention drift over her shoulder to this enchanting scene outside. But I most confess I was unsuccessful, as finches and squirrels darted back and forth from a bird feeder, as a team of monarch butterflies fluttered drunk through the purple haze of a butterfly bush. It was all so much more attractive than the gloom of Madame Verdun's private parlor, where Paul's death hung heavy in the air, where the stone floor was cold and the lights dimmed for a house in mourning.

"I will never forgive him, and when Our Lord calls me home, I will make Paul pay for what he has done. I promise you, that impossible husband of mine, he will get an earful. Or worse."

Her bony white fingers gripped the swoop of the teapot's handle. "One lump or two?"

"Two lumps, and milk, please."

The widow handed me my cup, poured her own, and for several awkward moments we sat in silence, the only sound in the room the grating of our silver spoons as we both wordlessly stirred our tea.

"They are still unclear as to what happened? He didn't leave a note? One didn't show up later?"

"No," Madame Verdun said bitterly. "A will, yes, executed a few years ago, but no suicide note. Maybe he took his life. Maybe he didn't. We will probably never know for certain."

I pursed my lips. Madame Verdun's old-fashioned way of talking always sounded to me like a deliberate attempt to let Paul's friends know that she was of "better" stock than her self-made husband.

"But I think I know why Paul died."

"Oh. Really?"

"Yes. The inspectors of *Gault Millau* and *Le Guide Michelin* killed him. They have blood on their hands. . . . If the police rule Paul's death a suicide, and I am denied the payment of his life insurance policy, then I will sue the guides for every penny. I am consulting with my lawyer now."

"I am sorry. I don't understand."

Madame Verdun stared at me—blankly—before placing her cup and saucer atop a coaster, next to a coffee table book on Etruscan gardens. She leaned forward and rubbed the coffee table with the palm of her hand, as if she had just located a wet spot.

"Well, Chef," she finally said, "you seem to be the only one of Paul's friends who doesn't know the next edition of *Le Guide* was going to reduce Paul to two stars. The day before he died he received a call from a reporter at *Le Figaro,* asking for comment. There were rumors, of course, but the reporter confirmed our worst fears: Monsieur Barthot, the Michelin guide's *directeur général,* personally approved his inspectors' decision. So it was this completely unwarranted and capricious act by Barthot and his committee that directly or indirectly led to Paul's death. Of this I am sure. He was powerless to fight their judgment, of course, and you should have seen him these last few weeks, since *Gault Millau* reduced him to fifteen points. He was gutted. Utterly without hope. And you know, the restaurant's occupancy rate immediately fell when the new *Gault Millau* rating became public. . . . When I think about it, I just become so angry. But just you watch. I will teach *Gault Millau* and that Barthot fellow a lesson or two. I hold them personally responsible for Paul's death."

"I did not know. I am so very sorry."

The room was again filled with our silence.

But Madame Verdun's arched, finely penciled eyebrows, and the plaintive look on her face, suggested she wanted me to say something more, so I nervously added, "Of course, the critics were entirely wrong. No question. If I can be of help in this matter, please let me know. You know how much I admired Paul. . . ."

"Oh, how kind of you. Yes. Let me think. . . . We are assembling testimonials from his peers. Part of the complaint's preamble."

But it was clear, in the curvature of her lips, that my two-star status was not quite of sufficient elevation for such an important task, and that she really had in mind some other assignment. "But I am not sure that would be the best use of your talents," she finally said.

I looked at my watch. If I left within the next ten minutes, I would hit rush hour but could still be back at the restaurant for the evening's sitting.

"Madame Verdun, I believe you asked me here for a specific reason, no? Please speak freely. We are friends and you must know I want to be of service to Paul in any way that I can."

"I did ask you here for a reason, Chef. How insightful of you."

"Please ask."

"We are going to have a memorial service for my late husband."

"Of course."

"It is Paul's wish. He left specific instructions in his will, which states he wants a hundred friends for dinner after his passing. He even had the funds set aside in a special account for this memorial meal. You must know Paul was always a little odd, and 'friends,' well, we must interpret this word liberally. The list of guests attached to his will is really just a Who's Who of French haute cuisine, with all the top-rated chefs, gourmand clients, and critics invited to send him off, even though he couldn't stand most of them. . . . Honestly, such an odd request."

The mask slipped and Anna Verdun was suddenly overcome by the tragedy of her husband's death. She had to stop talking altogether for a few moments.

"Tell me, Chef, would you invite all your enemies to your memorial service? I simply don't understand it. It must be a kind of showing off from beyond the grave, but I don't know. I just don't know. Truth be told, I never really understood my husband. Not in life. Not in death."

It was the first and only time I caught a glimpse of what lay behind the woman's frigid veneer, and the perplexed look on her face, the pain of her incomprehension, touched me deeply, and I instinctively reached over the coffee table to pat her hand.

She did not like this, not at all, for she promptly pulled her hand back, startled by the physical contact, and then covered up her embarrassment by looking for a tissue up her sleeve.

"But these were Paul's final wishes, so I will honor them."

She dabbed at the corners of her eyes, blew her nose, and then reinserted the tissue back up her chiffon sleeve. "Now, in all these specific instructions for the memorial, Paul wants, I quote, 'the most talented chef in all France to send me home.'"

She looked at me. I looked at her.

"Yes?"

"Well, apparently he thought that was you. I am, if I may be frank, not quite sure why he was so taken by you—you have only two stars, no? But he did once say to me that you and he were the only genuine articles in all France. When I asked him what he meant, he said something to the effect that you two were the only chefs in France who really understood food, and only you two could possibly save French cooking from itself."

A much-overblown and ridiculous remark, of course, so typical of Paul, but his widow smiled tremulously, and this time, against her better judgment, reached across the table to touch my hand.

"Hassan—may I call you that?—would you oversee Paul's memorial dinner? Would you do this for me? It would be such a relief to know the dinner is in your capable hands. Of course, you mustn't be in the kitchen yourself—you must be out front with the rest of us—but it would be *merveilleux* if you could oversee the menu, as Paul would have wanted. Is this too much to ask?"

"Not at all. I would be honored, Anna. Consider it done."

"How kind of you. I am so relieved. Imagine, dinner for one hundred gourmands. What a burden to impose on a widow. I am simply in no state to organize such a thing."

We stood and hugged each other stiffly, and I again expressed my condolences before moving, as quickly as I could without appearing rude, toward the front door.

"I will let you know the date of the memorial," she called out.

I scuttled across the gravel to my battered Peugeot, but she kept on talking from the doorstep as I searched for my keys.

"Paul really had affection only for you, Hassan. He once told me that you and he were 'made from the same ingredients.' I thought that a rather clever turn of phrase for a chef. I think, when he looked at you, he saw his younger self. . . ."

I slammed the car door shut, awkwardly held up a hand in a final farewell, and then sped off with such force I think I sprayed her with bits of gravel. But in the stop-go drive back to Paris— through the back roads of Normandy, through the *banlieue* suburbs of Paris, along the *périphérique,* and then down through the string of lights of the city center—I could only think about Paul, consciously or not, taking his own life.

"I am nothing like you, Paul. Nothing at all."

Restaurateurs from all over France—twenty-five thousand estimated the press—came to the capital that fateful day of the demonstration, and we initially gathered at the Arc de Triomphe. The atmosphere was festive, even as media and police helicopters hovered overhead like gathering storm clouds. Young and handsome chefs in toques, oversized and towering above us on stilts, were the charming front line of our demonstration, and we aligned ourselves in orderly rows behind them.

Colorful banners—cartoons of piggish politicians and emaciated chefs, red slashes through the value-added tax rate of 19.6 percent, simple NON PLUS placards—they were hoisted here and there by the rapidly gathering crowd, while the organizers in red aprons, holding megaphones, barked orders at us from the sidelines.

We had good cause. McDonald's meals were, for some twisted bit of political reasoning, entirely tax-free, but quality French restaurants like Le Chien Méchant had to add a 19.6 percent VAT to every customer's bill. So in the end, dinner at my two-star restaurant, without wine but including the labor-intensive service haute cuisine is rightly famous for, cost an average 350 euros a head. The universe of customers prepared to pay that amount for a meal was, as you can imagine, rather limited and rapidly dwindling. Dropped for a few years, the VAT charge had been reinstated. So the VAT, on top of the recession, was killing our business, and already several well-known restaurants—such as the celebrated Mirabelle over in the 8th—had gone bust.

Enough. We had to fight back.

Le Chien Méchant was that day well represented throughout the twenty-five-thousand-strong column. Serge and Jacques, my right and left hands, both were near the front, arm in arm, ready to roll down the Champs-Élysées like a meaty tanker. But I was also touched to see my pastry chef, Suzanne, plus two sous chefs and four waiters, all ready to do their part. Mehtab refused to come— we were all Bolsheviks, according to her—but the accountant, Maxine, arm in arm with our waiter Abdul, was there, repeatedly looking over at me, through the crowd, with hungry eyes. Even the young apprentice Jean-Luc was willing to be counted on his day off, and, touched to see his earnest face, I went out of my way to shake the boy's hand and thank him.

"Chef!" yelled Suzanne, waving over the protesters' heads. "What fun!"

I was not entirely sure. Immigrants, by instinct, we like to keep our heads down. Not make waves. Furthermore, my unease was fanned that morning when I met Le Comte de Nancy Selière. The count and his West Highland white terrier were heading off to their daily rendezvous in the Jardin des Plantes when I bumped into them at the corner of Rue des Écoles, just as the dog finished his business in the gutter and was triumphantly burying imaginary dirt on his mess with aristocratic flicks of his hind legs.

The aged count was bent over and cooing—*"C'est formidable, Alfie!"*—when he removed the linen handkerchief from his breast pocket to dab and tidy up around his dog's bottom. It was of course a rather awkward moment to engage the gourmet banker, but I thought it would be even ruder to pretend I had not seen him, so I cleared my throat and said, *"Bonjour, Monsieur Le Comte."*

The aristocrat straightened himself and looked around.

"Aah, Chef, it is you . . . I suppose you are off to march with the proletariat."

"Don't put it like that, please, Monsieur Le Comte. We want lower taxes."

"Well, I really can't blame you," said the count, patting his pockets, pretending to look for a plastic bag. "Perhaps we should all be doing the same. You know, it was my ancestor, Jean-Baptiste Colbert, the finance minister of Louis XIV, who once noted, very sensibly I should add, that taxation was the art of 'plucking the most feathers with the least amount of hissing.' Totally lost on this lot. They've proven themselves to be rough and greedy, like provincial butchers."

The count ignored the dog's mess, despite the fact that a sign ordering Parisians to clean up after their animals was directly before us, and added, rather thoughtfully, as we continued to stroll down the street, "Do be careful, Chef. This government will mismanage the demonstration. Be sure of it. Absolutely no feel for finesse."

At ten thirty that morning the morphing mass of demonstrators around the Arc de Triomphe seemed to solidify and congeal, and with a few barks from the megaphones, and some African drumming and whistles, we were off, arm in arm and chanting. I looked around as our sea of banners made its way down the Champs-Élysées, and found both Alain Ducasse and Joël Robuchon in the lines around me. I was literally surrounded by France's restaurant establishment, and the sense of bonhomie was palpable.

Le Comte de Nancy's warning suddenly seemed excessively dark and theatrical and misplaced. The sun was shining and the police looked bored; with the gawking Parisians stood wealthy Saudi and Kuwaiti families, the women in burkas, scores of children at their feet, standing along the Champs-Élysées and waving.

Less than an hour later, the forward ranks of the demonstration reached the other side of the Seine, in front of the Assemblée Nationale. It was there a phalanx of helmeted riot police with shields blocked our progress, as expected, with a makeshift pen created from a crescent of steel grilles preventing our protest from actually climbing the steps of the Assemblée Nationale and disrupting Parliament. But a stage, podium, and microphone had been set up within the pen, and a series of speeches was the next stage of the planned event.

Those of us in the middle of the human colony were intent on moving into the center of the action, but as we passed the Place de la Concorde, about to cross the bridge, scores of anarchists emerged from the Jardin des Tuileries behind us, kerchiefs pulled up over their faces, slipping into our ranks.

I am not sure what precisely happened next, but rocks and Molotov cocktails and cherry bombs were suddenly whizzing through the air. The riot police, armed with batons and shields, instantly and defensively surged forward and pressed down at us from the other end of the bridge.

There was tear gas smoke and screaming, torched cars erupting in flames, and the horrible crunching sound of police bringing batons down hard on heads.

We were trapped by the police on one side, the anarchists on the other.

The battle didn't last that long and none of my staff were hurt, nor, in fact, was anyone I knew personally; the press said, in the end, ninety demonstrators and eight police were taken to the hospital, out of a total of twenty-five thousand demonstrators, while eleven cars were torched and destroyed.

But the terror—the bloody heads and the blinding smoke and the high-pitched screaming—that was earthshaking and powerful and sobering right down to the very core. It awoke in me primordial fears from the past, of torchlit mobs bearing down on the Napean Sea Road. And when I saw the policemen on horses charge into the crowd, swinging their batons, this bubbling bile of animal panic rose in my throat and I grabbed the arm of my neighbor, the apprentice Jean-Luc, and forced him to turn with me, to run back against the crowd, toward the Place de la Concorde and the advancing anarchists.

Ultimately the anarchists pushing back forced us off to the side, down the steps leading toward the river, where, by chance, a barge was docked under the bridge. The elderly hippie couple on board were at that moment loosening their ropes to pull away as quickly as possible from the trouble overhead, eager to avoid the fiery debris that was falling from the bridge into the water below and onto their deck. But the couple saw our panic and yelled, *"Ici, vite,"* and somehow we jumped, Jean-Luc and I, with two or three other people, hitting the deck with a thud, just as the barge pushed off.

"Merde. Merde," was all the shaking boy could say for some time.

The riot on the bridge slowly retreated in the distance, and I recall the smooth sense of movement, of travel, of breeze. The couple had gray frizzy hair and soft voices and they made us sit on the deck under heavy horse blankets, the sun on our faces, while handing us shots of eaux de vie, for the shock, they said.

And I remember how we glided, glided silkily down the Seine, past the Eiffel Tower, past the Maison de Radio France, under Pont d'Issy, until at long last we reached the Île Billancourt out in the suburbs of Paris. And there, at long last, the couple docked their barge and let us out on the local pier, where we thanked them profusely and took their names and where I called Mehtab to come pick us up.

While we were waiting for my sister, Jean-Luc and I sat on a low wall and dangled our legs over the ledge that ran alongside a dusty park. Shards of broken wine bottles littered the parking lot. A few feet down below our ledge, to the left, an Algerian immigrant family was spit-roasting lamb on a park grill fashioned from an old oil drum. The father was off praying on a rug in the shade of a linden tree, while the women cooked and the children played soccer. The smell of searing lamb's flesh and cumin and bubbling fat came to us in the wind, and the simplicity of it all—the roasting meat, the mint tea, the cheerful familial chatter—it took my breath away.

And it was then, when I gazed back out across the quicksilver Seine, that I caught sight of the elderly woman on the promenade on the far bank. She wore a shawl and seemed to be calling me, waving, urging me forward.

She was the spitting image of Madame Mallory, I tell you.

But perhaps I imagined it.

Chapter Sixteen

*C*hef?"

"*Oui, Jean-Luc.*"

The apprentice licked his lips nervously.

"Monsieur Serge asked me to tell you the ptarmigan have arrived."

I looked over at the wall clock, next to the Ndebele wall hanging picked up in Zimbabwe, depicting village women roasting a quartered buffalo. There was just an hour and forty minutes before the restaurant opened for lunch.

I had been reading one of Madame Mallory's favorite cookbooks—*Margaridou: The Journal of an Auvergne Cook*—but at Jean-Luc's beckoning, I gently closed the old book shut, its simple recipes from a bygone era, and stood to put it safely away on the bookshelf.

It was, as I turned, the sight of the Credit Suisse "tombstone" in Plexiglas, the advertisement announcing the initial public offering of Recipe.com, an Internet start-up selling recipes and of which I was an outside director, that made me pause. My office, in that mote-filled light pouring in from the window, suddenly looked ridiculous to me. Wooden-and-brass plaques and awards littered every available surface in the office, the strangest of which was a gold-plated soup ladle from the Brussels-based International Soup Society. My long-cherished treasures suddenly looked like worthless bric-a-brac.

Something undeniable had happened since Paul's death. It was as if his spiritual malaise had jumped bodies and entered me, like some flesh-eating parasite from a Hollywood horror film. I was restless, irritable, had trouble sleeping. I did not know what was going on, only that a feeling of doom was bearing down on me. And I hated it, this unfamiliar sensation, for this was not me at all. I have always been quite a sunny fellow.

But Jean-Luc was still studying me from the door frame of my office, unsure whether some other prank was about to befall him. So it was ultimately the look on the boy's face—painful insecurity—that finally brought me out of myself.

I stood up and said, "*Bien*. Let us go to work, then."

Jean-Luc led the way down the spiral staircase, and we returned to the clatter and scrape and whoosh of Le Chien Méchant's kitchen gearing up for action; to waiters slamming through the swinging doors, polishing silver and filling cigar boxes and folding linen rosettes, their jackets off as they dashed between kitchen and dining room and back.

Chef de Cuisine Serge was on the far side of the kitchen with two sous chefs, standing over open flames. Suzanne, my pastry chef, was bent over a tray of tarts. There was excited palaver about soccer match this and that, but Jean-Luc and I made our single-minded way to the wooden crate standing in the cold kitchen, found on the counter every day in season, between late September and December, and flown in daily by game wholesalers in Moscow.

The boy forced open the wooden box with a crowbar, and together we carefully unpacked the braces of ptarmigan wrapped in tissue paper. Two other apprentices were hard at work, and I discreetly kept an eye on them as we unwrapped the birds. The girl on the far side of the sink was carefully sponging a string of red mullet with a wet cloth. I insist on this method; wash mullet under a tap and its subtle taste and color disappears down the drain. The senior apprentice brandishing a sharp knife on the meat counter—soon to don his own toque as a *commis,* now that we had Jean-Luc—was removing the nerves from the spine of the Charolais, the breed of French cattle that I prefer to Scottish Angus.

I took a plump ptarmigan in my hand. The arctic grouse's white-feathered head and black eyes lolled lifelessly backward, a downy weight in my palm. With a satisfying whack of the cleaver I took off the grotesquely overdeveloped claws, and the bird's legs disappeared into the vat of stock bubbling away on the burner to my side. I signaled to Jean-Luc that he should clean and pluck the rest.

I had to pluck forty game birds at a time when I started at Le Saule Pleureur, but happily for modern apprentices, automated plucking machines do the job quite nicely today, and I interrupted Jean-Luc to run my bird through the machine. The ptarmigan's white feathers—still ruffled and blood-speckled from the hunter's shot—were peeled off by the rotating rollers and then shot off on an airstream into a disposable bag to the side.

I took the plucked carcass over to the stove's open flame to singe off the bird's remaining quill stubble. A slice opened its crop and I took a few generous pinches of the bitter tundra herbs and berries that were still in the bird's throat pouch. I washed the herbs at the sink, so similar in appearance to thyme, and set them aside in a ceramic bowl.

This was my trademark dish of late fall: Siberian ptarmigan, roasted with the tundra herbs taken from the bird's own crop, and served with caramelized pears in an Armagnac sauce.

"I am not good with words, Jean-Luc. I talk best through my hands. So just watch how I do it."

The boy nodded. I gutted the bird, washed it, and carefully blotted away all moisture with paper towels. There was some shuffling of feet but otherwise the kitchen staff was mostly silent as they concentrated on their own work or watched my demonstration. The only real noise came from the lids of copper pots rattling atop the stove, and the white-noise whir of washing machines and refrigerators and ventilating ducts in the background.

The bird's meaty breasts came off with two clean swipes of the knife, and I seared the crimson pads of flesh in a hot pan.

A few minutes later I turned off the flame and looked up at the clock.

Just thirty minutes until we opened. The staff was watching me, waiting for the traditional presitting instructions.

I opened my mouth, but the usual platitudes, they choked.

They would not come anymore.

Because my head was flooded with torrid images, of Paul at the point of mangled death, surrounded by platters of his ornate dishes, loaded with goose fat and foie gras and rivers of his own congealing blood. I saw boarded shop fronts in the streets of Paris, the riot and bloodied heads and screaming on the Pont de la Concorde. And through these unsettling images loomed the supranaturally tanned face of Chef Mafitte, his bizarrely antiseptic lab-kitchen pumping out with great industriousness the most extravagant and decadently deconstructed meals.

And then, when I couldn't stand it anymore, when I gave in to all these unsettling images, when I was empty and couldn't find energy to fight and thought I might faint, they disappeared as quickly as they had come, and what poured into that empty space was a chiaroscuro vision of old Margaridou, that Auvergne cook, sitting at a farmhouse window, quietly writing her simple recipes in her journal. But when she turned her head to look directly at me, I realized with a jolt the aged woman was in fact my grandmother Ammi sitting at the upstairs window of our Napean Sea Road property in old Bombay. And she was not writing at all, but painting, and when I looked hard at the canvas in her hand, I recognized it as Gauguin's deceptively simple painting *The Meal*.

"You, in the kitchen, and you in the front room, all of you. Listen up.

"Tomorrow we throw out our menu, everything we have done for the past nine years. All the heavy sauces, all the fancy dishes, they are finished. Tomorrow we begin afresh, entirely. From now on we are only going to serve simple dishes at Le Chien Méchant, dishes where the most beautiful and freshest ingredients speak for themselves.

"That means no cleverness, no fireworks, no fads. Our mission, from now on, is to make a simple boiled carrot or a clear fish broth sing. Our mission is to reduce every ingredient down to its simplest, deepest nature. We will draw on the old recipes for inspiration, yes, but we will renew them by stripping them back to their core, removing all the period embellishments and convolutions that have been added to them over time. So I want each of you to go back to your hometowns, back to your roots across France, and bring to me the best and simplest dishes from your communes, made entirely out of local ingredients. We will put all your regional dishes in a pot, play with them, and together we will come up with a menu that is delicious and refreshingly simple. No copying the heavy old brasserie dishes, no emulating the deconstructionists and the minimalists, but our own unique house built on the simplest of French truths. Remember this day, because from now on we will cook meat, fish, and vegetables in their natural essences, returning haute cuisine to *cuisine de jus naturel.*"

And so, just a few weeks after this radical about-face in my kitchen, the day of Paul Verdun's memorial dinner finally arrived. I remember clearly that a saffron sun was setting in a filmy way over the Seine that November night, and France's culinary establishment—portly men in black tie and reed-thin women in sparkly gowns—climbed the Musée d'Orsay's stairs, the paparazzi at the ropes snapping their pictures.

All very pish-posh. Everyone who was anyone in French haute cuisine was at the memorial dinner that crystal-clear and chilly night, as even the papers reported the following day. Lists were ticked, mink coats and wraps taken, the guests making their way in stiff taffeta and soft silk to the museum's first floor, for champagne under Monet's *Gare Saint-Lazare* and Seurat's *Circus.* The excitement of a Cannes Film Festival was in the air, despite the sad occasion, and the cocktail chatter, reverberating between the museum's walls, eventually reached the roar of an airport arrivals hall. Finally, just as it was getting to be too much, a bell gonged, and a magnificent baritone announced dinner was served. The guests floated toward the grand salon, to the sea of white tables and long-stemmed irises in glass, to the Baroque murals and Rococo mirrors, to the tall windows offering a panoramic view of Paris dressed in expensive pearl strings of nighttime lights.

Anna Verdun, hair bouffant and loaded down in diamonds, sat regally at the head table in a column of blue cobalt silk.

Much had changed since I had visited her, because the silver-haired *directeur général* of *Le Guide Michelin*, Monsieur Barthot, now sat to her right, entertaining her guests with his amusing tales culled from the lives and adventures of the culinary greats.

Paul's legal adviser—also at Madame Verdun's table that night—had in the preceding months successfully convinced the widow that a lawsuit would drain her purse, be a source of continuous emotional turmoil, and would inevitably fail to produce the desired results. He instead recommended negotiating a face-saving arrangement directly with Monsieur Barthot.

We saw the outcome a week before Paul's memorial dinner, when *Le Guide,* as we simply called it, took out full-page ads in the major papers of the country, saluting the life's work of "our dearly departed friend, Chef Verdun." The deal-clincher—so my gossip-gifted sister informed me—was Monsieur Barthot's promise to deliver Chef Mafitte, who not only sang Chef Verdun's praises in the Michelin guide's ad, but was also at the dinner, sitting to the left of Paul's widow and pawing her hand.

Paul would have been furious.

Anna Verdun had shunted me to table seventeen in the back of the room. As it turns out, however, the table was under one of my favorite paintings—a still life by Chardin called *Gray Partridge, Pear, and Snare on Stone Table*—and I took this as a particularly good omen. Besides, my seat next to the kitchen entrance was immensely practical—I could keep one eye firmly glued on the staff coming and going with the night's fare—and the company at table seventeen was, I thought, far more entertaining than what was on offer at the more "elite" tables in the room.

We had, for example, my old friend from Montparnasse, Chef André Piquot, as cherubic and spherical and inoffensive as a *boule* of ice cream. Also at our table, the third-generation fishmonger Madame Elisabet. While it is true the poor woman suffered from a mild form of Tourette's syndrome, which at times proved rather awkward, she was otherwise so very sweet, and she of course owned the formidable fish wholesaler that supplied many of the top-rated restaurants of northern France. So I was delighted to find her at our table.

To her left, meanwhile, Le Comte de Nancy Selière, my landlord on Rue Valette, so at peace with his aristocratic superiority he was beyond concerns of class and caste, and, it must be added, such a sharp-tongued curmudgeon he was not tolerated at many of the 'finer' tables in the room. Finally, to my left, the American expat writer James Harrison Hewitt, a food critic for *Vine & Pestle,* who, despite his decades living in Paris with his Egyptian boyfriend, was deeply distrusted by France's culinary establishment because of his uncomfortably penetrating and well-informed insights into their insular world.

We all took our seats as a picture of a smiling Paul Verdun in toque was projected up onto screens. White jackets streamed from the kitchen: the *amuse-bouche,* a shot glass filled with a bite-sized baby octopus cooked in its "natural essence," extra virgin olive oil from Puglia, and a single caper on a long stem. The wine—in the partisan context of French haute cuisine and endlessly commented on in the papers the following day—was considered a shot across the bow: a rare 1959 Château Musar from Lebanon.

James Hewitt was a first-rate raconteur, and the American was, like me, quietly studying the odd ménage of characters at Madame Verdun's head table.

"You know she had to drop the lawsuit," he said softly. "All sorts of saucy details would have emerged had she persisted."

"Saucy details?" I replied. "Like what?"

"Paul was overextended. Poor man. His empire was about to collapse."

It was a preposterous suggestion. Paul had been an entrepreneurial tour de force. He was, for example, the first three-star chef ever to list his holding company, Verdun et Cie, on the Paris *bourse,* and to use the eleven million euros of his initial public offering to completely renovate his country inn and create a string of fashionable bistros under the name Les Verdunières. It was well known he had a ten-year contract with Nestlé, creating a series of soups and dinners for the Swiss food giant's Findus label. That contract alone was reportedly worth five million euros a year and resulted in Paul's beaming face plastered all across the billboards and TV screens of Europe. Then there was the small fortune he earned as a consultant to Air France, plus the steady stream of fees that came from the manufacturers of linen, jams, pots and pans, cutlery, crystal, herbs, wine, oils, vinegars, kitchen cabinets, and chocolates, all of which had been eager to pay the famous chef large sums of money for the right to use his name.

So when Hewitt made that ridiculous suggestion that Paul's empire was on the verge of collapse, I said, "Nonsense. Paul was a great businessman and ran a very profitable operation."

Hewitt smiled painfully over his glass of Château Musar.

"Sorry, Hassan. Verdun myth. He had not a sou left. I have it on good authority Paul was leveraged up to his bald spot. Been taking out loans for years, but off the balance sheet, so none of his shareholders at the publicly traded company knew what was going on. The drop in his ranking at *Gault Millau* hurt—Le Coq d'Or's bookings had been falling fast since his demotion and Air France was about to drop him as a consultant. So he was in a classic squeeze, struggling to find the cash to service his debts as his empire began to decline. No doubt about it. The loss of a Michelin star would have brought the whole thing down. I shudder even to think about it."

I was stunned. Speechless. But a stream of waiters suddenly emerged from the kitchen, and I had to concentrate as they brought out a simple oyster in clear broth, followed shortly by a salad of Belgian endive garnished with chunks of Norwegian smoked lamb and quails' eggs.

From the corner of my eye, I could see Chef Mafitte leaning over to whisper in Anna Verdun's ear; she turned girlishly in his direction, laughing, her hand lifting to touch the shellacked crust of her hair.

I flashed to that time when my former girlfriend and I visited Maison Dada down in Provence. Toward the end of the meal, handsome Chef Mafitte came by our table to say hello. He was, in his whites, the bronzed and dazzling picture of a culinary celebrity, immensely charming, and I was instantly reduced to nothing in his presence. Perhaps it was this boyish subservience on my part that in some way emboldened him, for the entire time he and I talked shop, Chef Mafitte had his hand in Marie's lap under the table, where she was heroically fighting off his inappropriate gropings.

When Mafitte finally left our table, Marie said, in her blunt Parisian way, that the great chef was nothing but a *chaud lapin,* which sounds rather endearing but in actual fact meant she thought he was a dangerous sex maniac. Later I learned Mafitte's voracious appetite extended to all ages and species of *viande.*

I was suddenly disgusted with Anna Verdun. There was something craven and corrupt in having Paul's artistic nemesis at her table, on this of all evenings. Where was her loyalty? But Hewitt must have read the look in my face, because he again leaned over and said, "Pity the poor woman. She's got to get out from under the financial mess Paul has left her. I hear Chef Mafitte is considering buying Le Coq d'Or—lock, stock, and barrel—part of his expansion plans for northern France. A deal with Mafitte would certainly save whatever there is left."

A waiter began to take away my salad plate, and I used the interruption to wave over the head caterer and whisper in his ear that he should tell Serge in the kitchen to slow down, that he was rushing the courses a bit. When I turned my attention back to the table, Hewitt was leaning forward and peering around me, a glass of the 1989 Testuz Dezaley l'Arbalete raised in salute, saying, "Isn't that true, Eric? Chef Verdun was in trouble. Hassan doesn't want to believe me."

Americans have a remarkable gift for running roughshod over other nations' caste systems, and Le Comte de Nancy Selière, normally never one to suffer fools gladly, simply raised his glass in return and said dryly, "To our dearly departed Chef Verdun. A train wreck that was, sadly, just waiting to happen."

The poached halibut in champagne sauce was served with a 1976 Montrachet Grand Cru, Domaine de la Romanée-Conti. André Piquot and I discussed our personnel problems; he was having trouble finding a "cold kitchen" sous chef he could rely on, and I was having trouble with a waiter who seemed to be deliberately slowing down the speed with which he executed his assignments, in order, we suspected, to clock up overtime—the costly bane of the restaurateur's existence since France had instituted the thirty-five-hour workweek.

Hewitt then regaled the entire table with a story about the time he and Le Comte de Nancy had been guests at a twelve-course meal at La Page, a "gastronomic temple" in Geneva. Apparently, the famous restaurant overlooking Lake Geneva was as severe as "a Calvinist church on Sunday," full of pompous waiters and aged couples who didn't say boo to each other. "There was absolutely no laughter in the room but the laughter coming from our table," Hewitt recalled. "Am I right, Eric?"

The count grunted.

Somewhere between courses six and seven at La Page, Hewitt had a hankering for Calvados, the apple brandy from Normandy that was his preferred palate cleanser, but the La Page waiter haughtily told him that wasn't possible. The American would have to wait until an hour or two later, after the cheeses, when a sweet brandy was appropriate. The waiter would happily bring him a liqueur then.

"Bring him his Calvados *immédiatement* or I will slap your face," snapped Le Comte de Nancy. The ashen-faced waiter raced off and returned, in record time, with the requested brandy.

We all roared with laughter at this story, all but the count, who, reminded of this evening in Geneva, seemed to get angry all over again, and muttered, "Such impertinence. Such incredible impertinence."

And while I laughed, the moment wasn't entirely carefree, because in the back of my mind I kept thinking about what Hewitt had told me about Paul's finances and the terrible predicament my friend had been in when he ran off the cliff. The notion that even one of the best businessmen in the field of gastronomy couldn't make a financial success of his three-star restaurant was almost too upsetting to contemplate.

"Are you all right, Chef?" asked the sensitive Madame Elisabet, before making us all jump to attention with a "motherfuck!"

I straightened my dessert spoon and fork on the table above my plate.

"I was thinking of Paul. I just can't believe the mess he was in. If it happened to him, it could happen to any of us."

"Now, look, Chef, don't mope," said Le Comte de Nancy. "Verdun lost his way. That's the lesson in all this. He stopped growing. End of story. I was at Le Coq d'Or six months ago, and, I tell you, the fare, it was mediocre at best. The menu was the same as it was ten years ago. Hadn't changed a bit. In his ambition to build his empire, Verdun took his eye off his kitchen—the source of his wealth—and then, when he was so distracted by all the noise of the circus, he took his eye off the basics of the business as well. So, yes, he was running both the creative side and the business side, very admirable, but in reality, each had only his superficial attention. He was running and running but had no focus. Any businessman will tell you that is a recipe for disaster. And sure enough, he paid the price."

"I suppose you are right."

"My friends, the hardest thing, when you reach a certain level, is to stay fresh, day in and day out. The world changes very fast around us, no? So, as difficult as it is, the key to success is to embrace this constant change and move with the times," said Chef Piquot.

"That's just blah blah. A cliché," snapped Le Comte de Nancy.

Poor André looked as if he had just been boxed in the ears. To make matters worse, Madame Elisabet unhelpfully added, "Stupid bitch fuck!"

But Hewitt, seeing how hurt the chef was by this two-pronged attack, added, "You are right, of course, André, but I do think you have to change with the times in a way that *renews* your core essence, not abandons it. To change for the sake of change—without an anchor—that is mere faddishness. It will only lead you further astray."

"*Exactement,*" said Le Comte de Nancy.

Normally an outsider fighting for a seat at the table occupied only by French insiders, I usually kept my opinions to myself, but that night, perhaps due to the strain of the performance, perhaps because of my recent turmoil, I blurted out, "I am just exhausted by all the ideologies. This school and that school, this theory and that theory. I have had enough of it. At my restaurant we are now only cooking local ingredients in their own juices, very simply, with one criteria: Is the food good or not? Is it fresh? Does it satisfy? Everything else is immaterial."

Hewitt looked at me oddly, like he was seeing me for the first time, but my outburst seemed to liberate Madame Elisabet, for she added, in that sweet voice so incongruous to her blasphemous eruptions, "You are so right, Hassan. I am always reminding myself why I got into the game in the first place." She pointed both hands, flat-palmed, out across the room. "Look at this. It's so easy to become intoxicated by all this flimflam. Paul was seduced by the Paris *bourse* and all those press clips hailing him as a 'culinary visionary.' That is what he had to teach us—all of us—in the end. Never lose sight—"

At that moment, however, the lights were dimmed and an expectant hush fell over the tables. Then, from the back, a simple candlelight procession, followed by a dozen young waiters holding aloft silver platters loaded down with roast partridge. The room rumbled and there was a smattering of applause.

Paul's Partridge in Mourning, as I named the dish, was the highlight of the evening, as the papers reported the following day. Up until that point, I was, I must confess, trying to hide my terror of performing before such a demanding audience, but the generous comments I received from my table suggested that my risky menu had paid off. In particular, I took great joy in seeing Le Comte de Nancy—who always called things as he saw them, was in fact incapable of an insincere remark—tearing a bread roll apart with great gusto before lunging in to mop up the last smears of juice.

"The partridge is delicious," he said, waving his bread stub at me. "I want this on the menu at Le Chien Méchant."

"*Oui, Monsieur Le Comte.*"

The dish that famously put Chef Verdun on the culinary map thirty years earlier was his *poularde Alexandre Dumas.* Paul filled the chicken's cavity with julienned leeks and carrots, then surgically perforated the bird's outer shell so truffle slices could be delicately inserted into the bird's skin. As the bird roasted in the oven, the truffles and chicken fat melted together, their essences seeping deliciously through the meat and leaving a uniquely earthy flavor. It was Paul's signature, a dish always found for a princely sum of 170 euros on the menu of Le Coq d'Or.

The night of his memorial, wanting to pay Paul an homage, I took the basic techniques of his *poularde,* and applied it to partridge, well known to be his personal favorite game bird. The result was a powerfully pungent bit of fowl, just this side of being feral. I stuffed the birds with glazed apricots—instead of julienned legumes—and then so blackened the fowl with black truffle slices inserted in their skin they looked like birds dressed for a Victorian funeral—hence the name Paul's Partridge in Mourning. Of course, my sommelier then had the inspired idea to twin the partridge with the 1996 Côtes du Rhône Cuvée Romaine, a robust red redolent of dogs panting and on point in the lushness of a summer hunt.

Several distinguished critics and restaurateurs—including one of my idols, Chef Rouët—personally came by our table later in the evening, to congratulate me on the menu and, in particular, my interpretation of Paul's signature dish. Even Monsieur Barthot, *Le Guide Michelin directeur général,* descended from the Olympian heights of the head table to shake my hand and to say, rather loftily, "Excellent, Chef. Excellent," before striding off to speak to someone of more importance. And in that moment I finally understood why Paul had orchestrated this posthumous dinner.

I looked over to the head table, to make grateful eye contact with Anna Verdun, but Paul's widow was at that moment looking vacantly out across the room, a smile of sorts frozen across her face, while Chef Mafitte was leaning in on her from the left, one hand under the table.

No, I would not tell her, I decided. She had enough on her plate.

Besides, it was enough that I knew why Paul had planned this evening.

The memorial dinner was not for Paul, you see, but for me. With this meal my friend had signaled to France's culinary elite that a new *gardien* of classic French cuisine had burst on to the scene. I was his anointed heir. And so I think it is safe to say that before that night I was a relatively faceless figure lost among the scores of competent and talented two-star chefs all across France.

After that night, however, I was propelled to the top ranks, my good friend ensuring—even from beyond the grave—that the country's gastronomic elite made room for a forty-two-year-old foreign-born chef he had personally chosen to protect the classic principles of France's *cuisine de campagne,* which he and Madame Mallory had fought so hard to protect.

Chapter Seventeen

Winter drove us to the wall. The recession dragged on right through the coldest months, and fabled restaurants such as Maxim's and La Tour d'Argent, they finally fell to the economic malaise. It was a shock, to walk down the Rue Royale and see Maxim's windows boarded up. No one in France, not since the war, had seen such a thing. The government again repealed the 19.6 percent VAT charge, but it was too little, too late; in the end none of us were immune to the new economic climate, and my own financial problems hit with great force in late February.

My biggest problem was a personnel issue that would not go away. The waiter Claude was tidy and pleasant-looking and had come to us, with glowing references, from Lyon. We found him quick to learn, energetic, and so unfailingly courteous and attentive with the customers that Jacques, my maître d'hôtel, wrote in his initial review that the young waiter conducted himself with the "highest professionalism."

But this you must know about French labor law: during the initial "trial period" we could dismiss Claude without too much difficulty; after six months on the books, however, the waiter was considered a full-time employee, with a long list of ironclad legal rights. Getting rid of him thereafter was extremely difficult and costly.

Our honeymoon with Claude lasted precisely until the day after the young man's six-month "trial" was over. What previously took Claude thirty minutes—polishing the silver candelabras, for example—suddenly took him an hour and a half. Or longer. Jacques, a stickler for proper deportment, coldly suggested Claude hurry up, but the nasty little fellow simply shrugged and said he was work-

215

ing as fast as he could. When Claude submitted his first time-and-a-half overtime work sheets, Jacques, normally coolly elegant and composed, threw the forms back in the boy's face and called him a *"connard."* But the boy had nerves of steel. He didn't flinch. He simply picked the papers off the floor and gently left them on Jacques' desk, knowing full well the law would protect him from us "capitalist exploiters."

Claude had not only calculated his overtime to the minute, but included a demand for 6.6 days in extra paid vacation to offset the fact we were violating his legal right to work only thirty-five hours a week. The restaurant business is of course all about long hours—that's just the nature of our work—and, not surprisingly, all my other hardworking staff soon began to complain about Claude, who was not pulling his weight and forcing the more conscientious members of the staff to pick up his slack.

This untenable situation finally came to a head when Mehtab handed me Claude's payroll records. In the year he had been on staff, Le Chien Méchant had paid Claude seventy thousand euros in salary, plus three times that amount in various social security and pension taxes. Le Chien Méchant still owed him ten weeks' paid vacation.

Claude was not a waiter, but a scam artist.

I called the Lyon restaurants, spoke to the owners, and they finally confessed Claude had done the same thing to them, and in the end they had written him glowing reviews simply to get him off their backs. So I told Jacques to fire him. And he did.

But then the boy returned—with his union representative.

"It's very simple, Chef Haji. The young man's dismissal is not legal."

Mehtab used all the poetic flourishes of Urdu to curse the union representative's entire family lineage. Jacques erupted in French.

But I held up my hand and hushed them both.

"Explain yourself, Monsieur LeClerc. This man is a cheat. A crook. How can this not be grounds for legal dismissal?"

Claude looked entirely serene as usual, and wisely didn't say a word, but let his union representative speak for him. "Your allegations are unfair and unwarranted," LeClerc said mildly, making a steeple of his hands and thoughtfully pursing his lips. "And perhaps more to the point, completely without proof."

"That's not true," Jacques interjected. "I have documented very carefully how Claude deliberately drags his feet on assignments, how even simple tasks—like setting a table—takes him four times as long as it takes the others."

"Claude is not the swiftest of workers, we concede, but that is not sufficient grounds to fire him, particularly since your own records commend him as a worker of the 'highest professionalism.' *Non, non, Monsieur Jacques.* This is not right what you have done. He took so much time to execute your orders simply because of this professionalism you previously commended. Tell me, were you ever dissatisfied with the quality of his work, after he completed the assignments? Was the work somehow sloppily done? I could not find any complaints in his file about quality of execution, simply about the amount of time it took him to complete his work—"

"Well, yes, that's true—"

"So, in a court of law, we could convincingly make the argument that it was precisely because *he cared so much about the quality of his work* that he took longer than the others—"

"This is outrageous," Jacques said, his face an alarming beetroot tint. "We all know exactly what Claude is doing and what this is all about. He is holding us ransom. He inflated his work sheets. Monsieur LeClerc, you are colluding with a crook. I cannot believe you are taking his side."

The burly LeClerc smashed his fist on the table. "Take that back, Monsieur Jacques! You have fired Claude illegally and now you are attacking my personal integrity to cover up your tracks. Well, you won't get away with it. The laws are very clear in these matters. You must reinstate Claude *immédiatement.* Or, if you want to release him, you must negotiate a proper severance package as stipulated under the law, not the paltry sum you gave him yesterday."

I looked over at Mehtab, who was furiously making calculations on a pad.

"And if we refuse?" she asked.

"Then the union will be forced to bring you before the *Conseil de prud'hommes* on charges of wrongful dismissal, and it will be horrible. This I guarantee you. We will make sure the press is in attendance at the *tribunal* and that your restaurant is rightly exposed as an 'exploiter of workers.' "

"This is blackmail."

"Call it what you like. We are simply making sure our union members are not taken advantage of by you *propriétaire,* and that you pay them what they are entitled to by law."

I stood up.

"I've heard enough. Give them what they want, Mehtab."

"Hassan! That's two years' pay plus vacation. It will cost us a hundred and ninety thousand euros to get rid of the little pig!"

"I don't care. I've had enough. Claude is stirring up bad blood with our decent staff, and if we keep him, it will cost us much more in the long term. Pay him. He's figured out all the angles."

Claude was smiling sweetly, and, I think, just about to thank me for the generous settlement, when I spoke deliberately and quietly to Monsieur LeClerc.

"Now get that piece of dirt out of my restaurant."

Paul Verdun was among the first of the top-rated French chefs to truly understand that the economics of our business had changed entirely, and that the great restaurants of France were, like cancer patients, living on a drip of borrowed time. The French state had, in all its wisdom, finally made it impossible for us to survive a downturn. The thirty-five-hour workweek; the pension liabilities and dozens of "social" taxes; the incomprehensible bureaucratic filings requiring a half-dozen accountants and lawyers to complete. The rules and restrictions and added costs, they all pushed us to the brink that winter.

Paul, of course, had seen all these financial problems looming on the horizon well before the rest of us, and he had fought back well before they had reached their catastrophic tipping point. In particular he studied the French fashion houses that had gone through a similar shakeout fifty years earlier and he learned their lessons well: he noticed, for example, the labor-intensive haute couture, at the top of the fashion pyramid, built world-class reputations on their innovative designs, but few women in the modern age could actually afford or bought these costly creations. Result: the haute couture ateliers all lost money.

It was instead the ready-to-wear lines and perfume licenses further down the pyramid that made money for the fashion houses. The astute fashion impresarios—such as Bernard Arnault over at LVMH—effectively used such product lines to monetize the valuable reputations established by the money-losing haute couture operations at the top of their business empires.

Paul intuitively understood that Le Coq d'Or was the culinary equivalent of Christian Dior's haute couture, and he similarly moved down the gastronomic pyramid to make money. He cut licensing deals in everything from linens to olive oil. Paul showed us how it could be done and he was quite simply the entrepreneurial inspiration for a generation of us lesser chefs trying to build our own gastronomic businesses during this difficult age.

So you can understand why I was so shocked when I finally understood Paul's success was an illusion. He was both bankrupt and dead. It almost suggested—even if no one yet was admitting it—that there was no longer a place on French soil for haute cuisine, as we previously knew it.

And if I clung to any delusional fantasies about my own restaurant, then the severance package we paid Claude efficiently tore the veil from my eyes. The restaurant's *bénéfice* the previous year—net profit, that is—was all of 87 euros on a turnover of 4.2 million euros. The year before that Le Chien Méchant actually lost 2,200 euros. Now forced to fork over 190,000 euros to Claude—something that hadn't been budgeted for—we were destined to have a big loss at the end of the year. Here was the bottom line: Le Chien Méchant's break-even point had just jumped to a 93 percent occupancy rate; our occupancy rate was running at an 82 percent average for the year.

So I suddenly understood how Paul had started down the slippery slope of quietly borrowing money to bridge year-end short-falls: a little here, a little there, because next year will be better. And if there was any chance I might not fully understand the implications of where Le Chien Méchant was heading, there was always my sister to remind me, at the restaurant—where she did the accounts—or at the flat, where she lived in the back room.

Indeed, that night, after work, I returned to the apartment behind the Institut Musulman Mosque. I dropped my keys and phone on the hall table and went into the kitchen; my nighttime snack plate—a spoonful each of my sister's baingan bharta and dum aloo, mashed eggplant and potatoes in yogurt—was waiting for me on the kitchen counter. But Mehtab was not in her bed, as was normal at this late hour, but sitting in her nightgown at the counter before a pot of chai, her eyes red-rimmed and sagging in their fleshy pouches.

She got up, poured me a glass of sparkling water from the fridge, and handed me a napkin. "Very serious," she said. "I see it now. We will be back to selling bhelpuri by the roadside in no time."

"Mehtab, please. I am very tired. Don't get me riled up before I go to bed."

She sucked pensively on her lower lip for a few minutes, but I could tell she was in one of her pugilistic moods. The next thing she said was, "And what happened to that Isabelle? Why she doesn't ring anymore?"

"We broke up."

"Aiiieee. You dumped her. You are like a teenager, Hassan."

"I am going to bed, Mehtab. Good night."

Of course, my sister had gotten under my skin—it was her comment we'd soon be selling bhelpuri at the side of the road that did me in—and I tossed and turned that night. Somewhere in the middle of the blackness I flashed to a trip I had made just the month before, to a greenfield site outside Paris. One of my poultry suppliers had opened a new factory, and, very proud of his state-of-the-art plant, he had invited me for a tour. It was the size of an airport hangar, smelled of hot feathers and guano, and inside this cavernous space I was greeted by chickens flying down a chute to a pen, where North Africans in hairnets, white coats, and rubber boots stood waiting. The men, burly but oddly graceful, grabbed the squawking birds by their scaly legs and rhythmically slotted them, one by one and upside down, into clips moving along a conveyor belt overhead, a magic carpet heading straight to a black flap in the wall.

Pulled through the opening in the wall, the chickens—dangling upside down, their hearts pounding, wattles trembling— were plunged into a dark and warm and confined space, their automated journey lit softly by a soothing purple tube light overhead. The birds were instantly calmed, their shrieking wing-flap suddenly reduced to a cluck now and then. The belt headed— smoothly, inexorably—up to another flap. As the belt turned the corner, the silent birds' dangling heads brushed against an innocent-looking wire. The electric jolt to the head instantly stunned them. Then another wire, again, as they went through the last flap.

So they never saw the rotating blade, like an electric can opener, coming in to slit their throats, or heard their spurting blood hit the steel walls. They never saw the butcher leaning in, with his steel-gloved hand, knife at the ready, slitting further any chicken neck not completely opened up, the slop trays underneath filling up with tapping fluids. But I did. And I saw how the dead birds continued on their automated journey into a block-long metal box, where they were dragged through boiling water to loosen feathers and where rollers peeled off their white coats, so they emerged pink and naked and ready for the rows of men and women sitting at their posts, ready to quarter and package and ship.

This was the vision that visited, in that restless space between sleeping and waking, and it greatly soothed me. For this vision of the chickens heading to slaughter reminded me that there are many points in life when we cannot see what awaits us around the corner, and it is precisely at such times, when our path forward is unclear, that we must bravely keep our nerve, resolutely putting one foot before the other as we march blindly into the dark.

And it was just before I fell asleep that I remembered one of

Uncle Mayur's favorite expressions, often repeated as we walked, hand in hand, through the slums of Mumbai when I was a little boy. "Hassan, it is Allah who gives and takes away," he liked to tell me, with a cheerful wobble of his head. "Always remember this: His will is only revealed at the right time."

And so, finally, I arrive at the last pivotal event of those strange days. Following Claude's dismissal, Jacques and I searched for a front-room replacement. We interviewed I don't know how many prospects—a Welshwoman with a ring through her nose; an earnest Turk who seemed promising but spoke very poor French; a Frenchmen from Toulouse who looked superb on paper until we found out, during a background check, that he had been arrested three times for torching cars during student riots. In the end, we hired the half brother of Abdul, one of our best waiters, who promised he would take personal responsibility for his younger sibling.

It was toward the end of this wearisome process, late one afternoon, that Jacques stuck his head in my office to announce that there was a chef downstairs asking to see me personally.

I looked up from the stock sheets I was studying.

"What's this? You know full well we don't need another chef."

"She says she used to work with you."

"Where?"

"Le Saule Pleureur."

I had not heard that name for some time, but hearing it again on Jacques's lips was like a bolt of lightning. My heart began to pound.

"Send her up."

I don't mind admitting, in that peculiar mental state I was in, I was strangely frightened and half-expecting Madame Mallory to walk through the door.

But of course it was not the old woman.

"Margaret! What a wonderful surprise."

She stood hesitantly at the door frame of my office, shy and retiring as she had always been, waiting for me to invite her in. I instantly came from behind my desk, we hugged and kissed, and I gently led my old culinary comrade and lover by the hand into the center of the room.

"I am so sorry to barge in on you like this, Hassan. I should have called."

"Nonsense. We are old friends. Here. Sit. . . .What are you doing in Paris?"

Margaret Bonnier, in a fleur-de-lis dress and cardigan, calfskin Kelly bag at her shoulder, nervously fingered the crucifix around her neck, bringing it up to her lips, just as she had done so many years ago when Madame Mallory used to terrorize us. She was more matronly, of course; her hair was now bottle-blond. But through the thickening of age, she had somehow managed to hold on to something soft, and even through the marks of time I could see my old friend from long ago.

"I am looking for a job."

"In Paris?"

"I married. The mechanic, Ernest Borchaud. Do you remember him?"

"Yes, I do. My brother Umar was mad about cars. Ernest and Umar, they used to work on engines together. Doing I know not what."

She smiled. "Ernest owns the Mercedes and Fiat dealerships now. We have two children together. A boy and girl. The girl, Chantal, she is eight. Alain, he is just six."

"That's marvelous. Congratulations."

"Ernest and I divorced. The papers came through two months ago."

"Oh," I said. "I am sorry."

"The children and I, we have moved to Paris. I have a sister here. We all needed the change."

"Yes, I understand."

She looked at me, steadylike. "Perhaps, it is something I should have done long ago. Moved to Paris."

I did not say a thing.

"Of course, the city is so expensive."

"Yes, it is."

Margaret looked out the window for a moment, gathering herself, before turning her eyes back on me. "Forgive me for being so bold," she said, in a voice so battered of its self-confidence, only a whisper came out. "But . . . do you need a sous chef? I will work any position. Hot kitchen. Cold kitchen. Desserts."

"No, I am afraid not. I am sorry. I cannot afford to take on more staff."

"Oh," she said.

Margaret looked around the office in a panic, trying to figure out what she should do next. Her shoulders, I noticed, were tensed and bunched under her dress, but then abruptly dropped in defeat. And then she was standing to say good-bye, clutching her Kelly bag for balance. She smiled, but her lip was trembling a little.

"I am sorry to have troubled you, Hassan. I hope you won't hold it against me. But you see, you are the only restaurateur I know in Paris, and I didn't know whom else I could—"

"Sit."

She looked at me like a frightened girl, her crucifix dangling from between her lips.

I pointed at the seat. "Nah?"

Margaret sank back into her chair.

I picked up the phone and called Chef Piquot.

"*Bonjour, André . . . Hassan ici. . . .* Tell me, did you fill that cold-kitchen opening? . . . He didn't work out. . . . Yes. Yes. I know. Terrible, the way they carry on these days. Such prima donnas. . . . But you know, it's excellent news the fellow didn't work out because I have the perfect candidate for you. . . . Yes. Yes. Not to worry. I worked with her at Le Saule Pleureur. First-rate sous chef. Hardworking. Very experienced. I tell you, my friend, you will be thanking me. . . . No, I don't think so. She's just moved to Paris. . . . I will send her right over."

When I put the phone down I discovered, much to my horror, Margaret was not joyous that I had found her a position at Montparnasse, but was sobbing into a tissue, unable to talk. I did not know what to do, where to look, as the office filled with her weeping. But then, still shaking with emotion, head still down,

Margaret's left hand reached out across the table, fingers blindly searching the air for contact.

And that's when I understood she had had a very hard time.

That this was the best she could do—for the moment.

So I reached over with my right hand and we silently met halfway.

Chapter Eighteen

March's feeble sun retreated behind the city's rooftop guttering. It was that time of day when the restaurant was brooding in its dismal place, that strange twilight between matinee and evening's curtain call. The returning members of the staff were exhausted and snappish after the two-hour break, unsure whether they could once again pull themselves together for the late performance. And the dining room itself, so lively in the bright lights of the evening performance a few hours hence, appeared shopworn through the stale haze left over from lunch. It was difficult not to become despondent. Late winter shivered in the folds of the velvet drape; a bread roll, like a dead beetle, lay on its back under a chair.

I was in the kitchen as usual, sweating onions and garlic in a skillet, sliding into that trance that overtakes me when I cook. But for some reason, on this dark March evening I did not surrender myself completely, but hovered at the edge, halfway between here and there, as if I knew something momentous was about to occur.

Through the kitchen's swinging doors—as I shook the spitting skillet—I heard the returning waiters stamping their feet in the hall. I heard the Hoover's drone and the banging of the espresso machine as it was knocked free of old grounds by an apprentice. Bit by bit, din and duties stepped into the cold space that had occupied the restaurant just moments before: knives were sharpened, fresh linen was snapped, we heard the industrious back-and-forth of the accountant's printer coming from upstairs. And before long, the gloom was gone.

France Soir, the evening paper, came roughly through the letter flap, clapping to the mat. It was an old habit that Jacques stubbornly would not part with, even in the digital age, and he picked the paper up and took it to the back table where his front-room staff was sitting down to a quick dinner of grilled *andouillettes* before the evening service began.

Newspaper under his arm, Jacques took his seat in the back, among the others. He helped himself to a portion of the chitter-lings with rice, and tomato salad, reading the paper as he ate. But suddenly there was this odd gurgling in the back of Jacques' throat and he violently dropped his fork. Before the others could find out what was the matter, however, he was up on his feet, through the door, and dashing across the dining room. And the scoundrels, enjoying nothing more than a good fight, jumped up and ran after him, hoping to witness what was looking like a first-rate row.

That was how they arrived in the kitchen: out of breath, highly agitated, slamming through the swinging doors. We in the kitchen were innocently shelling peas and dicing shallots and trimming fat, but now we froze in midchop and looked carefully about us as Jacques thrashed the air with the evening paper and bellowed.

I thought, Oh, hell, not again—for the previous night Jacques and Serge almost came to blows, as each had blamed the other for a botched order. And from the corner of my eye I could see Serge gripping the end of a lamb joint like it was a club, quite prepared to wallop Jacques or any other member of the front staff foolish enough to provoke him. I was, I don't mind admitting it, utterly exhausted and at the end of my strength; I could not take another fiery confrontation between staff members.

"*Maître! Maître!*"

Jacques accusingly pointed the rolled-up newspaper at me.

"The third star! Michelin has just given you the third star!"

The first roars of excitement subsided and the staff stood three-deep around the butcher block, clinging to my every syllable as I read aloud the five-paragraph story. It was all about who was up and who was down. And then it came—the half sentence—inform-ing *le tout Paris* Le Chien Méchant was among just two establish-ments in all France elevated to the third star.

I was stunned, numb, while a kind of Bastille Day raged all around me.

The staff banged pots and yelled and leaped about the burners. Jacques and Serge were in each other's arms, almost like lovers in a passionate embrace, and there were tears and back-clapping and hoots of joy, all followed by more rounds of the most heartfelt handshakes.

And what was I thinking?

I cannot tell you. Not rightly.

My emotions were stirred up. Jumbled. Bittersweet, you know.

The excited staff stood in a line—the black jackets of the front room and the whites of the kitchen, like chess pieces lined up in a row—each wanting to personally congratulate me. But I was not warm, not effusive in my thanks. It might even have appeared as if I didn't care as I observed all this joy unfolding about me from a great distance.

But consider: only twenty-eight restaurants in all France had three stars, and my journey to this point had been so long and arduous that I could not rightly believe it had finally arrived. Or, at least, I could not believe it simply on the basis of a half sentence in a mass-market evening paper. And Suzanne, near the end of the line, appeared to read my mind, for she suddenly said, 'What if the reporter got it wrong?'

"*Merde*," Serge yelled from across the kitchen, angrily pointing at her with a wooden spoon. "What is it with you, Suzanne? Always something bad to say."

"That's not true!"

Fortunately, at that moment we were distracted by Maxine descending from the upstairs office, wringing her hands, informing me Monsieur Barthot, the *directeur général* of *Le Guide Michelin* was on the phone and urgently wanting a word. My heart thumped as I took the spiral stairs two by two, the staff's cries of good luck ringing in my ears as I disappeared up the turret.

I took a deep breath and picked up the phone. After the usual feigned politesse, Barthot asked, "Have you read the evening paper?"

I informed him I had, and asked straight out whether it is true we were to get the third star. "Damn papers," he finally said. "Yes, it is true. Congratulations are in order."

Only then did I allow the news to sink in, the enormity of it all. Destiny had finally paid me my visit.

Monsieur Barthot rambled on about procedural matters and I struggled to stay focused on his florid talk. It seems I was expected to appear at an awards dinner in Cannes. "You know, Chef," he said, "you are the first immigrant ever to win the third star in France. It is quite an honor."

"Yes, yes," I said. "Quite agree. A great honor."

"I had to fight for you, you know. Not all my colleagues think chefs with—how can I put it?—with exotic backgrounds have the proper feel for classic French cuisine. This is a new thing for us. *Mais c'est la vie.* The world is changing. The guide must change as well."

He was lying, of course, and I didn't rightly know what to say to the man. It wasn't Barthot who championed my cause, this I knew; he would have been among the last to vote for me. It was the inspectors' fiercely independent reports, filed after their secret visits to the restaurant and discussed at the committee level twice a year, that undoubtedly carried the day. They were uncompromisingly dedicated to the truth as they saw it.

"Monsieur Barthot," I finally replied, "I once again thank you and the Inspectors' Committee. But forgive me. I must go. The restaurant opens in under two hours. You understand."

Chapter Nineteen

That magic night in late March when I won my third star, there was, as the evening's sitting drew to a close, an about-face on the tongue, toward the light and sweet and meltingly good, toward the pistachio madeleines and the star anise *clafoutis* and my famous bitter-cherry sorbet. Only a soufflé or two in the oven, only Pastry Chef Suzanne working hard at bringing up the rear. I went to her station and side by side we spooned a Beaujolais compote into crisp pie crusts just taken from the oven, a dollop of mascarpone, the final touch to my *tarte au vin*. And you could feel it, the heat of the kitchen, as it was notched down, that time of night when Le Chien Méchant's stoves were silenced, one by one.

The guests outside, they slapped their linen napkins on the sides of their plates, hoisting the white flag. And I saw, from my glass portico, their legs stretched out at odd angles under the tables, upper torsos collapsed over the tabletops like meaty soufflés.

Jacques and the staff still fussed, but not so intensely. Now it was the endless subtractions, the taking away of sauce-stained platters and wine-teared crystal, the crack and crumb of bread rolls scraped from tabletops. Reviving coffees and petits fours arrived; digestives in cut crystal and a good Havana, taken gingerly from the footstool's pocket.

"Jean-Pierre," I called, taking off my jacket. "Bring me clean whites."

An Australian couple seated in what we called "Siberia" saw me first, coming out of the kitchen's swinging doors, but were unsure. As I proceeded deeper into the next salon, however, a hush swept across the room, and Jacques, looking up from the books, came forward to meet me.

Le Comte de Nancy was at his usual table to the far right side of the restaurant, with two senior partners from Lazard Frères as his guests, and he raised his liver-spotted hand in greeting, the elderly aristocrat only with great effort coming to his feet. Before I knew it, the mayor of Paris, he and his guests, they, too, were on their feet; as was Christian Lacroix, the designer, and that great Hollywood actor Johnny D., shyly tucked away in a booth with his daughter. The front-room commotion, it pulled Serge and the others from the kitchen, and they emerged to stand in the back of the dining room to join the applause. And the clapping from guests and staff alike—it was deafening—as they congratulated me on my elevation to the uppermost echelons of French haute cuisine.

What a thing, I tell you. What a thing.

That moment, that moment was the pinnacle of my life, these famous and distinguished people on their feet, my *camarades de cuisine,* all showing me such respect. And I remember thinking: Hmmm. Rather like this. Could get used to it.

So I stood at the center of my restaurant, taking it in, bobbing my head in return, as I gave my thanks to everyone in the room. And I tell you, as I looked out at those good people—red-faced and stuffed with my food—I suddenly felt my father's mountainous presence at my side, beaming with pride.

Hassan, I imagined him saying. *Hassan, you killed them. Very good.*

Maxine came downstairs from the office to say good night. "It's incredible, Chef," she said, flushed with excitement. "We took seven hundred reservations this evening, the e-mails are flooding in, and the phone is still ringing—from the Americas now, as the news spreads across the Internet. We're already booked solid through to April of next year. At this rate, we'll have a two-year waiting list by the end of the month. And, look, you have urgent messages from Lufthansa, Tyson Foods, and Unilever. They must be calling about some business deals, *non*? . . . What, Chef? Why are you looking so sad?"

Lose a Michelin star and business falls off by 30 percent, but gain a star, and the business jumps 40 percent. A Lyon insurance company—selling "loss of profits" coverage to restaurateurs in danger of losing their rankings—had just proven this fact through an actuarial study.

"Ahh, Maxine. I am sad because I am thinking of Paul Verdun. My friend, he could not save himself. But he saved me."

The young woman put her arms around my neck and whispered, "Come by for coffee later. I will wait up."

"Thank you for the offer. Very tempting. But not tonight."

I said good night to two waiters and Serge. He was the last to depart that evening, and only did so after we had kissed and congratulated each other one more time, and he had thumped me several more times on the back. But finally I eased shut the door, once again alone.

And that was it.

My special night gone, forever, passed into history.

With the definitive click of the back-door bolt slotting into place, I began spiraling down from the intoxicating height of the evening's great performance. The low spirits, they rushed in, that familiar depression only a tenor coming triumphantly off the stage at La Scala could rightly understand. But that was how it was in the kitchen.

"*Tant pis,*" as Serge always said. Too bad.

We must take the bad with the good.

I reassured myself the windows were bolted and the pantry padlocked. Upstairs, up the turret, I made sure all the computers and my office lights were off, picking up my mobile phone and key ring from the side table as I made my way back downstairs. Dining room lights, off. One last look at the restaurant, at the faintly luminous orbs hovering in the black, the white Madagascan tablecloths shedding their last vestiges of light. Alarm, on. And then I shut the door.

The ivy around the restaurant's barking bulldog shingle was wet with evening dew, but it had not hardened into frost, and for the first time that year I felt the balminess of an approaching spring coming through the night. It was just a hint, but it was distinctly there. I looked up Rue Valette, up the hill, as I did every night. It was my favorite view in all of Paris, looking up at the dome of Le Panthéon, caught in the yellow glow of spotlights like a soft-boiled egg in the night. And then I locked the front door.

It was the small hours, but you know, night in Paris, it's an intoxicating affair. Always the life: an amorous middle-aged couple, arm in arm, coming down Rue Valette, as a Sorbonne medical student roared back up the hill, in the opposite direction, on a red Kawasaki. I think they felt it, too, the coming spring.

I made my contented way home, by foot, through the darkened passageways of the Quartier Latin, to my flat behind the Institut Musulman Mosque. It was not a long walk home, past Place de la Contrescarpe, down through the gauntlet of cheap North African restaurants on narrow Rue Mouffetard, a few windows to the street eerily lit by a greasy souvlaki carcass under a red light.

But somewhere down the middle of the sloping lane of Rue Mouffetard, I stopped in my tracks. I was not quite sure at first, not quite trusting my senses. I again sniffed the moist midnight air. Could it be? But there it was, the unmistakable aroma of my youth, joyously coming down a cobblestone side passage to greet me, the smell of machli ka salan, the fish curry of home, from so long ago.

So I was helpless, pulled down the dark passageway, drawn by this haunting odor of curry, to a narrow shop front at the end of the lane, where I found, squeezed between two unsavory Algerian restaurants, Madras, newly opened but now closed for the day.

A streetlamp buzzed overhead. I shielded my eyes to cut the glare of the light and peered through the restaurant's window. The dining room was dotted with a dozen rough wooden tables, covered in paper sheets and set for the following day. Black-and-white photos of India—water-wallahs and loom weavers and crowded trains at a station—were framed simply and hung on bright yellow walls. The front lights of the restaurant were out, but the harsh fluorescent overhead tubes of the back kitchen, they were on, and I could just see what was going on down the long hall to the kitchen.

A vat of fish stew bubbled away on the stove, the special for the following day. Before the stove, a lone chef in a T-shirt and apron, sitting on a three-legged stool in the narrow back passage, his head lowered in exhaustion over a bowl of his spicy fish curry.

My hand, it rose on its own accord, hot and flat like a chapatis pushed against the glass. And I was filled with an ache that hurt, almost to breaking. A sense of loss and longing, for Mummy and India. For lovable, noisy Papa. For Madame Mallory, my teacher, and for the family I never had, sacrificed on the altar of my ambition. For my late friend Paul Verdun. For my beloved grandmother, Ammi, and her delicious pearlspot, all of which I missed, on this day, of all days.

But then, I don't know why, standing before that little Indian restaurant, in that state of intense longing, it suddenly came to me, something Madame Mallory told me one spring morning many years ago. It was, as I look back, among the very last days I was at her restaurant.

We were in her private rooms at the top floor of Le Saule Pleureur. She wore a shawl about her shoulders and was sipping tea in her favorite bergère armchair, watching the warbling doves in the willow tree outside her window. I sat across from her, studiously absorbed in the *De Re Coquinaria,* taking down notes in my leather-bound book which to this day follows me everywhere. Madame Mallory returned her teacup to its saucer—with a deliberate rattle—and I looked up.

"When you leave here," she said acidly, "you are likely to forget most of the things I have taught you. That can't be helped. If you retain anything, however, I wish it to be this bit of advice my father gave me when I was a girl, after a famous and extremely difficult writer had just left our family hotel. 'Gertrude,' he said, 'never forget a snob is a person utterly lacking in good taste.' I myself forgot this excellent piece of advice, but I trust you will not be so foolish."

Mallory took another sip of tea before pointedly turning those eyes on me, which were, even though she was an elderly woman, uncomfortably blue and piercing and glittery.

"I am not very good with words, but I would like to tell you that somewhere in life I lost my way, and I believe you were sent to me, perhaps by my beloved father, so that I could be restored to the world. And I thank you for this. You have made me understand that good taste is not the birthright of snobs, but a gift from God sometimes found in the most unlikely of places and in the unlikeliest of people."

And so, as I looked at the exhausted proprietor of Madras, grabbing a bowl of simple but delicious fish stew at the end of a long day, I suddenly knew what I would tell that impossible man, the next time he told me how honored I should be, the only foreigner ever to earn a place among France's culinary elite. I would pass on Mallory's comment about Parisian snobs, perhaps letting the remark settle a moment before leaning forward to say, with just a touch of flying spittle, "Nah? What you think?"

But a nearby church bell chimed one a.m. and the duties of the next day beckoned, pulling at my conscience. So I took one longing last look at Madras and then unceremoniously turned on my heel, to continue on my journey down the Rue Mouffetard, leaving behind the intoxicating smells of machli ka salan, an olfactory wisp of who I was, fading fast in the Parisian night.

Chapter Twenty

Hassan? Is that you?"

From the penthouse kitchen, the clinking of dishes getting washed in the sink.

"Yes."

"It's amazing! Three stars!"

Mehtab had her hair done smart that day and she came into the hall, kohl-eyed like our mother, in her best silk *salwar kameez*, smiling up at me, arms outstretched.

"Not so bad, yaar," I said, slipping back into the patois of our childhood.

"Oh, so proud. Oh, I wish Mummy and Papa were here. I tink I might cry."

But she looked nowhere near to crying.

In fact, she gave me a very hard pinch.

"Ow," I yelped.

The gold bangles up her arm jangled violently as she shook her finger. "You stinker! Why you not call and tell me? Why you embarrass me with the neighbors? I have to hear from strangers?"

"Ah, Mehtab. Wanted to, you know, but so busy, yaar. Learn just before restaurant open and phone ringing all the time and guests arriving. Every time I try and call you I have one big thing to deal with after another."

"Huh. Just excuses."

"So, who told you?"

Mehtab's face suddenly softened.

She put her fingers to her lips and beckoned that I should follow.

* * *

Margaret was in the living room, sitting upright in the middle of our white leather couch, her eyes closed, her head slowly dropping back as she dozed, only to snap forward at the last moment. A hand each rested on her son and daughter, both sound asleep, both with their heads on her lap, their legs curled under the blankets that I recognized came from Mehtab's personal chest. And I recall that the children's faces were wiped of everything but the most profound and touching innocence.

"Aren't they adorable?" Mehtab whispered. "And so good. Ate up all my dinner."

The look on my sister's face, it was the utter joy of finally having children in her home, that destiny she always thought would be hers but was never meant to be.

But then she scowled, just like Auntie, with that bitter-lemon look. "She the only one of your friends bother to tell me you get the star."

She pinched me again, but not so hard this time.

"Brought me the paper, *France Soir*. Such a nice girl. And told me all about her husband, you know. What a brute. They have suffered terribly, her and the little ones . . . and why you not tell me she move to Paris?"

Luckily, at that moment, I was saved from another barrage of Mehtab mortar attacks, because Margaret opened her eyes, and when she saw us peering at her from the door, she smiled, her face sweetly lit up. She held up a finger, signaling us to wait, and she slowly, delicately extricated herself from the dangly limbs of her children, both still sound asleep.

We hugged and kissed warmly, out in the hall.

"I couldn't believe it, Hassan. It's so exciting."

"Shock to me. Come out of the blue."

I grasped both her hands and squeezed, looking into her eyes.

"Thank you Margaret, for coming here. For informing my sister."

"We came right as soon as we heard the news. It was just so fantastic. We just had to see you and congratulate you. *Immédiate-*

ment. What an incredible achievement. . . . Madame Mallory, she was right!"

"I am sure, up in heaven, she is telling Papa that right now."

We laughed.

Mehtab, in her auntie mode, fiercely shushed us with a finger to her lips, and pointed we should go to the other side of the flat, to the kitchen counter, to talk. In the kitchen, we pulled out the stools from the marble counter, as Margaret told me how things were working out at Montparnasse, how decent Chef Piquot was, not at all a yeller and a tyrant, like so many of the other leading chefs.

"I will never forget, Hassan. We owe you everything."

"I did nothing. I made one phone call."

From the SieMatic fridge, I retrieved a bottle of chilled Moët et Chandon, popped the cork over the sink, and poured us glasses in amber antique flutes. Margaret, refreshed by her nap, was talkative.

"It was lovely to see your sister again, after so many years. She was so good to us, when we just showed up unannounced at the door. So kind to the children. And my, can she cook! *Ooh la la*. Just as well as you. She gave us dinner. *Délicieuse*. A spicy beef stew, thick and gooey, perfect for the chilly night. And so different from our *boeuf Bourguignon*."

Mehtab, her cooking suitably relished and appreciated, was looking very regal, very aloofly pleased, even though she was pretending not to listen to our conversation. She was setting my place for my late-night snack.

"Margaret, come," she said, pushing a dish of sweets across the counter. "You have still to try my carrot halva. And we must discuss Hassan's party. The menu. And who we should invite."

My sister turned to me and in a tone close to barking said, "Go. Go wash up."

When I put my face down under the running water, the phone rang. A few moments later, the sound of padding feet, and Mehtab's voice coming through the bathroom door.

"It's Zainab. Pick up."

The line crackled. Far away. Like talking under the sea.

"Oh, Hassan. They would have been so proud. Papa and Mummy and Ammi. Imagine. Three Michelin stars!"

I tried to change the subject, but she would have none of it. Had to give her all the details.

"Uday wants a word."

Uday's baritone boomed down the line.

"Such incredibly good news, Hassan. We're terribly proud of you. Congratulations."

Zainab's husband, Uday Joshi.

No, not the Bombay restaurateur who set my father's teeth on edge.

The son.

Uday and Zainab, the two of them, they were the talk of all Mumbai. They had turned the old Hyderabad restaurant into a pish-posh boutique hotel and restaurant chain. Very Mumbai chic. Turned out, of all of us, little Zainab was most like Papa. An empire-builder. Always with the big plans, just more competent.

I remembered that time when Uday and Zainab married in Mumbai, shortly before Papa died. It was very awkward at first, when Papa and Uday Joshi, Sr., finally met up at the wedding. Papa talked far too much, carrying on with his show-off palaver, old man Joshi looking bored, stooped and gripping the handle of a cane. But later the two aged fathers posed together for the *Hello Bombay!* photographer, a couple of paternal peacocks, for a wedding spread that eventually took up five pages of the popular magazine, and after that the old men both softened up and talked together late into the night.

When Papa and I met up later, he said, "That old rooster. I look much better than he does, yaar? Don't you tink? He is very old."

And I remember standing with Papa, late in the night, when the festivities were in full swing, as a jeweled elephant carried the newlyweds across the grass, while the white-jacketed servants, bearing aloft silver trays covered in champagne flutes, professionally threaded themselves among the twelve hundred glittering guests. And there, in the center of the main tent, a silver vessel filled with beluga, the politicians elbowing their way forward, plopping soup ladles of the caviar onto their plates, two-thousand-dollar dollops at a time.

But Papa and I just watched, standing off to the side in the shadow of the night, under a string of fairy lights, eating kulfi, the Indian ice cream, from the *kulfi-wallah*'s simple earthenware pots. And I remember the taste of the cold blanched almond cream as we marveled at the women's emerald earrings. Big as plums, Papa kept on saying. Big as plums.

"We must talk business," my sister's husband again said down the phone. "Zainab and I, we have a business proposal that you might find interesting. Now's the time to open tip-top French restaurants in India. There's lots of money sloshing about. We already have financing."

"Yes. Yes. Let's schedule a time to talk. But not tonight. Let's talk next week."

"He has a very light dinner, or none at all, but always a nighttime snack after he comes home from work," Mehtab was telling Margaret when I returned to the kitchen. "It helps him relax. And he usually has a mint tea. With a spoonful of garam masala in it. Or sometimes a bit of my vegetables. And sparkling water."

"Ah. I know this pastry."

"They are not from the pâtisserie, of course. I make them myself, using the recipe of his old teacher. A pistachio paste, and in the glaze, yaar, a little vanilla essence. Try it."

"Better than Madame Mallory's, I think. Certainly better than mine."

My sister was so flushed with pleasure at this compliment, she had to turn back to the sink to cover up her embarrassment. I had to smile.

"Mehtab. Did anyone else ring?"

"Umar. He is going to drive the whole family down for the Three-Star Party."

Umar still lived in Lumière, the proud owner of two local Total garages. He also had four stunning boys, and the second oldest was coming up to Páris next year, to join me in the kitchen of Le Chien Méchant. The rest of the Hajis, adrift and scattered across the globe. My younger brothers, the rascals, both chronically restless, had wandered the world for years. Mukhtar was a mobile phone software designer in Helsinki, and Arash, he was a law professor at Columbia University in New York.

"You must call all your brothers tomorrow, Hassan."

"*Mais oui*," said Margaret, lightly touching my elbow. "Your brothers must hear the fantastic news from you directly."

Umar, my sister continued, said he would also see if Uncle Mayur was game, but he didn't think the retirement home would allow him to make the journey to Paris, because Uncle Mayur was so wobbly on his legs these days. Uncle Mayur, eighty-three, was the last one we thought would make it this long. But when I looked back, Uncle Mayur, he never worried about anything, was always stress-free, perhaps because Auntie fretted enough for the two of them.

Mehtab patted her hair. "And what do you tink, Margaret? Who else of Hassan's friends should we invite? What about that strange butcher with all the shops, the one who owns the chateau in Saint-Étienne?"

"*Ah, mon Dieu*. Hessmann. A pig."

"Haar. I think so, too. I never know what Hassan sees in that man."

"Put him on the list," I said. "He's my friend and he's coming."

The two women just looked at me. Blinked.

"And what do you think of the accountant? Maxine, the nervous one. You know, I think she has a crush on Hassan."

I let them get on with it, their plots and machinations for my party, as I drifted, restless, from room to room through the flat, as if there were some unfinished business I had to attend to, but couldn't remember what it was.

I opened the door to my study.

Mehtab had placed the copy of *France Soir* on my desk.

It came to me, then. At my desk, with great purpose, I picked up a pair of scissors and neatly trimmed the page-three article. I slipped the cutting into a wooden frame, leaned over, and hung the announcement of my third star on the wall.

In that hungry space.

Of generations ago.

Acknowledgments

All writers, particularly those with journalistic training, culti-
vate the impression they know far more than they actually do.
My inclination is to create an aura of wisdom by expertly pilfer-
ing the knowledge and experience of my betters and presenting
their insights as my own. So while there are countless people and
sources that enhanced this work and lent it credibility—too many
to name and thank here—I do hope you will bear with me as I
thank a few key people and resources that made significant contributions to *The Hundred-Foot Journey*.

This book is an homage to the late Ismail Merchant, the talented
and irrepressible film producer behind Merchant Ivory Produc-
tions, who died unexpectedly in 2005. Ismail and I both loved eating well and banging pots in the kitchen, and one day, as we dined
at the Bombay Brasserie in London, I urged Ismail to find a literary
property that combined his love of food with his love of filmmak-
ing. I would help him in this endeavor, I promised. Sadly, Ismail
died before I finished writing this book, but it is my sincere hope
that one day *The Hundred-Foot Journey* will make it to the screen,
a fitting memorial to my late friend.

My desk is cluttered with culinary references; I relied heavily
on their expertise to portray as accurately as possible the technical
mysteries of the kitchen. Here a few resources: *Life Is a Menu,* by
Michel Roux; Ismail Merchant's *Indian Cuisine; French Chefs Cooking,* by Michael Buller; *Flavours of Delhi,* by Charmaine O'Brien;
The Cook's Quotation Book, edited by Maria Polushkin Robbins;
Cuisine Actuelle, Patricia Wells's presentation of Joël Robuchon's
kitchen; *The Decadent Cookbook,* by Medlar Lucan and Durian
Gray; *The Oxford Companion to Wine,* by Jancis Robinson; *The

Sugar Club Cookbook, by Peter Gordon; culinary essays of the incomparable *New Yorker*; and, last, Scribner's classic *Joy of Cooking*, by Irma S. Rombauer, Marion Rombauer Becker, and Ethan Becker. There were of course countless other sources, from websites to articles and novels, that inspired me during the writing of this book, but my special thanks to *Forbes* for my journalism career that has allowed me to visit foreign places and learn about the world.

In India, Adi and Parmesh Godrej deserve my thanks. They kindly introduced me to the restaurateur Sudheer Bahl, who invited me to spend half a day in the kitchen of his first-rate restaurant, Khyber, a key piece of research that greatly enhanced my understanding of India's robust cuisine. In New York, meanwhile, my friend Mariana Field Hoppin used her charm and connections to similarly get me into the kitchen of the esteemed fish restaurant Le Bernardin. In London, through our friend Mary Spencer, I was able to spend quality time in the bowels of The Sugar Club, when Peter Gordon was that restaurant's star chef. But let the record show that it was Suraja Roychowdhury, Soyo Graham Stuart, and Laure de Gramont who kept me honest by reading my work and calling me on the accuracy of my cultural transgressions, besides correcting the many examples of mangled Franglais and Hindi-Urduisms.

Also: thanks to my friends Anna Kythreotis, Tony Korner, Lizanne Merrill, and Samy Brahimy for their unfailing good humor, friendship, and support. V. S. Naipaul, whom I don't know well, was nonetheless uncommonly kind and generous to me during a key period, as was his wife, Nadira, who regaled me with colorful stories of her upbringing, some of which I pinched.

Most of all, however, I must thank my dear friends Kazuo Ishiguro and his wife, Lorna. I cannot recount the number of times, despairing at the latest rejection, or stumped by a technical writing problem, that Ish picked me up, dusted me off, and sent me on my way again with a kind word and some stimulating insight. No one could have asked for a better friend and role model than I had in Ish.

Tom Ryder, fellow chowhound and publishing legend, has been an immensely generous promoter of my fiction. His advocacy cleared many paths and I owe him a damn good meal. And a martini or two. My thanks also to Esther Margolis, for representing my book in its early incarnation.

It is Richard Pine of InkWell Management, however, who has brought about much of my recent publishing success. Richard has fantastic genes: his father, Artie, was my agent when I started my career. But Richard is undeniably in a class of his own—with a keen editorial eye and a creative flair for deal-making—and it is Richard who paired me with the sensitive and gifted editor Whitney Frick at the storied U.S. publishing house Scribner. Whit is the consummate pro: she sweetly stroked my ego one moment, while firmly poking and prodding me to improve the manuscript the next. I am in fact grateful to production editor Katie Rizzo and all of the Simon & Schuster/Scribner staff for their professionalism and hard work publishing my book. My growing number of publishing deals overseas are, meanwhile, almost entirely the result of one tireless and much-valued advocate: Alexis Hurley, foreign rights guru at Inkwell Management.

Last, I must bow deeply in reverence to my wife, Susan, and my daughter, Katy, both of whom were elated by my successes and anguished by my stumbles, and who still stood by me through all the ups and downs that are the writer's lot. And to my parents, Jane and Vasco, who gave me courage, and to my older brothers (John, Jim, and Vasco), who instilled in me an instinct for survival. The youngest must quickly learn how to be wily and eat very fast—if he is to eat at all.

And to you, dear reader, for purchasing and savoring this book, my sincerest thanks and best wishes. May you, when times are hard, always find a moment for a restorative meal in the company of true friends and a loving family.

Richard C. Morais
Philadelphia, USA